DEAR SANTA,

Flash and me have been extra good this year, so we have a really big wish. Could you fix it so Mommy and Daddy live together again? Daddy's at our house until Mommy gets the new baby, so he'll be here when you come down the chimney. Could you make him stay all the time? We think he wants to stay because he likes making cakes and gourmay food in our kitchen, and he's making friends with all the grown-ups in town. I don't know about Mommy, but sometimes I think she wants him to stay because that's when I feel happy.

I love you, Santa.

Amy

and Flash

Meet two of the seven winners of the American Romance Christmas Is For Kids Photo Contest, whose likenesses appear on the cover of *Dear Santa*. They are Andrew Nosbusch of Brookfield, Wisconsin, and Lauren Lee Bronson of Boise, Idaho.

Andrew's mother, Kathy Nosbusch, wrote to tell us of his joyous preparations for Christmas.

> Picking up toys . . . helping whenever . . . secrets about gifts . . . letters to Santa . . . school projects hung on walls . . . loudly proclaimed wishes . . . cookies and milk for Santa, carrots for the reindeer . . . lots of hugs and kisses . . . questions full of wonder whether everything will fit down our chimney . . . how many hours until Christmas morning?

Lauren's mother, Joan Bronson, told us that:

> Lauren is the kind of child who exudes joy through every pore in her body. On Christmas Eve she's like a butterfly flitting from here to there and back again. She has so many exciting, happy thoughts in her head, she can't concentrate on just one thing. Lauren's our sunshine!

DEAR SANTA

MARGARET
ST. GEORGE

Harlequin Books

TORONTO • NEW YORK • LONDON
AMSTERDAM • PARIS • SYDNEY • HAMBURG
STOCKHOLM • ATHENS • TOKYO • MILAN

To Trey and Tracie

Published December 1989

First printing October 1989

ISBN 0-373-16323-1

Chapter One

The frosty air turned Penny Martin's cheeks pink as she stood in the open door, holding a bowl of candy against her swollen waist, blinking incredulously at the man standing under the porch light.

She had to be hallucinating. It couldn't be him.

Some events were too shocking to immediately assimilate. Such as a letter from the IRS. Or missing a period. Or finding one's soon-to-be ex-husband standing on the front porch when he should be two thousand miles away.

"I thought you were a trick-or-treater," she whispered. The jolt of seeing him robbed her of her voice. Four of the six children who lived in the rural subdivision had been to her door. When she answered the bell, she had expected the last two. Instead, John Martin stood before her, staring at her with an expression as stunned as her own.

"Good God," he murmured, briefly closing his eyes.

Penny could guess what he was thinking as surely as if his thoughts were stamped on his forehead. Drawing a deep breath, she looked past him to the Porsche parked in the driveway under the yard light. A small U-Haul trailer was hitched to the back of the car, an incongruity that reminded her of one of those captions: What's wrong with this picture?

Giving him a moment to recover, feeling the intensity of his shocked stare, she raised her eyes to the cold dark sky. Because the mountain air was thinner and without competition from city lights, she could see the Milky Way carpeting the sky with glittering brilliance. Smoke curled from the chimneys of several houses in the valley and the pleasant smell of woodsmoke permeated the night air.

A puff of silvery vapor formed in front of John's lips as he swore softly. He collapsed against the doorjamb, then with obvious effort forced his eyes up from her waist. "Tell me you're wearing a Halloween costume, Penny. Tell me this is a joke."

"Amy and Flash told you, didn't they?" Irritation deepened the pink in her cheeks. She had spoken to Amy and Flash individually and together and made them promise on their scout's honor not to tell. Her irritation vanished as quickly as it had come, ending as a sigh. Some secrets were too big for eight- and six-year-olds to keep.

"You're pregnant!" He returned his stare to her middle with wide dazed eyes. "I thought Flash and Amy were joking, I didn't believe them. No, that's isn't true, I believed them, I just didn't ..."

Deep inside she really hadn't believed the kids could keep the evidence of a new baby secret. But she had hoped they wouldn't blurt it out until she was ready to tell John herself.

"Penny... you ... you are *pregnant*!"

"I know."

"I..." He rubbed a hand across his face. "How far along are you?"

"Beginning the eighth month." Immediately, she sensed his mind racing, thinking back to the previous March and what seemed in retrospect to be a foolish attempt at a reconciliation.

When he opened his eyes, he gave her a thin smile. "It seems we have a lot to talk about. Are you going to invite me inside? It's cold out here."

"Yes, of course." A blush of embarrassment tinted her cheeks. She wasn't thinking straight. "I'm sorry, come in."

When he stepped forward, close to her, the sudden moment of awkwardness caused Penny to frown and bite her lip. What was the etiquette in situations like this? Did they kiss as they would have less than a year ago? Did they politely embrace? Shake hands? For a moment they looked at each other, then both turned aside abruptly and cleared their throats.

Stepping backward, Penny gestured to the pegs along the entry wall and watched John hang up his coat and driving cap. She couldn't believe he was really here, in Aspen Springs. Then she gave herself a small shake and waved the candy bowl toward the stairs leading up to the living room, kitchen and bedrooms. "The other set of stairs go down to the recreation room and the kid's rooms. Mom and I have the upstairs bedrooms. Amy and Flash wanted to be downstairs. They call it their apartment."

She was babbling, stalling while she wondered what on earth they would say to each other. They would discuss her pregnancy, of course. And John's work. The upcoming divorce. She flicked a glance at him from beneath her lashes. Of course. That was why he was here. Most likely he wanted to discuss the divorce settlement. Maybe he was regretting his generosity and wanted to renegotiate.

"Nice place," he murmured automatically at the top of the stairs, after a cursory glance toward the rock fireplace and floor-to-ceiling windows. Penny was aware he hadn't looked away from her stomach for more than two seconds.

"I forgot. You haven't been to Mother's house." She hadn't forgotten, but it was a sore subject. When they were living together, she had tried several times to persuade John to visit Colorado, but somehow it had never worked out. In the early years they hadn't had the money; later, they hadn't had the time. Instead, Penny's mother visited them in Los Angeles.

After putting the bowl on the counter and self-consciously brushing imaginary crumbs from her smock, Penny lifted a hand. "The view is spectacular. I don't know if you can tell in the darkness, but the house sits on the side of a hill overlooking the valley. We can see the Blue River, and there's a breathtaking view of the back range. A month ago, when the aspens turned color, it was absolutely—"

"Penny. You and I have to talk."

He spoke from directly behind her. When Penny realized how close he was standing, she drew a sharp breath. For an instant she responded to his solid warmth, to the familiar lingering scent of his spicy after-shave. It would have been so easy simply to turn into John's arms and rest her head against the hollow of his shoulder, that special place she had once thought of as being fashioned just for her.

But she didn't, of course. A woman didn't cuddle up to a man she was divorcing. Instead, she stepped around the counter into the kitchen and managed to smile across the counter. "Coffee? It's a fresh pot."

"First the kids. I'd like to see them. Are they here?"

Penny looked at him for a long moment, thinking uncharitable thoughts. John had been very good about phoning Amy and Flash regularly, but he had not been good at actually seeing them. He had been too involved with work to take them for the summer, too busy to fly out for a weekend. If she had not taken the children to L.A. last March during spring break, he wouldn't have seen them then, either. Of course, if she hadn't taken the children to L.A. over spring break, she would not now be pregnant. Before she had realized a reconciliation was impossible things had gotten out of hand.

"Mom took the children to the Halloween carnival at school." Aside from a tremor in her fingers, the normalcy of the conversation amazed her. "They plan to do a little trick-or-treating in town afterward. I expect them home about nine o'clock."

It was seven now. They had two hours of privacy. A new thought occurred and she looked up at him. "John, did the kids know you were coming?"

"Not really. I told them I'd try to make it for Christmas. But..." He ran a hand through hair as ash blond as Amy's. "I'm sorry to keep staring, but...Penny, we're going to have a baby!"

"I've noticed." His expression was much as her own must have been the day Dr. Adler confirmed her condition. Now her smile was wry but genuine. "Believe me, a woman who is approaching her eighth month of pregnancy knows it."

"I expected this." His eyes dropped again to her rounded smock. "But seeing you makes it very, very real. How can you be so calm about it?"

"I've had time to get used to the idea." As much as that was possible. Being pregnant at this particular point in her life was one of fate's little jokes. And not very humorous.

Since her stomach got in the way of getting close to the counter, Penny approached the coffeepot sideways and poured two cups. Responding to habit, she added sugar to John's cup, milk to hers, then pushed his cup across the counter.

"It's not French Roast, and not made from freshly ground beans," she murmured, then wondered why she was apologizing. She hadn't expected John; he hadn't been invited. Even if she had expected him, she probably wouldn't have found the time to buy French Roast coffee beans, his favorite.

Beginning the conversation by getting defensive about her brand of coffee did not strike her as a good sign. Determined to keep their discussion civil, she stepped past John and entered the living room, choosing the sofa, because it was the firmest place in the room. Her mother's chairs were deep and inviting, but at Penny's stage of pregnancy soft, upholstered furniture was a trap just waiting to snare her.

She sat on one end of the sofa and John sat on the other.

"Good coffee," he said politely, taking a sip, then looking toward the fire crackling in the fireplace.

His comment indicated he was as nervous as she was. John was particular about his coffee. According to her soon-to-be ex-husband, the absolutely right way to make coffee required grinding precisely measured beans seconds before brewing. In his opinion, this method assured the richest, most flavorful taste. Once upon a time, Penny had agreed.

Now she wasn't sure if she could tell the difference between coffee from a can and coffee from freshly ground beans. Suppressing a sigh, she admitted there were a lot of things she wasn't sure of anymore.

"I don't know where to start," John said after a moment, looking at the mound where her waist used to be.

Penny glanced at the clock over the television set. If he was here to renegotiate the divorce settlement, then they had a lot of ground to cover and not much time before her mother and the children returned.

"Did you receive the latest packet from my lawyer?" she asked, opening the conversation, struggling to keep her voice carefully polite and neutral.

Suddenly she felt as if she must be dreaming. This could not be real. She and John—her John—were sitting here discussing a divorce. It was crazy. Impossible. So far everything had been handled long-distance through the attorneys or the mail. Until now she had not been forced to directly face what was happening.

Blinking at the heat behind her eyes, Penny looked at him, sitting where she had imagined him a hundred times. Finally John was here, but it was too late. In ninety days she would walk into a courtroom and a few minutes later their marriage would be dissolved. How was that possible? she thought in bewilderment. How had they arrived at this point?

"I heard from your lawyer, and I want to talk about it, but first..." Placing his elbows on his knees, John leaned forward over his coffee mug, then turned his head to look at her. "Penny, for God's sake, why didn't you tell me you were pregnant?"

His dark eyes seemed darker in the firelight, his California tan more deeply golden. He was as handsome now as the day she had met him, maybe more so, Penny thought. Dressed in a cashmere sweater and wool slacks, the firelight glowing in his golden hair, he might have stepped from an ad depicting the smart set enjoying themselves before a cheery fire on a cold Colorado night. The realization made her feel very bulky and very unfashionable. The maternity smock and slacks she wore was a set she had purchased when she was carrying Flash. That was six years and a hundred washings ago. And the outfit hadn't been particularly fashionable even then.

It occurred to Penny that she had never seen a fashionable maternity outfit. There was no such breed. Granted, there were designers who tried, who gave it their best. But the result was always the same. You ended looking like a lump wearing fashionably padded shoulders. Or a lump sporting evening sequins. Or a lump wearing beautiful material but with a peculiar hemline that hiked up in front and dipped in back. It was rather like putting a head and limbs on a basketball than draping it stylishly. It could not be done. No matter how well-intentioned, you ended as a lump wearing a tent.

And while the mother-to-be was getting lumpier by the minute, her husband remained slim and great looking. There was no justice.

"Penny?"

She pushed a hand through her hair. "Being pregnant doesn't change anything."

"The hell it doesn't." Anger darkened his eyes.

"Let me put it this way. It shouldn't change anything. At least not for you."

"I'll let that comment pass for the moment. I want to know why you didn't tell me you were pregnant. Asking the kids to do it seems small and irresponsible."

"I intended to tell you. And I asked the kids *not* to say anything." Crimson flamed on her cheeks. "But the right moment just didn't arrive." She met his eyes. "Plus, I thought you might be tempted to make some kind of heroic gesture if you knew. I thought you might decide to quit your job, and move here. You and I talked about moving to a small town with small-town values from the beginning of our marriage. But I wanted you to make the move for the right reasons. Because this was where you wanted to be. Not because you felt pressured, not because you felt you had to be here or that the decision was not your own."

"Did you—"

"Get pregnant on purpose? No. When I took the kids to L.A. during spring break, I had no idea you and I would get carried away." Crimson again flared on her cheeks. "If I had anticipated what would happen, I would have taken precautions."

"That isn't what I was going to ask." He was controlling the anger she identified in his steady gaze, but it was there. "Did you stop to think that I had a right to know? This is my baby, too. When were you planning to tell me? When the baby was a year old? Ten? Ready to start college?"

Suddenly Penny felt tired. Lately she had been trying to juggle too many balls at once, and the effort was beginning to show.

"The truth?" she asked, leaning back against the sofa cushions. "I don't know." Closing her eyes, she rested her coffee cup against her stomach, feeling the warmth through her smock. "When I first learned I was pregnant, I was stunned. I didn't want to accept it. Then I got depressed thinking how hard it was going to be: trying to make it as a divorced mother with three children, one of them an infant. I felt overwhelmed. I've been taking it one day at a time, not thinking too far into the future. I guess I would have told you about the baby after the divorce was final."

"That's big of you." When he realized what he had said, a humorless smile lifted his mouth. "But you know damned well you don't have to worry about making it on your own. If there's one thing that isn't a factor in this mess, it's money."

"Isn't it?" Penny asked quietly, then looked toward the steps as the doorbell rang. After a minute John offered to take the Halloween candy to the door, but Penny shook her head and struggled to rise from the sofa. "That will be the Galloway kids, and—"

"You want to see their costumes," John finished, his expression softening. "Remember the year before Amy was born? You and I dressed up like clowns and went trick-or-treating in our apartment building?"

"We put ice cubes in a couple of glasses and went trick-or-treating for booze."

"We were too poor to buy decent liquor, remember?"

"I remember we kept collecting people, and we were all getting giggly and having a great time. That was the night we met Betty and Fred. We ended up in their apartment with a collection of adult trick-or-treaters we'd picked up along the way."

They smiled at each other.

Then Penny cleared her throat as the doorbell rang again. "Well. Excuse me a minute." After getting the candy bowl, she descended the short flight of stairs to the foyer, opened the door and exclaimed over the Galloway kids. "Oh dear, who could this be? A pirate and Darth Vader. Pretty scary."

Susan Galloway waited at the end of the porch. When she caught Penny's attention, she lifted her head from her coat collar and tilted a nod toward the Porsche gleaming under the yard light, then raised a questioning eyebrow. Penny shook her head, indicating they would talk about it later.

She remained in the frosty doorway, watching the Galloway kids run back to the car. Susan waved, then backed out of the driveway and onto the dirt road that looped through the subdivision. The word subdivision was a misnomer, more of an optimistic forecast than an actuality. So far there were only eight homes, and four of them belonged to summer or weekend people. On long nights when Penny couldn't sleep and had the lonely feeling that she was the only person in the world, it was good to look out the window toward the Galloways' yard light and know that other people were only half a mile away. It was a measure of how much she had changed that she could consider a half-mile distance as close.

But it was a nice change. She could no longer imagine living as she had before, in a condominium with people above and below her and on both sides, packed in like upscale ants living in a luxury anthill. The solitude and quiet of country living appealed to something basic. No matter how tired she was, no matter the turmoil of the day, she had only to gaze toward the snow-capped peaks to calm her thoughts.

When she returned to the living room, John had lit candles in the jack-o'-lanterns. They grinned at her now from the kitchen counter, the hearth, the top of the low bookcase that ran along the north wall. The pungent scent of heated smoke against damp pumpkin filled the room. It was a scent Penny liked, an autumn scent, a scent that conjured memories of her own childhood.

"So," she said a little too brightly, "tell me about you." After placing the candy bowl on the counter, she returned to the sofa, lowered herself carefully onto the cushion, then shifted to smile at John. "Are you on vacation? How long will you be staying? Do you have a telephone number where the kids can reach you?"

When she had reappeared at the top of the stairs, fresh shock filled his eyes at the sight of her.

"We haven't finished talking about the baby."

"If you don't mind, let's put that subject aside for a little while. We'll come back to it." They needed some time to adjust to the idea of being together again.

Although he obviously disagreed, John made an effort to do as she asked. "Okay. One thing at a time." Dropping back on the sofa, he turned to face her. She noticed he had refilled their coffee cups. "I've taken a leave of absence until the baby is born. I guess I'm on vacation."

"Now I'm staring," Penny said. "That doesn't sound like you. Are you sure Blackman Brothers can function without you?" Immediately, she regretted her sarcasm. She wanted to handle this encounter in a civilized manner. But old wounds lay close to the surface.

"Maybe I deserve that crack," John said quietly, "but is it so hard to believe that I want to share the holidays with the kids? Also, I was present at Amy's and Flash's birth, I'd like to be present for the birth of this one."

"Look, I'm sorry." She felt a flush of discomfort. "I'm just surprised that anything could drag you away from Blackman Brothers." And not sure how she felt about having him nearby until the baby was born. A silenced opened.

Leaning forward, he propped his elbows on his knees again and looked into the fire. "The timing is perfect, actually. I built up enough vacation days to cover four months away from the office at full pay." When she winced, he managed a smile. "I know you hate reminders that I rarely took vacations." Before she could comment, he turned his gaze back to the fire. "After you and the kids left, I promised myself I'd wrap up the Claxon Cat Food takeover, then resign and follow you."

"Oh, John. You've been promising you would resign after one deal or another since Amy was born."

He nodded, still without looking at her. "You probably won't believe this, but I thought I'd go crazy after you left. I discovered I didn't just lose a wife, I lost my best friend." Now he looked at her, a glance and then away. "Anyway, to fill the time, to keep from thinking about you and the kids, I worked harder."

"I can see what's coming," Penny said with a sigh. "Working harder meant you were always in the middle of one deal or another."

"Right." He turned to look at her. "The problem is, I like what I do. At least most of the time. After all, investment banking has been pretty good to us, Penny. It's what allows us to support two households comfortably, drive new cars—"

"I think I've heard this song before," Penny commented. The bitterness had crept back. Biting her tongue, she dropped her head and moved her coffee cup in circles on top of her stomach.

She knew how addictive investment banking could be, how seductive. There was no high on earth as exhilarating as guessing right and winning. She would never forget the first time *she* had made a million dollars for a client.

From then on she had been as committed, as addicted, as John. She ate, drank, slept and breathed the market. Her conversations were liberally peppered with references to greenmail, mergers, buy-outs, hostile or friendly takeovers. Then she had gotten pregnant with Amy and her perspective had changed abruptly. A sense of balance had returned to her life. She had continued working part-time, but working was no longer the be-all and end-all.

"If only you could have agreed to three more years in L.A., investment banking would have made us wealthy."

"We're already wealthy."

"Have you forgotten the crash of October '87? No one is ever as secure as they think."

"I can't figure it out," Penny said, frowning. "You're a huge success in one of the highest-risk businesses in the world, but you won't take a risk in your personal life."

"By moving here? Come on, Penny. Where's the opportunity in Aspen Springs?"

The had been together less than an hour and already voices were rising and expressions tightening.

"Why on earth do you need opportunity? Why do you think you have to amass another million or so before you can risk making a move?" They were both getting angry. Penny felt the tension growing in her chest, could see it in John's expression.

"I simply can't grasp why you won't see the enormity of what you're asking." Leaning forward, he pushed a hand through his hair in a gesture of frustration. "You want me to abandon a successful career and all the perks that go with it, give up the security of an extremely lucrative profession, and spend the next forty years sitting on my thumbs going crazy with boredom!"

"I'm not as stupid as you make me sound!"

"Dammit, Penny, I've never said you were stupid. I said it's hard to understand why you can't see—"

"People do make changes, John. I have. I'm not sitting on my thumbs bored to death. Other people in this town have found something productive to do with themselves. The point is, the pace of life is slower and better! What I can't grasp is why you prefer an artificial high-octane life where people aren't judged by who they are inside, but by what they're wearing, eating, or driving and by the status of their job title or bank account!''

''That's how it is. Like it or not, Penny, the people who run this world don't live in small towns, no matter how terrific you think those small towns are. Taking risks has nothing to do with it. Lack of opportunity has to do with it. Living in a backwater has to do with it. Being out of the mainstream. Can't you understand that?''

''I understand this conversation is going nowhere,'' Penny said between her teeth.

''Look,'' he said after a minute. ''I didn't mean for us to say hello then start fighting. I apologize for losing my temper.'' He gave her the smile that once had melted her toes. ''Let's not push things. We'll have plenty of time to discuss all this.''

''There's nothing to discuss, isn't that obvious?'' She bit her lip and looked away from his determined smile. ''You and I are never going to agree. You want the run-run-run excitement of a big city. I want a relaxed pace and the solid value system small towns are famed for.''

Straightening against the sofa, he extended his arm along the back cushions and studied her with a curious expression. ''Is that how it's working out? Is moving to Small Town, Colorado, everything you thought it would be?''

Penny didn't respond immediately, though the question was one she had pondered frequently.

''I'm not sure,'' she admitted finally. Then her chin lifted. ''Mostly the answer is yes. But nothing is perfect. I didn't expect that. There are problems here, too.''

''Such as?''

"I'm still looking for a slower pace to allow me to spend more time with Amy and Flash, more time to pursue all the things I put off during the busy years." The words emerged slowly. "Somehow it hasn't happened yet. I'm confident it will, but it just hasn't yet. But then I'm still getting established," she added. To her surprise, she sounded defensive. "Once I feel solid in my job, I'll—"

"Your job? You're working?"

She nodded. "I'm an assistant manager at Santa's Village."

Santa's Village was not Aspen Spring's primary attraction—that was skiing—but it ranked near the top. As the name suggested, Santa's Village was a park built around a Christmas theme. There were rides in the summer, sledding and ice-skating in the winter. A small theater ran holiday movies, a dozen gift shops featured toys and ornaments and Christmas-related gifts. There was a bi-weekly newspaper that printed the letters to Santa collected in the mailboxes located around the park, and Santa's workshop, and games galore. And Santa, of course, available all year around to hear the hundreds of daily requests.

John listened in silence to the description, studying her expression as she spoke.

"Penny, why are you working? Wasn't the whole point of this move to escape the corporate grind? To spend more time with the kids? Am I sending too little money? Is that the problem?"

Fresh color rushed into her cheeks. "You've been very generous. But I don't want to be one of those women who remains solely dependent on her ex-husband." She spread her hands. "I need to feel I'm taking charge of my own life." When his expression stiffened and turned stormy, she added, "this has nothing to do with you. I worked and carried my part during our marriage. I don't want to become dead weight now that we're divorced."

"We aren't divorced yet."

"I need to start rebuilding my life, John, and a job is part of that process."

After a moment of uncomfortable silence, John leaned forward, staring at her intently. Before he spoke they both heard the front door bang open.

Alice Sage, Penny's mother, called from the entry in a cheery voice, "Does the Porsche with the California plates mean we have company?" The lack of surprise in her voice brought a frown of suspicion to Penny's brow. "Wait a minute." Now Alice was calling to the kids. "The surprise I mentioned will keep until you've hung up your coats."

Penny turned angry blue eyes toward John. "You arranged this visit with my mother!"

"I figured I'd have better luck with Alice." He grinned. "You would have said no." When her glare deepened, he spread his hands. "Will it make you feel better if I tell you I brought your dining room set in the U-Haul, and the boxes of stuff you'd left under the staircase?"

The kids reached the top of the stairs and stopped in their tracks, their mouths dropping, their eyes wide.

"Daddy!"

"It's Daddy!"

A miniature Rambo and a fairy princess flew across the living room and hurled themselves on John. His laughter was as eager and delighted as theirs as he swung Flash up on his shoulder, tucked Amy under one arm.

"Be careful with my crown, Daddy."

"We got lots of candy. Do you want to see?"

"I sure do. But first, let me say hello to Grandma."

After setting the children on their feet in a whirl of excitement, he hugged Alice and kissed her cheek. "You look wonderful." Then he lifted an eyebrow. "You didn't tell me how cold it is in Colorado."

"No comment," Alice said, smiling. "It's good to see you, John." Her cheeks were pink with cold, her blue eyes sparkled. Firelight glowed in her short white curls.

Penny scowled at her.

Mothers never stopped mothering. They always believed they knew what was best, no matter how old their children were, Penny thought. The recognition diminished her anger and wrested a sigh from her lips. Alice—she had always called her mother Alice—had joined in the secret of John's arrival because Alice hoped for a reconciliation. She had made her feelings known from the beginning. Alice encouraged Penny and the kids to remain with her and discouraged Penny from seeking a place of her own because, despite everything Penny said to the contrary, Alice insisted the separation was only temporary.

"Isn't this a nice surprise?" she said to Penny, her face bright and falsely innocent.

"It's certainly a surprise," Penny answered with a look that said, We'll discuss this later. Both she and her mother watched the kids spill their cache of candy over the kitchen counter for John's inspection.

Amy tossed a braid over her shoulder and turned pleading eyes toward Penny. "Can we eat some now, Mom? Please, please?"

"Right before bedtime? I don't know..." Penny said, teasing, knowing she would relent.

"Please, Mom?" Flash's sticky mouth and cheeks indicated he had already enjoyed a liberal sampling of the night's plunder.

"Please, Mom?" John said, smiling at her. "Halloween only comes once a year..."

"All right," Penny decided, ignoring him. "Choose three things. Then it's time for your baths and bed."

They protested.

"Can we have five pieces?"

"Can we stay up late? We want to talk to Daddy."

"Four pieces," Alice said, leaning over the kitchen counter to *ooh* and *ah* over the collected goodies.

Penny decided it was time to take charge. Pushing against the sofa cushions, she heaved herself up and moved to the counter. "Three," she said firmly, frowning at Alice. She didn't remember her mother being this indulgent when she was six or eight.

"Do I have to have a bath?" Flash asked, looking up at her with John's mischievous dark eyes. His reddish gold hair resisted taming by the Rambolike bandanna twisted over his forehead and tied in back. An unconscious smile curved Penny's lips. She didn't recall that Rambo had freckles. Or the mustache Flash had insisted she draw with her eyebrow pencil. And she suspected it would have diminished some of Rambo's macho appeal to have chocolate laced around his mouth and chin.

"Yes, you have to have a bath."

Amy grabbed her hand. "But we can stay up late, can't we, Mommy?" She gave her father a radiant smile. "Daddy's here!"

"You can see Daddy tomorrow. Maybe he'll pick you up from school..." She glanced at John for confirmation and addressed her next question to him. "Where are you staying?"

Amy looked astonished. "He's staying with us. Aren't you, Daddy?"

"Of course he is," Alice said quickly, stepping into the sudden silence.

"Mother!"

"Let's see. I'll put you in my room unless you and Penny..." She examined Penny's thunderous expression, then smiled and shrugged. "I guess not. So, you take my room, John, and I'll sleep in Amy's room."

"This is crazy," Penny protested hotly. She was being railroaded. "It's bad enough we've taken over your house and your hospitality without us putting you out of your bedroom. I won't hear of it. John? Say something."

The something she wanted him to say was that he would find a hotel room.

"Penny's right, Alice." He dropped an arm around Alice's shoulders and gave her a hug. "Thanks, but I wouldn't feel right taking your room. How about I sleep with Gordon?"

They all looked at him.

"Gordon?" Amy asked, puzzled.

"He means me," Flash said proudly. It was only in the past two months, since beginning first grade, that he had learned Gordon was his real name. After two days of agonizing indecision, he had decided to stay with Flash. Flash sounded cooler than Gordon.

"Why don't you sleep with Mommy, like always?" Amy asked. She and Flash gazed at them, bewildered by the conversation.

John flicked a look at Penny from the side of his eyes, hesitating, waiting to hear her response. Penny didn't look at him or at her mother.

"Now, Amy, you and Flash remember what we discussed. Mommy and Daddy don't live together anymore." It was more painful to say it in front of John that it had been when she'd first told the children. She drew a deep breath and made herself smile. "People who aren't married don't sleep together." Not quite true, but suitable for the discussion of the moment. Alice cleared her throat, lifted an eyebrow, but said nothing.

"But Daddy's here now," Amy insisted. "That means you're married again, doesn't it?"

Her children's hopeful expressions tugged Penny's heart and she glanced away.

Finally John spoke. "Are you trying to get rid of me? Kick me upstairs to Mommy's room?" He grinned at them. "I want to see this apartment of yours."

The excitement of having him to themselves displaced Amy's and Flash's concern about the sleeping arrangements. "You could stay in my room," Amy suggested, pulling on his hand. Immediately Flash protested and an argument erupted.

"Flash's room it is," Penny said, ending the bickering. Flash beamed; Amy's small face puckered with disappointment.

"Okay, kids. Off we go. Bath time," Alice said, herding them toward the stairs. "I'm sure Mommy and Daddy have some things to talk about." Ignoring the flood of protests, she followed them downstairs. "You'll have plenty of time to talk to Daddy. He'll be along in a few minutes."

When they had gone, John leaned on the kitchen counter and asked softly, "Angry?"

"Angry and feeling steamrolled," Penny said, her expression grim. Plus bewildered and confused. And suddenly very tired. "I can see you're right. We need to talk further." But this wasn't the moment. The kids were waiting for him, and she felt exhausted, assaulted by too many conflicting emotions. "What are you doing?" she asked after a minute, watching him spill Flash's and Amy's trick-or-treat sacks onto the counter.

"Checking the candy."

Carefully he set aside the apples and oranges, and all pieces of candy that weren't store wrapped.

Penny's eyebrow lifted, then she touched his wrist as he prepared to sweep the isolated pieces into the waste can he'd removed from under Alice's sink. "That isn't necessary."

Her comment surprised him. "Better safe than sorry. There's no way to know what might have been done to this fruit and candy. Last Halloween the papers were filled with stories about crazies putting razor blades in apples or poisoning soft candy, or injecting it with drugs."

She stared. "John, for heaven's sake. This is Aspen Springs. The people who gave the kids treats are people Alice has known all her life. People I grew up with. They aren't monsters."

"Come on, Penny. It's a nasty world out there. You can't trust anyone." He swept the candy and fruit into the trash.

Silently Penny watched him replace the waste can then push the remaining candy back into the kids' trick-or-treat bags.

"What happened to us?" she asked softly, genuinely bewildered. "We didn't used to think the world was a nasty place. Or look at life with a cynical eye. Or believe we couldn't trust anyone." The use of *we* was an effort to be polite. She didn't feel those things. To her the world was a nice place and she couldn't imagine living without trust.

"We grew up," John said, as if that explained everything. As if the world and the people in it had always been threatening and unpleasant, but they had been too young and too naive to notice.

"I don't believe that," Penny said, shaking her head.

But there was a time when she had started to. That was when she had understood she couldn't wait any longer for John to resign; when she had to leave the big city and return to her roots and a positive value system. They had always planned to leave Los Angeles when they began a family. They had promised they would raise their children in a small town, if not Aspen Springs then another much like it. It had been important to them both to raise their children in a place where people weren't afraid to walk alone or in a strange neighborhood. Where people knew their neighbors and knew they could rely on them in an emergency. Where a man's handshake was as good as a contract.

"Small towns can't be that different," John said.

"So you've said." Every time she pointed out that the children were growing and they were still in Los Angeles. "But you're wrong, John. It is different here." She met his eyes, saw he didn't believe her.

"Not different. Just smaller and slower."

Before they resumed an argument they had already had a hundred times before, she smoothed her hands over her stomach and managed a thin smile. "I'm very tired, and the shock of finding you on the doorstep... If you'll excuse me, I think I'll have a bath and turn in early."

Another awkward moment opened between them. Their eyes met and held, then Penny cleared her throat self-consciously. "When you see Alice, would you tell her I'd like a word with her?"

"Good night," he said quietly. "Penny, I—"

Before he could say more, she lifted a hand. "Good night, John." Turning, she fled toward the staircase.

Chapter Two

John stood at the kitchen counter watching Penny walk toward the stairs leading to the upstairs bedrooms. Her beauty took his breath away. As she had with Amy and Flash, she carried her pregnancy with quiet pride and a stately dignity, which she probably didn't recognize. For reasons he had never comprehended, Penny believed she was bulky and clumsy when she was pregnant. She was not.

Her skin glowed with radiant health. The golden hair, tied back in a ribbon, was rich and shining with warm red highlights. The serenity he associated with her earlier pregnancies was missing from her expression, but he attributed that to the shock of his unexpected arrival. With very little effort, he could imagine her naked. Her breasts would be full and firm, the faint bluish veins visible through her translucent skin. Her stomach would be taut and rounded and lovely, though she had never believed him when he told her so.

He unwrapped a piece of taffy and put the candy in his mouth, shifting his gaze to one of the grinning jack-o'-lanterns. The thing he most regretted was that the impending divorce was largely his fault. Penny had been more patient than he'd had any right to expect. She had waited eight years for him to honor the promise they had given to each other on their wedding night.

For a time their life together had worked out as planned. During the early years they had both worked for Blackman Brothers. They had joked about seeing each other on the run, about sleeping together but not really living together. The situation had been tolerable, because they were building toward a future in which there would be a lifetime of evenings and weekends together.

But he'd kept delaying the move to Small Town, America. Finding reasons to do it later. Amy was born, then Flash, and then John had been offered a partnership in the firm, which prompted the most serious argument of their marriage. Penny realized if he accepted the partnership, they would never leave Los Angeles. He had accused her of being unsupportive, of resenting his success. She had accused him of letting his ambition obscure his values. They had argued into the night, then she had accused him of breaking his promise. He'd had no answer for that one. The truth was he thrived on life in Los Angeles. He liked the big city, liked his job, their friends, all of it. The idea of moving no longer had appeal. He wasn't really sure it ever had.

Three months later Penny and the kids were gone.

Tilting his head, he listened to Amy and Flash laughing and shouting downstairs as they put on their pajamas, listened to the sound of Penny's bath running. God, he had missed these homey noises. Nothing was more silent than a bachelor apartment.

Standing in front of the fire, he inhaled the pleasant pungent smoke of the candles burning inside the jack-o'-lanterns, anticipated the good soapy scent of his children fresh from their baths. The faint sweet smell of Ivory and flannel pajamas and damp curls. The minty scent of toothpaste hiding candy breath. He smiled.

From where he stood, he could see into the kitchen, could see the refrigerator door plastered with crayoned portraits of witches and goblins. One of Flash's battered sneakers peeked from beneath the sofa. Amy had left her crown and wand on one of the stools beneath the counter. A stack of schoolbooks sat on top of the bookcase. These were the sights and scents of family and home. His chest constricted with the familiar pain of missing them.

During the drive to Colorado he had decided to test Penny's decision not to return to Los Angeles. He needed his family; he wanted them back. Learning about the new baby increased his determination. He didn't want his children growing up without him, didn't want to watch them mature in yearly increments.

Alice's smile appeared at the top of the stairs. "Two wild Indians are waiting for you," she announced, nodding toward the basement. "I made up the bunk bed in Flash's room. If you need extra blankets, you'll find some on the shelf in the closet."

"Bunk bed?" He groaned and rolled his eyes. "What have I let myself in for?"

"It gets worse," Alice said, returning his grin. "You get the top one." John lifted his hands in mock despair. "Young Rambo longs to sleep on top, but he's afraid of falling out."

"So am I." As he headed toward the steps, he stopped and pressed Alice's arm. "Thank's for having me, Alice. I appreciate all you've done and everything you're doing."

She kissed his cheek. "I've loved having everyone here—it hasn't been any trouble. I hope you and Penny get things worked out."

The water was shut off upstairs and he looked toward the upper staircase, and the silence that followed. It felt strange and wrong to be going downstairs when Penny was upstairs. "Well," he said, turning to the steps leading to the basement. "I'm off to the North Pole."

"The North Pole?"

"About as far away from anything soft and warm that a man can get."

Alice laughed and waved good-night. A few minutes later she rapped on Penny's bathroom door, then poked her head inside. "May I come in? John said you wanted to talk to me."

Penny sat in a tub full of bubbles, her hands laced together over her stomach. She stared straight ahead at the steamy tiles.

"Playing innocent, Alice, isn't going to work." She bit her lip. "I've been sitting here trying to think what to say to you."

"I brought a peace offering." Alice set a glass of white wine on the side of the tub, then sat on the lid of the commode and sipped from a glass of her own. "An amusing little wine," she said, parodying Penny's Los Angeles friends. Usually Penny laughed. Tonight she didn't.

"How could you?" After hesitating, Penny tasted the wine then raised blue eyes dark with anger. "How could you conspire against your own daughter? You should have told me he was coming!"

"I thought about it," Alice agreed, nodding. She looked at herself in the mirror on the other side of the tub, pushed at her tousled white curls. "But I figured you would object."

"Thanks for the wine—it's just what I needed. And damned right I would have objected."

"Now Penelope, you can't have it both ways. You can't castigate John for being too busy to see the kids, then refuse him when he misses them so much he drives twelve hundred miles to be with them."

"Of course you're right." Penny glared at her wineglass, then a huge intake of breath lifted her stomach above the bubbles. "Do you think that's what his sudden appearance means?" she asked softly. "He's missing Amy and Flash?" She didn't ask the obvious question—if John had mentioned anything about missing her.

"What did he tell you?"

"I didn't ask. What did he tell *you*? When the two of you were hatching this plot?"

Alice peered more closely at the mirror. "The steam in here is wrecking my hair." Standing, she finished her wine, then made a show of glancing at her watch. She covered an exaggerated yawn. "Do you want me to get you anything before I turn in?"

"You're avoiding an answer."

"Right." Alice laughed and patted Penny's head. "I admit I like to meddle, but only to a point. I've done my part. The rest is up to you and John."

Lifting her chin from the moat of bubbles between her throat and her stomach, Penny studied her mother. Alice Sage was a youthful fifty-six. Regular exercise kept her figure slim and attractive, and the wrinkles deepening around her mouth and eyes reflected a sunny nature and decades of smiles and easy laughter. The fashionable slacks and angora sweater subtly stated Alice's pride in her contemporary outlook. No old-fashioned attitudes for her.

"Mom...I heard it again last night."

"Uh-oh," Alice said at the door. "When you call me Mom, something serious is coming."

"Did you hear anything?"

"Hear what?"

"A car in the driveway. About two o'clock."

"Good heavens." Alice blinked. "What are you doing awake at two in the morning?"

"I woke up worrying whether I'd ordered enough star ornaments for the Holly Shop." Penny shifted in the tub. "I could swear I heard tires on the gravel. Then a scratching noise against the side of the house." She frowned. "I looked outside, but it was too dark to see anything. No moon, and there were heavy clouds."

"With any luck we'll get some snow. Jim Anderson said they'll start making snow in the ski areas if we don't get a base started by next week."

Penny raised her hands. "Alice, we are talking about people driving up to the house in the middle of the night!"

"I wouldn't worry about it, honey. You know how sound travels in the country, especially at night. I heard that Mort Cantrell is working the night shift at the Henderson Mine. Maybe you heard Mort come home. Sometimes when conditions are just right, you can hear Mort and Mildred waxing their skis." She smiled.

"You're probably right," Penny said reluctantly, as she always did when they had this conversation, then added as she always did, "But it sounds like a car in *our* driveway. And I swear something is bumping against the outside wall."

"There's a trellis on that side of the house. Maybe the wind is bumping it against the siding."

"I can't believe you haven't heard anything. This has been happening off and on since I arrived."

"Well, you know me. Out like a light the minute my head touches the pillow. Speaking of which . . ."

After Alice left, Penny continued to think about the odd sounds because she didn't want to think about John. The first time she had awakened to the sound of a car in the driveway—about a week after she and the kids arrived—it had frightened her badly. She was certain something sinister was afoot. But following the equally peculiar bumping noise on the side of the house, silence had returned and nothing further had happened. That had been the pattern since. Every few days she awoke to the sound of a car in the driveway, a bumping, then silence.

She supposed Alice was right. What she was hearing was Mort Cantrell coming home from work. The sounds no

longer frightened her—this was Aspen Springs, after all—
but they continued to puzzle her.

Putting the small mystery out of her mind, she opened the
drain, then heaved her swollen body up and out, noting the
task was becoming more difficult with each passing day.
After toweling and patting herself with baby powder because she liked the scent of it, Penny dropped a singularly
shapeless flannel nightgown over her head. For a moment
she stared at her reflection in the mirror against the back
wall of the tub.

"We call this creation Lump in Flannel," she murmured, striking a pose. "Note the gathered yoke, ladies and
gentlemen, the very gathered yoke. Once baby has arrived,
an enterprising mother can dismantle this creation and use
the flannel to make pajamas for all the children of India,
with enough material left over to upholster New York City."

Then her thoughts changed abruptly. John was downstairs with the children. A few feet away. Never before had
they been in the same house and slept apart. It didn't feel
right.

Don't think about it, she told herself.

It was hard not to. And it was a hell of a thing to encounter one's almost ex-husband looking the way she did.
Squinting her eyes, she studied herself in the mirror and
tried to remember what she had looked like when she had a
waist. Pressing her hands to the approximate site, she caught
the billowing yards of flannel and tamed them against her
sides. Squinting until her image was a blur, she tried to see
the barest suggestion of a waist. There was none. Her waist
and hips had vanished.

Was John thinking about her? Or was he reading Amy
and Flash a bedtime story?

Don't think about it. Keep the hurt at arm's length.

Since her body was hopeless, she turned her attention to her face, leaning close to the mirror over the sink and studying her skin with an unforgiving eye.

But there was nothing to forgive. Pregnancy did great things for her skin and breasts. Seen in the warm light from the heat lamp overhead, her skin looked creamy and flawless, still dewy from her bath.

As for her breasts . . . One of the really great things about pregnancy was what it did to one's breasts. Normally she was small-breasted with a small-breasted woman's secret envy of full-figured women. All through high school and college she had yearned to look down and see a crease. She had longed to walk into a lingerie department and nonchalantly say, "I'll take the D cup, please."

Now, for a brief time, she had been granted a lifelong wish and wore an adult size C cup, but no one could tell because her stomach had expanded to size Z. Her figure was lost in a slope that began beneath her throat and ended near her thighs. Right now she didn't want to even think about her thighs.

Switching off the bathroom light, she turned into her room, the one she had as a child, and climbed into bed. After Penny finished college and married John, Alice had converted Penny's room into a guestroom. The canopied four-poster had been moved to the basement and a queen-sized bed had appeared in its place.

Penny touched the empty pillow beside her. And thought of John downstairs. She closed her eyes. John had always liked her small breasts. It had taken him three years to convince her that he was telling the truth. If he was. Hollywood and Hugh Hefner had cast permanent doubt on the issue.

She thought about the U-Haul parked behind the Porsche and what a pain it must have been to pull a trailer twelve hundred miles. When she first saw it, her heart had jumped.

She had thought perhaps he was moving to Aspen Springs. Maybe with the idea of a reconciliation.

Anger and hurt constricted her chest. When *she* wanted to attempt a reconciliation, John hadn't budged an inch. If anything, he had become more entrenched, more insistent that he was being a realist and she was just kidding herself that they could build a life in a small town and find something they couldn't find in Los Angeles.

It infuriated her that he believed he was being realistic and she was not. Anyone could see how phony and superficial their life in California had been. Except John.

If he had the faintest hope that she would return there, he could forget it. She knew who the realist in the Martin family was. Enough of a realist to know a reconciliation was out of the question.

But it hurt. It hurt so much. Penny turned her face into the pillow and pressed the cool material against the tears standing in her eyes.

BECAUSE HIS INNER CLOCK was still ticking on Los Angeles time, John rose an hour earlier than anyone else. After making coffee—out of a can—he sat at the kitchen table, which was placed before floor-to-ceiling windows that extended into the living room. Entranced by the view, he watched a rising sun drape the snow-capped peaks in shades of pink and gold.

He had awakened filled with a familiar cramping anxiety, forgetting for a moment where he was and that he didn't have to rush to the office. When he remembered, he studied the narrow configuration of the bunk bed and smiled, listening to his son roll over below him. Then he thought about the rush-hour traffic he wouldn't have to fight today, about the shrill phones he wouldn't have to answer, about the lonely sterile condo he wouldn't be going home to. All this sounded unpleasant, and much of it was, but there was also the exhilaration of the city, the steel mountains to climb.

The hectic pace Penny objected to suited him well. Rush hour didn't annoy him; he'd had some of his best ideas while stalled in traffic. Ringing phones meant something was happening. Others could claim the rush and bustle of big cities created an artificial excitement, but to him the excitement was genuine.

Penny couldn't accept that he honestly valued their life in the city. To her, their entire problem centered on his ambition. Yes, he was ambitious, but he didn't see it as a crippling fault. Lacking ambition, man would still be living in caves eating dinosaur burgers.

Now, sipping his morning coffee and watching the sunlight on the mountains, listening as the house began to stir, his thoughts shot toward Blackman Brothers. Already he missed work, wondered what was happening to his accounts. It frustrated him to read yesterday's quotes in the morning paper instead of being on top of things as they occurred.

He was on vacation, he reminded himself, hoping to resolve his personal life. But he decided to phone the office later, just to keep in touch. For the moment, it surprised him to realize that looking at the mountains relaxed him. As he generally equated relaxing with slothfulness, the realization brought him immediately to his feet.

Because he knew how frantic mornings with the kids could be, he explored the kitchen, deciding to make himself useful. The pans he found were home size, not restaurant size as he preferred, but serviceable. The stove was the right height for most women, a bit awkward for a man. Penny had always laughed when he insisted their dream house would have his and her stoves and restaurant-size utensils. He wondered if she still had the file of dream-house clippings and drawings they had started to collect shortly after they were married.

Whistling, he heated a skillet, cut a chunk of country butter into it, and started bacon in another skillet while he waited for the butter to melt. Enjoying himself, he stirred up a batch of hotcakes, pouring juice for the kids, placed a bowl of eggs on the stove top ready to go the minute someone appeared.

"Good grief!" Alice exclaimed, following the scent of coffee and bacon into the kitchen.

"Scrambled or sunny-side up?"

"Plus hotcakes? You have enough food to feed the whole county." Smiling, she poured a cup of coffee. "Over easy. And thanks. This is a treat."

"You look wonderful." Alice wore a green wool skirt, a Paisley blouse and fashionable knee-high boots.

"I volunteer at the library three days a week. Keeps me busy and I get first shot at the new books. Do you need any help?"

"Nope. Everything's done."

Amy and Flash ran up the stairs and slid into their chairs. They watched their father moving about the kitchen with the kind of astonishment they might feel if they had just discovered he could step off the balcony and fly.

"I didn't know you could cook," Amy said. Her blue eyes widened as if she wasn't certain this new side of Daddy was a good thing.

"A lot of men are terrific cooks," John said, smiling. "I'm one of them."

"I want Fruit Loops," Flash announced.

"Tough," Alice told him with a grin. "Today you get eggs and/or hotcakes. Your daddy has gone to a lot of trouble to make you a great breakfast, and you are going to eat it, mister."

Flash pulled up on his knees and leaned on the back of the chair so he could watch John cooking his egg. "Grandma likes to sound mean, Daddy," he explained. "But she isn't. She just likes to sound that way."

Alice rolled her eyes. "Listen, Rambo. I'm plenty mean and don't you forget it." Both the children giggled.

"Look, Mommy," Amy shouted when Penny appeared in the kitchen. "Daddy can cook!"

"You're still pregnant," John said, staring. "I thought maybe I'd dreamed it."

Penny smiled and accepted a cup of coffee with a nod of thanks. "As a matter of fact, your daddy is a better cook than I am. His degree is in Hotel and Restaurant Management, even though he decided to be a broker instead." She gave John a quizzical look. "Now that I think of it, this is a surprise. I don't recall that you've done any cooking in years, have you?"

"I thought you did deals, Daddy."

"I do deals when I'm not on vacation." Draping a kitchen towel over his arm like a waiter, he inclined his head to Penny in a half bow. "What would the very pregnant *madame* like for breakfast? Eggs and hotcakes? One or the other?"

"Just coffee and vitamin pills." She glanced at her watch, resisting his charm. "I'm running late. Alice, can you drop the kids at school? They're going to miss the bus."

"No problem."

John frowned. "You should eat some breakfast." He cast a pointed glance at the soft gray plaid stretching over her swollen stomach. The blue stripe matched her eyes. She was every man's private vision of a mother-to-be. Radiant, healthy, fragile and lovely. Looking at her, he experienced a caveman urge to protect her.

"Eating for two is an old wives' tale. Eating right is better. Where on earth did I leave my car keys?"

Flash spilled his milk, which dripped on Amy's slacks and raised a howl of blame and protest. Alice shouted, while John dived for a roll of paper towels.

"Eating right is coffee and vitamins?" he called over his shoulder as he mopped the table, Amy's slacks, Flash's jeans.

Grinning, Penny watched the scene, overcoming an impulse to jump in and take charge. "You can't guess how many times I have imagined you coping with the morning madness." In the frenzy of mopping up and jumping out of the way, someone knocked over Amy's milk. Penny's grin widened as John tore off more paper towels and tried to catch the stream of milk flowing toward the table edge and the floor. Naturally he would fail. The first law of physics stated that milk could run faster than parents.

"Gotta go," she said, grabbing the kids long enough to plant a kiss on top of their heads. "Don't forget your homework." She wiggled her fingers at John, still grinning. Milk was streaming off the table edge, dripping onto the floor.

"Penny, wait. Will you have lunch with me?" John asked.

"I have a pretty crowded schedule," she said, hesitating. The commotion over the spilled milk magically quieted.

"We need to talk," John said.

Three heads nodded. One white, two small and gold.

"Can't argue with that," she said lightly, feeling outnumbered. Clearly she was the victim of a conspiracy. "How about twelve noon at Santa's Village? I'll meet you at Mrs. Claus's Kitchen." After glancing at her watch again, she edged toward the stairs. "Take Highway 9 through town, the entrance to the Village is about two miles further south. You can't miss it. 'Bye, everyone. See you tonight."

"Tonight?" John asked Alice when Penny had gone. Soggy paper towels littered the table and counter.

"This is the busiest time for Santa's Village, from now until Christmas," Alice explained after sending Flash and Amy off to brush their teeth. "The staff arrives at eight. The park closes at nine at night, and sometimes Penny doesn't get home until ten. Hours are supposed to be staggered, but it doesn't always work that way."

"That's an appalling schedule! Can't they see the woman is pregnant?"

"A blind man could see Penny is pregnant." Alice laughed.

A thought occurred to him as he poured a cup of coffee. The mess could wait. "What time do the kids get home from school?"

"Not to worry. I'm here when the bus arrives. It works out nicely." She saw the clock over the stove and started. "Good grief. Kids? Hurry up! We're all going to be late."

A flurry of confusion ensued. Coats and caps had to be found, Flash needed some Halloween candy for his pockets, Amy wanted to stay home with Daddy. There were goodbye kisses. The door opened and closed, then opened as Amy dashed back inside for her homework. She left, then Alice ran inside waving a rubber-banded stack of mail.

"John, would you drop these bills by the post office on your way to lunch? I'm not going to have time."

"I'd be glad to."

"Oh, dear, I feel like I'm forgetting something. Well, never mind. 'Bye. Sorry to leave you with the cleanup."

He heard Alice's car crunch across the frost-coated gravel, then he stepped outside onto the balcony and waved as the car passed below, on the road looping through the subdivision.

When he came back into the kitchen he stopped short and smiled. Penny was right when she teased him that men dirtied more dishes than women. It looked to him like every dish and pan in the house was on the stove and table. Soggy paper towels littered every surface.

Reminding himself there was no reason to hurry, he poured another cup of coffee and sat down at the table. Already he was beginning to feel slightly proprietory about Buffalo Mountain, the rounded peak framed in the window. He suspected that staring at mountains might be as conducive to thinking as being stalled in traffic.

He really should jump up and clean the kitchen, then unhitch the U-Haul and unpack Penny's table and boxes.

The thought passed through his mind, then evaporated like the wisps of cloud floating about the top of Buffalo Mountain. For the first time in years he had a morning with absolutely nothing pressing to do and hours in which to do it. A guilty feeling of laziness stole over him as he sipped his coffee and watched the clouds flirting with Buffalo Mountain.

He thought about the kids spilling their milk and the confusion of getting everyone out the door and on their way, and he laughed. It was good to be home.

HELEN SCRANSKY, Penny's secretary, was already at her desk when Penny hurried into the office. Looking up from her typewriter, Helen pointed to the hallway leading to the manager's office. "The department heads just left."

"Damn!" Running late made her crazy. She had a feeling she would be a step behind all day. "Is Lydie there?" Helen nodded and gave her a sympathetic look. After tossing her coat inside her office, Penny ran down the hallway toward Allenby's door. Waddled was more the word. Pregnant women didn't run; they did a fast waddle.

It was no secret that both she and Lydie Severin were being considered to replace Ian Allenby. Allenby's promotion to corporate headquarters would take effect after the first of the year. His replacement had not yet been named, but he had let it be known the choice was between Penny and Lydie Severin.

She knocked once then stepped inside Allenby's office and dropped into the seat beside Lydie. "Sorry to be late," she murmured. "Have I missed much?"

"Is everything all right?" Lydie asked, her warm eyes dark with concern.

"Fine. I'll tell you about it later."

The rivalry between them was more a fabrication by the staff than genuine. Lydie Severin was a good friend.

"We're discussing the inventory problems at International House," Ian Allenby said. "Only half the Swiss angels survived shipping."

"There's no problem securing credit for the broken items," Lydie added.

"Except Helga will delay filling out the forms until it does become a problem," Penny finished. Ian and Lydie nodded. "I'll talk to her again. Part of the problem may be lack of help. Helga could use another clerk, especially between now and Christmas."

They discussed personnel problems, inventory warehousing, anticipated delays from the snow-removal crews, extending the parking lot, the print runs for the Village newspaper; then Ian asked if Penny had received the new cut of *Mary Poppins* for the theater. She gave him a blank look.

"Our copy is getting scratchy. You ordered a new cut, remember?"

"Oh, Lord." She pushed a hand through her hair. "I'm sorry, Ian, I spaced it out."

"You didn't put in the order?" He straightened behind his desk and looked at her. "Will you take care of it immediately, please? Perhaps you can put a rush on it."

"Of course. I'll see what I can do to speed things along."

After the meeting Lydie followed her back to her office for a quick cup of coffee. "Tough break about the *Mary*

Poppins flick." She perched on the edge of Penny's desk. "Allenby's keeping score on screw-ups."

"Don't I know it." A teasing smile curved her lips. "But I figure I've still got an edge on you. Forgetting to hire a replacement Santa when Kurt Pausch went on vacation did you in. I mean, what's Santa's Village without Santa?"

Lydie laughed. "I'm never going to live that one down. You're right. You can forget to order a lot of movies and still not equal one missing Santa." They drank their coffee in companionable silence, listening to the Christmas carols piped through the park and into all the offices.

Penny leaned back in her chair and touched her fingertips to her forehead. "There's just the two of us here, Lydie, no one to overhear...."

"Uh-oh."

"So tell me the truth. Do you have days when you think if you hear one more version of 'Rudolph the Red-Nosed Reindeer' you're going to scream and rip the speaker off the wall?" Lydie laughed and nodded. "Or that you can't bear to look at this candy-cane wallpaper for one more second?"

All the administration offices were papered in green wallpaper with vertical red stripes. Hundreds of tiny candy canes marched down the space between the stripes. The first time Penny had seen the wallpaper, she had thought it charming, if a bit overwhelming. Recently it had begun to lean more to overwhelming and less toward charming.

"It's the bowls of ornaments that get me when I'm feeling stressed out," Lydie confided. Beribboned baskets of shiny glass ornaments decorated every desk, every table in the reception area and were scattered throughout the park. "Do you ever want to tuck one of those baskets under your arm, then run after Allenby and see if you can hit his bald spot with a glass ball?"

Penny grinned. "Right now I'd like to take after Helga. Maybe if she knew she was going to be bombed with ornaments, she'd make an effort to fill out the damned forms."

"Possible, but doubtful," Lydie said. "Helga considers paperwork the scourge of the earth. So," she said, studying Penny, "how are you feeling? Is the baby still scheduled to arrive *after* Christmas, please, God?"

"I'm feeling great, and everything's on schedule as far as I know."

"You look tired." Tilting her dark head back, Lydie smiled at the ceiling and remembered. "Let's see. Right about now it feels like you have Muhammed Ali in your tummy and he's using you as a punching bag. Am I right?" Penny laughed, nodding. "You have to go to the bathroom all the time, and I mean all the time. It feels like you have to go even when you don't have to go. You feel like you have a twenty-pound bowling ball strapped to your stomach and there is absolutely no comfortable sleeping position. Am I close?"

"Right on the money."

"You hate your clothes, hate your figure, hate your exercises, hate stuffed furniture. You haven't seen your feet in so long you couldn't say for certain if you're wearing matching shoes. You want the whole thing to be over."

"Don't I ever!"

"You run into things, drive with your arms out stiff to reach the steering wheel, try to convince yourself it's all water weight and you're going to look great five minutes after the baby's born. You wish the guy who did this to you could get pregnant so he'd appreciate what he's done."

Penny laughed, then her expression grew more serious as she told Lydie about John's appearing on her doorstep.

"No kidding? He's in town?" Interest gleamed in Lydie's dark eyes. "Does this mean a reconciliation?"

"What you're really asking is, does this mean I'm out of the race for the manager's position?"

"Well, does it?"

Penny threw up her hands. "I keep telling you I don't want the promotion."

"Right."

"Honestly, Lydie. I don't want to get sucked into the corporate game any more than I already am. This is enough," she said, tapping the brass plate that identified her as assistant manager. "Curiosity is the only reason I haven't withdrawn my name from consideration. I'd like to know if I could have gotten it. And staying in the race has nothing to do with beating you. It's strictly a personal thing."

"If I believed you I'd understand, because that's how I'd feel in your place." Lydie smiled. "Meanwhile, back to the original question. Is a reconciliation in the wind?"

Penny picked up a pencil and frowned at it. "John is here to spend the holidays with the kids, that's all there is to it."

"You're sure? I mean, it isn't the usual thing to invite a man you're divorcing as a houseguest. Would it be pushy to inquire about the sleeping arrangements?"

"Very pushy," Penny said, feeling a rush of pink tint her cheeks. "But if you have to know, he's sleeping with Flash in the basement. He's going to move to a hotel."

"If he can find one. 'Tis the season, kiddo. There isn't a room to be had." Lydie finished her coffee and stood. "Need I say that I hope your ex sweeps you off your feet and carries you away from all this?" She waved at the candy-cane wallpaper and grinned. "Ambition has made me shameless. But, in case it doesn't work that way and you're still in the running, I'd better get to work."

Penny groaned. "What do I have to say to convince you? If Allenby offered me the promotion, I'd turn it down."

"Sure. And I'm the Christmas fairy. Don't forget to order *Mary Poppins*," Lydie called as she left. Penny envied her brisk step.

She looked at her phone messages and the paperwork hiding her desk, then glanced at the wall speaker as "Rudolph the Red-Nosed Reindeer" filled her office.

A person could get to hate Christmas, she thought with a sigh. She wondered at what point overkill set in.

THE POST OFFICE was unbelievable. For an instant John wondered if the real post office was somewhere else and this one was a Chamber of Commerce project created to charm tourists.

First, it was smaller and more attractive than any post office he had ever seen. Second, there were no long lines in front of the clerk's windows. Third, everyone present seemed to know each other. He had watched this scene in a dozen movies about small towns and had never quite believed it. People greeted each other by name as they passed in and out, chatted as they opened their postal boxes. Although the weather was definitely on the cold side, two old guys sat on a bench outside the front door, talking to everyone who passed. It was Small Town, U.S.A.

"That your car, son?" one of the old guys said to John when he came outside after mailing Alice's letters. "The one with the California plates?" He pronounced it calee-forn-i-a.

Ordinarily John would have ignored an overture made by a stranger, but it occurred to him that Alice and Penny might know this man. Effecting a compromise, he didn't ignore the inquiry, but didn't fully respond. He nodded, then waited to hear the pitch. There was always a pitch; everyone wanted something. Strangers didn't instigate a conversation for no reason.

"Nice piece of machinery," the old man said. Looking away from the Porsche, he smiled at John's driving cap. John waited. "Enjoy your vacation, son. Should have some snow for you by the end of the week. Probably not enough to ski on, though." Turning, he waved to a man emerging from the post office. "Mornin' to you, Tim. How's the missus feeling? Any better?"

It was a moment before John realized that was it. When he understood he was standing like a fool still waiting for the old man to ask for a handout or push some printed material into his hands, a rush of heat warmed his cheeks. Turning on his heel, he strode to the car, unlocked it and slid inside. After watching the old man for a minute, he put the car in gear and backed out of the space.

People weren't friendly to other people for no reason. The world didn't operate that way.

After deciding he'd steer clear of the old man if he came to the post office again, he put the incident out of his mind and drove slowly through Aspen Springs.

Small was the word that came immediately to mind. But he supposed some people might consider Main Street charming in a rustic sort of way. Historic buildings mixed with new construction built to resemble the older shops. As in most resort towns, the shops featured a display of goods ranging from the definitely upscale to more modestly priced souvenirs. The restaurants looked surprisingly top row.

Aspen Springs definitely possessed a laid-back atmosphere. A man draping the street lamps with chains of holiday greenery seemed more interested in artistic effect than in speed. No one leaned on the car horn when the town's three traffic lights turned red. The noise level was so low it was nearly nonexistent.

How did people stand it here? he thought, passing the town square slowly, turning south when he reached the pond at the bottom of Main Street. What on earth did they do to get the adrenaline going? Watch the lights on the old-fashioned barber pole? Taking his time, he explored the side streets, located the courthouse and the school, drove past rows of sturdy pine- and aspen-framed houses built to look as if they dated from the Victorian period.

On the outskirts of town he found houses more like Alice's, built of wood and stone and glass, mountain chalets, rows of condominiums, many of which were positioned to enjoy a view of Aspen Lake. The dock was deserted now, the lake covered by a thin layer of ice, which would be thick enough to drive on before Christmas.

All this was snuggled in a valley that offered spectacular views. A shrewd investor could make a fortune on those condominiums, he thought, parking on the side of the lake road. John looked back at the town, feeling a sense of déjà vu. He'd seen this town in a dozen Disney movies. Too good to be true. Or maybe he was thinking of the town in *The Stepford Wives*.

As he pulled back onto the road and continued south on Highway 9, he found himself wishing for a breath of good old smog to remind himself who he was. There was nothing like a powerful dose of exhaust fumes to put a man's perspective right.

The entrance to Santa's Village was through an arch formed by two interlocking candy canes that opened to a large parking lot. After staring at the giant candy canes a moment, he drove inside, parked and locked the car. Speakers at the end of each row played ''Frosty the Snowman,'' and fluorescent sleigh tracks led to an admissions booth manned by an elf.

John paid the park fee, then entered a village that Charles Dickens would have recognized. Or maybe it was only a fantasy of the Dickens era. It didn't matter. The village appealed to a nostalgic sense of how Christmas ought to look.

Before he let the kid in him run away with his thoughts, he reminded himself why he was here. He was here to test the waters, which so far appeared as icy as the lake he had driven past. Equally as troubling, was the possibility of losing his children. But beyond that ... He glanced down the main street of Santa's Village, then walked toward Mrs. Claus's Kitchen.

Chapter Three

The morning passed quickly until Penny noticed it was eleven o'clock. Then time sagged and seemed to move forward in slow motion. Her ability to concentrate evaporated, and she found herself gazing out the window thinking about her upcoming lunch with John and dreading it. What irritated her most was recognizing the chemistry that still flashed between them. Realizing she was still drawn to him flipped her thoughts into chaos. She didn't want this emotional upheaval, especially now when the demands of her job were greatest and she was uncomfortable physically. She wished John had remained in California.

At twelve o'clock she straightened her desk, then walked to Mrs. Claus's Kitchen. While she waited for John at a table by the window, she observed the restuarant's smooth operation with a critical eye. The waiters were dressed in black slacks and red velvet jackets; the waitresses wore red velvet jumpers over crisp white blouses. The menu offered a holiday feast, or, in smaller print, conventional burgers for those who might prefer them to turkey and plum pudding. At the end of the meal each diner received a tiny gift package containing a truffle.

Mrs. Claus's Kitchen was the main restaurant on the premises. The Village also offered a cafeteria, three soda shops, a pastry shop, two candy stores, a specialty fudge shop, and a cheese-and-sausage shop. Turn-of-the-century carts positioned along cobbled lanes offered roasted chestnuts, hot chocolate, hot dogs, and hot pretzels. No one went hungry at Santa's Village.

She spotted John the moment he appeared on the platform beyond the admissions booth.

It gave her an odd feeling to watch him when he didn't know, almost as if she were spying. But she couldn't help herself.

John Martin was catch-your-breath handsome, the type of man all women looked at twice. His driving cap and tailored overcoat marked him as a tourist; a local would have been wearing jeans and a jean jacket. But he was heartachingly handsome. It was no wonder they had such great-looking kids, Penny thought with a small sigh.

And his smile. It had been a long time since she had seen him smile like that. Open and genuinely delighted. It was a smile Penny noticed hundreds of times a day, when people saw Santa's Village for the first time. But it had been a very long time since she had seen that particular smile on John's lips. As she watched, his smile faded and was replaced by a look of loss, then determination.

For a moment she felt like crying, felt the sting of sudden tears behind her eyes. The tears weren't caused by John or their situation, she told herself. She was merely experiencing one of the hormonal swings caused by pregnancy.

Knowing that the staff at Mrs. Claus's Kitchen was very aware of her presence and that they continually glanced in her direction, she blinked the tears back and self-consciously smoothed the plaid smock over her stomach. It wouldn't do to turn sloppy over lunch. Ian Allenby would hear about it even before she left the restaurant.

She swallowed and forced a smile as John was shown to her table and seated with a flourish.

"The park is wonderful!" John said, taking the chair that faced her across the table linen. His dark eyes swept the gaily decorated restaurant. "It even smells like Christmas. How do you manage that? And do I get a tour after lunch?"

"If you like." Mentally she reviewed her appointment calendar, did a quick reshuffle. Lydie had agreed to take her one o'clock appointment if the lunch stretched into overtime. "So, what have you been doing all morning?" she asked, hoping he would answer that he had booked a hotel.

He told her about exploring Aspen Springs, told her about stopping by the post office and the old man on the bench.

"That would be Wesley Pierce," Penny explained with a smile of affection. "That's his bench. I don't mean he has it staked out—it's truly his bench. He bought it and installed it."

"You're kidding? Some guy bought a park bench and set it up on government property?"

Penny nodded. "Wes Pierce is one of the men who developed Vail. During the war, he and a small group trained in this area for cold-weather operations. They fell in love with the mountains. When the war ended, each man in the group bought land here. Several years later they decided to share their discovery by developing the area for skiing." She shrugged. "The rest is history."

"That old man on the bench in front of the post office is wealthy?" John looked astonished.

Penny smiled. "About as wealthy as they come. But I doubt Wes Pierce thinks about it very often. People are important to him, and community. You could say Wes Pierce is the town crier, so to speak. If you need something, you'll get quicker results by mentioning it to Wes than if you took out a classified ad."

"The man who developed Vail is a busybody?"

"Not exactly," she said, watching him curiously. "More like an information pipeline. By this time tomorrow everyone will know who you are." When John made a face, she added, "Does that bother you?"

"Anonymity is one of the blessings of a big city."

"No one is anonymous here. There aren't many secrets in a small town." They paused to give their order to the waitress. "That can be annoying sometimes—if there's something you want to hide—but it can be a comfort, too."

"Really? Frankly, that's hard to imagine."

She shrugged. "I like knowing everyone in town knows Amy and Flash. If one of them needed help, they could go to any house in town and the owner would know who to call." Her eyes twinkled. "And I kinda like knowing that Bobby Willis is meeting Jeannie Groton out behind the Elks Club. Or that Martha James changed her will again. To me, being involved with other people is what being part of a community means."

"I wouldn't like everyone knowing my business."

"No man is an island, John. People need people."

He met her eyes. "What about us, Penny? Do we still need each other?"

He said it quietly, but the impact was the same as if he had shouted.

"I think the time for that question is long past," she answered finally, feeling a twinge of resentment that he had opened a door they had agreed to close.

"We had something good for a lot of years."

For a long moment Penny stared at him. "What are you trying to say, John?"

"I'm not really sure." He turned toward the window. "Maybe I'm taking stock. Trying to discover how things stand now that we've had some time apart."

A cramp of anger tightened Penny's stomach. It wasn't fair for John to reappear in her life now. Now, when she had finally accepted the wreckage of their dreams, had finally and painfully accepted that it was over.

"If you're asking if a reconciliation is possible—"

"I didn't say that," he said quickly.

"—the answer is no." Drawing a breath, she waited until she could speak without sounding so harsh, until she could handle the pain of what she was saying. "Last March it might have been. That's why I flew to L.A. I was missing you so much and I hoped..." The words came in a rush bringing with them the same sense of rejection she had felt then, when her hopes had come to nothing. "But now I've accepted our situation. I'm rebuilding my life, and all in all, it's okay." Maybe that was stretching the truth a little, but not by much.

"You honestly don't feel the new baby changes anything?"

"Like what?" She spread her hands. "If anything, having another child confirms my decision. Aspen Springs is where I want my children to grow up."

He nodded, moved his coffee cup in circles on the table top, then looked up at her. "The change in my life will be significant. I'll have a child I'll never know. Is that fair, Penny?"

Of course it wasn't fair. It also wasn't fair to make her feel guilty about it.

"The choice was yours as much as mine," she snapped.

She wished they weren't seated in a public restaurant. The urge to slam doors and shout was almost as overwhelming as the tension clamping her chest. She wished John had stayed in California. She didn't want this.

"I guess what I'm trying to say, what I was thinking about during the drive here, is that perhaps we should use this time before the new baby arrives as a period of reassessment. We owe our children that much. And ourselves."

"Look, I'm genuinely sorry you'll have a child you won't know as well as you might have. But you're a little late with this line of thinking, aren't you?" Bitterness crept into her tone and her gaze. She would have given the world to hear him say these things a year ago. Now it was too late.

"My thinking hasn't changed," he answered sharply. Her tone of voice had triggered a flash of anger. "I never wanted to lose my family."

"You could have stopped it."

"So could you," he said, making a deliberate effort to keep his voice level.

When the silence became uncomfortable Penny lifted a wary gaze. "This reassessment you're suggesting, what exactly do you want to reassess?"

"I think we should consider whether it's possible to set aside our personal differences for the sake of our children."

"I've never believed in people living together just for the sake of their children."

"Neither have I. But maybe it's something we should reconsider. Maybe that belief is still valid, maybe it's not. All I'm suggesting is that we reexamine our positions during the next few weeks and make absolutely certain they still apply."

"I think I've made my feelings clear." As clear as she could, considering she was riding a hormonal roller-coaster that swept her up one day, down the next. At this point she couldn't take a stand on anything with any certainty. Except this. On this issue, she knew how she felt. "And I thought I understood your feelings. Are you saying you've changed your mind about the divorce?"

The anger receded from his gaze, and he pushed his coffee cup away. "The truth? I honestly don't know. I guess the answer is yes and no." He met her eyes. "I hate the thought of having a child I won't know and who won't know me. I miss you and the kids. Sometimes missing you is so painful that . . ." He looked away from her. "I imagine it's fair to assume there are occasions when you miss me." When he paused, she nodded in reluctant agreement. "On the other hand, I know we can both build a life without each other— we're doing that now. And I imagine you're discovering as I am that there are some benefits to living alone. The bottom-line questions are, is a life apart better than a life together and is that the best thing for our children?"

"We've already made those decisions."

"Agreed. But the situation has changed." He nodded toward her stomach. "We've been given a chance to take one last hard look at what we're doing. All I'm asking is that we agree to take a second look." He smiled. "We made a lot of major decisions in a very heated emotional climate, Penny. I realize there's still a lot of anger on both sides, but we're no longer in the eye of the storm. I'm suggesting we use this period to take a calmer look, that's all. Make sure we're doing the right thing."

"Suppose we decided, for the children's sake, to try again," she said after a lengthy pause, watching his face. "Would you expect us to return to Los Angeles to live?"

Surprise lifted his eyebrows. "Of course."

A bubble of hysterical laughter formed in her chest and pressed against her rib cage. Shaking her head, she pushed her plate aside, her appetite gone.

"Penny? What's wrong?"

"Me. You. Everything." Her shoulders dropped. "For one stupid moment I thought you were saying you would consider living in Aspen Springs. I was sitting here arguing the morality of that because obviously your willingness to reconsider came about solely because of the new baby. All the time you were talking about Los Angeles."

"That's where we live. That's where my job is." He lifted a hand. "I know what you're thinking. But I grew up in

L.A. and it didn't scar me. Kids can learn a decent value system in big cities, too. Millions of them do.''

"I should have known where this conversation was leading," she said angrily. "John, we agreed. We said we would raise our children here. In a small town."

"We weren't being realistic. Time has proven we were wrong to lock into such a promise. One of the mistakes we made was not accepting each other as we are. I'm a big-city kid. Always have been, probably always will be. Additionally, if we're honest, we both knew taking jobs with Blackman Brothers meant a long term commitment. You knew you were getting a big-city banker when we married, Penny."

"I have a longer memory than you appear to." She was leaning forward, her hands clenched on the table. When she remembered people were watching, she hastily thrust her hands into her lap. "When we made the decision to get married, you were about to get your degree in Hotel and Restaurant Management. Your dream was to manage and someday own a luxury hotel with a world-class restaurant. That dream was not incompatible with raising children in a small town. Aspen Springs has half a dozen excellent hotels catering to the ski crowd with restaurants as fine as you'll find anywhere in the world!"

"Whose managers are starving to death on less than thirty thousand a year! That isn't what we wanted, Penny. We wanted a shot at the brass ring. And we got it."

"Yes, we caught the brass ring. Now it's time to cash it in and start thinking about our children and about slowing down and about the rest of our lives."

Her voice had risen and people at the next table turned to glance at them. Embarrassed, Penny gestured to the waitress to remove their plates.

When the waitress had gone, she released a long breath. "Look. Let's stop this. We've fought this battle a thousand times. Neither of us can win. It's hopeless. All we're doing is making each other furious.''

John was as visibly upset as she was. When he reached for his coffee, his fingers were shaking. Seeing the tremble surprised her, for it was so unlike him.

Then her shoulders stiffened. No, she was not wrong to insist on her point of view. It was as valid as his.

''All I'm asking is that we take a second look at everything,'' he said finally, struggling to keep his voice level. ''That's all.''

''Too many things have been said, John. There've been too many hurts, too many heartaches.''

''On both sides. And maybe neither of us can forgive and forget. That's something else to consider. For Flash and Amy's sake I'm willing to make that effort. Are you?''

Blinking rapidly, wishing she were anywhere but here, she looked at her wristwatch. ''Good heavens, I didn't realize what time it was. I'll have to ask for a rain check on that tour. I have an appointment and I'm already late.'' Pushing to her feet, she fumbled for her purse, found it hanging from her shoulder.

Standing when she did, John stepped close to her and touched her cheek, brushing his thumb gently across the dampness beneath her eye. Penny stifled a gasp. His touch was electrifying, explosive with memory.

''All I'm suggesting is that we consider the future with an open mind. We have too much shared history to throw it away without taking a hard second look.''

They had discussed second chances last March; it hadn't gotten them anywhere then and it wouldn't now. She lifted an expression that mixed resentment and anger. ''Do you really think anything is going to change?''

He shrugged. His face was carefully expressionless. ''I just want both of us to be very sure.''

''Why does it always have to be on your terms?''

"If you're referring to location, there's no investment bank or brokerage house in Aspen Springs."

There was no rebuttal to that one. Penny clamped her lips together. Outside the restaurant, she glanced down the Main Street of the Village, automatically checking the traffic flow, then feeling the bite of the frosty air, wrapped her arms around her upper body.

Looking up, John extended his hand, palm upwards with a blink of exaggerated surprise. "Good Lord, what's this?"

One of the things she had loved about him was his ability to ease a tense situation. Penny smiled and felt the tightness ease in her shoulders. "Around here, stranger, we call that snow."

"So, this is what it looks like." He grinned down at her.

"Not much of that stuff in California. But here, we get about twelve to twenty feet of it every winter."

A mock shudder convulsed his body. "A horrible place to live. You have to agree even Eskimos have it better," he said with a wink.

"Afraid not," she answered lightly. "If you were a skier, you'd think Aspen Springs was heaven."

"Maybe I'll take some lessons while I'm here."

They looked at each other and an awkward moment opened. In the past they had always made a point of ending arguments with an embrace. It was their way of offering comfort and saying all was forgiven. Penny moved backward a step and rubbed her arms vigorously.

"It's getting cold."

"I've heard that happens when it snows," he said, still smiling.

"John...I really have to insist that you find a hotel." The words emerged in a blurted rush. "It would be easier on all of us."

"I don't agree," he said after a minute. "I have a lot of time to make up with Amy and Flash." His gaze reminded her there might not be another chance. "And I'd rather not disrupt their usual routine to do it. Unless the situation is absolutely intolerable, I'd like to accept Alice's invitation and stay at the house."

"It isn't absolutely intolerable," she admitted finally, wondering if that was really true. One thing was certain, she resented him for dismissing her feelings in favor of his own. It wasn't her fault he had been too busy to take the kids over the summer, hadn't spent as much time with them as he wanted. "I'm not convinced that having you stay with us is the best thing for the kids." When she saw she had hurt him, she touched his sleeve briefly, the gesture instinctive. "I'm sorry, but this is going to make it very tough on Amy and Flash. You can see that, can't you? Think how hard it will be on them to say goodbye again. We're sending them mixed signals."

"I hear what you're saying, and I regret any confusion this arrangement might cause. But would pushing and pulling the kids between their home and a hotel be better for them? Part of their things would be at my hotel. Their friends and part of their things would be at your house. You and I would be placed in a position of competing for the kids' time and attention..."

Everyone involved would hate it, Penny conceded with a frown. "Staying with us places complex pressures on a situation that's already complicated."

"I'm willing to do whatever you think is best, Penny. You decide."

"Dammit." Chewing her lip, she wrapped her arms around herself again, hating this, and looked down the Village's Main Street. He was right, of course. The kids' lives would be less disrupted if he remained at Alice's. It would be easier, more convenient, for everyone except her. "All right," she said finally, unhappily. "You can stay."

"Thank you."

He leaned forward as if to kiss her cheek and she hastily stepped backward and raised a hand. "Don't," she said quietly. "Please, John. If we're going to live in the same house for the next few weeks, we need some rules. The first one is...don't push. I'm not part of the deal, okay?" The snow was falling thicker now. She brushed at her shoulders, shook the flakes from her hair.

"Sorry, some habits are hard to break," he apologized. His dark eyes centered on her mouth and a shiver that had nothing to do with the cold trembled through her body.

"Please don't let it happen again."

He raised both hands and smiled. "Not a chance, ma'am. You could beg me to kiss you and I wouldn't do it. Me? Kiss my wife? No way. Not if you dragged me out of the North Pole and threw yourself on me."

"The North Pole?"

"A euphemism for a bunk bed in the basement."

She smiled in spite of herself. "The North Pole, huh?"

"Just out of curiosity, how long should I not kiss you? Is there a time limit on this? Suppose I run into you in a shopping mall ten years from now. You say, 'Well hello, John Martin, isn't it?' and I say 'If it isn't ole what's-her-name,' do we exchange a polite kiss then? Or how about this—we come out of the divorce court, smile and given each other a peck to show we're civilized people handling our troubles in a mature manner. Is that allowed? Suppose we run into each other some New Year's Eve, do we hide in the host's basement at the midnight hour or do we exchange a kiss for old time's sake?"

Penny smiled. "Let's agree to cross those bridges when we come to them." She tilted her head. "You're pushing and you agreed not to."

"Is cheek kissing allowed?" he continued, grinning.

"No."

"Shaking hands?"

"No."

"I'm merely trying to locate the perimeters. How about waving?"

She laughed and threw up her hands. "This is crazy. John, we're in the middle of a divorce. The court date is set. It's what we both want." Then her gaze dropped to his lips and she felt her mouth go dry. It had been a very long time—since March, to be exact—since she had been kissed. And John Gordon Martin was a world-class kisser.

"I know. I'm sorry things worked out as they did," he said softly, looking down at her.

"I am, too." Snow drifted between them, falling softly on his cap and on the top of her stomach.

"Well." He cleared his throat. "You need to get inside. It's cold out here."

"Yes." She moved backward a step. "I . . . I'll see you tonight."

The words rang in her head the rest of the day. The next weeks were going to be the longest in her life.

"And it's your fault, Whosit," she murmured, pushing back from her desk to place her hand on her rounded stomach. She suspected this child was going to be a handful. He or she was already causing complications she wouldn't have believed.

PENNY PLACED her cafeteria tray on the table, then sat down across from Lydie. "Why are we both scheduled to work late tonight? I thought the whole point of having two assistant managers was to stagger the workload and the closing schedules."

"It's your night to close. But I don't want to talk about work. I suggested coffee and pie for the sole brazen purpose of learning every gossipy detail about your lunch with John. He is one gorgeous guy, by the way."

Penny looked up. "You saw him?"

"Everyone in the Village saw him. A straw poll says you're an idiot to divorce that guy. He's great looking, has a smile to swoon for, drives a Porsche and he looks at you like he's crazy about you."

"That's ridiculous! We agreed to keep our behavior as amiable as possible for the sake of the children. Believe me, Lydie, John is as much in favor of the divorce as I am. You're mistaking civility for something more."

"If you say so. Remind me why you're divorcing this guy, will you? And it better be something worse than leaving whiskers in the sink."

Penny laughed. "John's a workaholic."

"A good provider."

"The best. Except the work he's addicted to is in L.A. He's a big-city boy and I'm a small-town girl. Plus, he'd be a workaholic no matter where he lived. I'd rather have a husband in the house instead of all the latest appliances. There's a downside to living with a good provider."

"If I had a choice between my ex-husband and a microwave, I'd take the microwave any day."

"Then you don't regret the divorce?" Penny asked curiously.

Lydie frowned, pushed the whipped cream off her pie. "I suppose there are always regrets when a marriage crumbles. How about you?"

Not really hungry, Penny pushed her pie aside and looked up at the ceiling. "I hate the feeling of failure. And guilt. My father died when I was eleven. I know a little about growing up without a father, and I can't bear to think about Amy and Flash and little Whosit not having a father." She lifted her gaze. "The problem is, they didn't really have a father when John and I were married. We didn't have time to do the family things. So which is worse? Not having a father and no father expectations? Or having a father who continually disappoints you by not having time to be there?''

"Look, Penny, you haven't asked my advice..."

"But you're going to give it anyway, right?"

Lydie grinned. "Right." Her smile faded while she thought about what she wanted to say. "What the kids think is important. So are their expectations, I'm not saying it isn't."

"But?"

"But the foundation of any marriage is the wife and husband, not the kids. You can't beat yourself with guilt about the kids if you and John can't be happy together. Kids are resilient—they'll cope. We adults are less resilient. You can't live your life based on what you might think is best for your children. Even that one," she said, nodding to Penny's stomach. "You have to marry or divorce based on your own feelings and expectations."

"I've always thought that, but lately..." The lunch with John had made a greater impact than she had realized. Frowning, she thought out loud. "Actually marriage is a family affair. Amy and Flash have a stake in this decision, too."

"If that's how you feel, then you're in for some tough times ahead." When Penny lifted an eyebrow, Lydie spread her hands. "Think about it. If you really see marriage as a family affair, then every family event that comes along when you're divorced is going to be agonizing. Because part of that equation is missing."

"Like the holidays," Penny said slowly.

"Kiddo, you haven't suffered until you've spent your first Christmas alone," Lydie commented grimly.

Penny raised her head and looked around the cafeteria at the beribboned wreaths, the strings of bright ornaments, the gaily wrapped packages under the cafeteria's Christmas tree. She frowned.

"Trust me," Lydie said, pushing away her plate and reaching for her coffee. "Christmas is for kids. And what they want most is a complete family. If you see a family as incomplete without a man to carve the turkey, you're in for a rough time of it."

Oddly, she hadn't thought about this year's upcoming holidays. She was surrounded by Christmas every day, but she hadn't let herself think about spending a real Christmas without John. Or about Christmas future.

JOHN PICKED UP THE KIDS from school, the first time he had ever done so. When the final bell sounded and a stream of children poured out the school doors, he watched them with a critical eye. In short order, he decided his were definitely the best-looking kids in the Aspen Springs school system. Glancing at the other parents waiting in the line of cars, he felt sorry for them, having to make do with ordinary children, hoped they didn't envy him too much when the best of the bunch jumped in his car and gave him excited kisses.

"It's snowing, Daddy!"

"Then it's probably too cold for ice cream, right?"

They grinned and assured him it was never too cold for ice cream. Since he happened to agree, they drove to Ye Olde Ice Cream Shoppe and spent fifteen minutes picking out flavors for double dippers, then they sat in front of the steamy windows and licked their cones, each claiming their flavors were the best.

He needn't have worried what they would talk about. Amy told him about her best friend, Diedre, and Flash showed him a page of large-figured arithmetic. They argued about who had the best teacher. Everyone, including him, dripped ice cream on their clothes and didn't care. Amy said she wanted to be a famous ice skater when she grew up. Flash said that was dumb; he wanted to cook eggs and hotcakes when he grew up.

"Like you, Daddy," he said, wiping at a chocolate mustache. "I want to be just like you."

John's heart lurched and melted, and he had to look away. "Got something in my eye," he muttered gruffly and reached for a napkin.

"Now who's being dumb," Amy said indignantly. "Daddy doesn't cook eggs and hotcakes for a living. He does deals." Her small brow furrowed and she tossed a braid over her shoulder. "Don't you, Daddy?"

"Then I want to do deals," Flash announced.

"You'd be good at it," John said. Leaning forward, he dabbed Flash's mouth with a fresh napkin. Some of the chocolate came away, but most of it looked like it was there to stay. He wondered if women knew some trick that he didn't. "Right now I'm on vacation."

"I know what you can do. You can stay home and take care of us and Mommy and Grandma Alice." Having disposed of his vacation time, Amy applied herself to licking the drips from her fingers.

"I'll think on that while I get a cup of coffee," he said, finishing his cone. While he was at the counter, he remembered to ask where he could buy coffee beans.

"You could try City Market," the man behind the counter said, pouring John's coffee. "I think they carry coffee beans."

"That's the only place?"

"As far as I know."

He would have expected a specialty shop in a resort town. Most groceries carried a limited selection and the beans weren't always fresh. Someone was missing a great business opportunity by not recognizing a market.

The kids looked up at him when he returned to their table, then looked at each other.

"Okay. What's going on with you two?" he asked, smiling.

"Do you still love Mommy?" Amy asked, speaking for them both. They clutched their ice-cream cones and looked at him, waiting.

Oh boy. How did he answer that one? "Love changes sometimes," he answered. "People change."

"But do you love Mommy?" Flash asked.

"Does that mean you stopped loving us, too?" Amy whispered.

Oh, my God! "No, no, honey, I'll always love you and Flash. Always!" The crucial thing was to reassure them. He drew a quick breath. "And I'll always love Mommy. It's just a different kind of love now."

"If you love us, why didn't you come with us to Colorado?"

He should have anticipated these questions, but he hadn't. "It's a long story..." They waited. "Well, the place where I do deals is in California—"

"Are you and Mommy going to get a divorce?" Flash asked.

"Diedre's mommy and daddy are divorced and she says it's okay. Sorta. Except her mommy and her stepmommy fight on the telephone and she misses her real daddy. Her stepdaddy is okay, but she says her real daddy is better. Her real daddy gives her lots of stuff, but most of it is for little kids, so she only pretends to really like it. She spends two weeks in the summer with her real daddy and her stepmommy and a week after Christmas." Amy's eyes were very round, very blue and very brave. "We don't want you to divorce us, Daddy, but if you do we want to know if we can spend the whole summer with you instead of just two weeks."

"Oh, God," John whispered.

"How many steps will we have?" Flash asked, pulling his knees up under him on the chair.

"Steps?"

"He means stepdaddys and stepmommys and step-Alice's and stepbrothers and stepsisters. Diedre even has a stepaunt."

"Look," John said, swallowing. His chest and throat were tight. Their faces devastated him. "It appears that Mommy and I will get a divorce." They looked at him with big eyes. "I'm sure she told you."

"Yeah."

"Yeah."

"It's important you understand that both Mommy and I love you. The divorce has nothing to do with you." But it would have an enormous impact on them. Guilt and regret clamped his teeth together. "Mommy and I both love you very much. We both wish we could all stay together. But sometimes mommys and daddys just can't live together anymore."

"Like Diedre's mommy and daddy."

He nodded, hating this. "Mommy and I have some problems we don't seem able to work out."

"Did we make you mad, Daddy?" Flash asked, licking at his cone, trying to present a six-year-old's version of cool and casual. He looked at his lap. "We don't want you to divorce us."

Us. There it was again. For a moment John closed his eyes against the pain. Penny had been coping with this from the beginning. How had she endured it? Each word was like a dagger to the heart.

"No, honey. You and Amy didn't do anything wrong," A thousand-pound weight pressed against his chest. "This is strictly a problem between Mommy and me. It's terribly important you understand the divorce is not your fault. It has nothing to do with you."

For the first time he noticed an older woman sitting at the next table, facing him. A flush of discomfort darkened his cheeks as he realized she had overheard the conversation.

When she stood up to leave, she smiled at him. "You're Alice Sage's son-in-law, aren't you?"

"Yes," he said, standing.

"I'm Winnie Greene. Greene's Antiques, just up Main Street." She pressed his sleeve. "Take my advice, John."

He blinked. She knew his name.

"This divorce is a big mistake. Forget about it and concentrate on winning Penny back."

"I beg your pardon?"

"You should romance her. Pregnant women need romance, too. Some candy and flowers wouldn't hurt. Right?" she asked the children. "Flash Martin, look at your face." She bent over Flash, and when she straightened, the chocolate mustache had disappeared. "Romance." She leaned near his ear. "You should bend a little. You've made a killing in the market, so you can afford to retire from that hotshot job and start over here. Stop being so stubborn."

His mouth dropped and he stared after her as she stepped through the door into the swirling snow.

ALICE LAUGHED when he told her about it. "That's Winnie for you. The woman doesn't have a shy bone in her body."

"Alice, you're missing the point. This Winnie Whoever—"

"Greene. Greene's Antiques. It's at the end of—"

"Main Street. Yes, I know. The point is, she knew our private business." Anger flashed in his eyes.

"Now, John." Alice sat forward on the sofa and patted his hand. "Winnie has known Penny all her life. She means well."

"Does everyone in Aspen Springs know about Penny and me?" Taking Alice's wineglass, he carried it into the kitchen and poured refills for them both. For the hundredth time he checked the wall clock, starting to worry.

"Probably," Alice admitted. "There may be a couple of tourists who haven't heard yet," she said smiling.

He stopped at the windows and peered into the darkness, trying to see past the falling snow. "What time—"

"She'll be here any minute. Stop worrying. Penny grew up driving on snowy roads. She's a careful driver."

The drank their wine in front of the fire, listening as the wind picked up.

"Alice, how often does Penny get home after the kids are asleep?"

"More often than she would like," Alice said lightly. "She's trying to carve a niche for herself. Things should ease up for her after the first of the year. At least, that's the plan."

"You're not convinced."

Alice hesitated. "Frankly, I'm worried about Penny. Leaving you has been very hard on her. I know what she's doing, of course. I did the same thing after Marshall died. She's keeping herself too busy to grieve, too busy to hurt. If she works until she's exhausted, then she'll sleep at night. She won't have to think about being alone or being lonely. She thinks she's working this hard to provide for the future, but . . . I think what she's really doing is running away from the present."

Knots formed in his jawline. "The present isn't too pleasant right now."

"John, I don't mean to meddle, but is there any way you two can work things out? If I ever saw two people who were made for each other . . ."

"I don't know." He frowned, thinking about his conversation with Amy and Flash. "You happen to have a very stubborn daughter."

Alice looked at him with affection. "And a stubborn son-in-law," she added mildly.

They heard a car in the driveway and John's face relaxed. He glanced at his watch. "A pregnant woman shouldn't be out on icy roads at this time of night."

A blast of snow and frosty air filled the entryway, then Penny appeared at the top of the stairs. Snow dusted her cap and the fur collar turned up around her face. Below the fur she resembled a wool ball.

She looked at them, at the wineglasses and the crackling fire, then burst into tears.

Alice took her coat and cap, John led her to the sofa before the fire, then knelt in front of her and rubbed her hands.

"Penny, honey, what's wrong? Are you all right? Are you hurt?"

"Don't 'honey' me!" The tears kept rolling down her cheeks, infuriating her.

"Sorry, it just slipped out."

She dashed at the idiotic tears with an angry motion. "I'm not crying."

"You are crying," Alice said, leaning down to stare at her.

"No, I'm not!" She was behaving like a pregnant woman, whose hormones were out of whack and running emotionally amuck. Which was exactly what was happening.

"Can I get you something?" John asked anxiously. He lifted a hand as if to smooth back her hair.

She slapped at his fingers. "No. I'm fine. It's just . . ."

Raising her hands, she pressed the heels of her palms against her eyelids, deeply embarrassed. "It took forever to close tonight, and then when I got out to the parking lot I discovered I had a flat tire. I couldn't find anybody to help, then I finally did, but . . . and all the time I wanted some lemon custard ice cream in the worst way."

"You craved lemon custard ice cream when you were pregnant with Amy." Standing, John started for the door. "I'll get you some."

"You can't. Ye Old Ice Creame Shoppe is closed. I drove by on the way home."

"Then I'll drive to Vail or Denver and get some."

"John, that's crazy. It's seventy miles to Denver. One way."

Alice stood. "We don't have a problem here. I have some lemon custard in the freezer."

"I don't want it now," Penny said, knowing how contrary she sounded and hating it. Alice sighed and sat back down. "It's snowing and I had to drive slowly, and I knew the kids were already asleep and the baby is kicking up a storm and I'm exhausted and I missed the turnoff and . . ."

And then she had hauled herself up the stairs and found Alice and John drinking wine and chatting before the fire, and they looked so comfortable and relaxed while she was feeling bulky and exhausted. She had taken one look at them and she had fallen apart.

"Honey . . . Penny. You don't need this job. Any job that makes you this upset and keeps you out this—"

"It's not the job, dammit!" Pushing her hands against the sofa cushions, she tried to thrust herself up. "It was just a bad day, okay?" The sofa cushion had turned vicious. Having gotten a grip on her, it refused to let go. She leaned over her stomach and tried to rock forward. "I forgot to order *Mary Poppins* again. And, in case you haven't noticed, I am very, very pregnant!"

The rocking wasn't working, and she was digging herself deeper into the sofa cushion. She could feel the soft upholstery closing over her like the arms of a woolen trap. Planting her feet beneath her, she slid forward, hoping to balance the bulk of her weight over her feet.

"Of course you're pregnant," said John. "And there's going to be emotional swings—"

"Don't be condescending!" Sliding forward had been a big, big mistake. Her feet slipped out from under her and now most of her weight was perched precariously on the outer edge of the sofa cushion. Seeking balance, she tilted backward. Too far backward. Her head slid down the back cushion. It occurred to her that she must look like a plaid whale wallowing helplessly on an upholstered beach. "And don't blame everything on my being pregnant. You used to do that and it made me crazy!"

Her head slipped further. Now she was talking to the ceiling. Frantically, she tried to find something firm to push against, but the evil sofa cushion swallowed her fists as easily as it had swallowed her body. Her stomach began a forward roll heading toward the sofa edge. Her hair pulled up along the back cushion as her head slipped down.

In an effort to halt the forward slide, she spread her legs and pushed her heels into the carpet. God only knew what she looked like, spraddle-legged, talking to the ceiling while her skirt slid up toward her thighs and she slid off the sofa.

"I hate this," she said to the overhead beams.

John reached for her, then changed his mind, afraid she would get upset if he touched her.

Her knees were doing the splits. She tried harder to dig her heels into the carpet in a last attempt to save herself. In her mind she pictured a plaid ball going over the side of a Herculean cliff.

"I really hate this." She sighed at her helplessness, felt like the world's biggest, bulkiest, clumsiest fool. "Are you going to help me or just let me fall on the floor?" she said, glaring, giving up.

John caught her under the arms a split second before she plopped onto the floor, then lifted her back onto the sofa. Immediately she felt the cushion grab her again.

"Up," she said between her teeth. "Clear up." Her voice was shrill. Once John set her on her feet, she straightened her skirt then lifted cheeks flaming with embarrassment and mustered what dignity she could before she waddled toward the stairs leading to her bedroom.

When she turned at the staircase, Alice and John were staring.

"I know what you're thinking. You're thinking the job is getting to me. You're thinking I'm working too hard and too long. Well you're wrong. It's not the job." After mounting the short staircase, she turned around and went back down. "And it's not because I'm pregnant, either!"

"Then what is it, dear?" Alice asked.

"It's just..." Appalled, she realized she was going to cry again. "I'm just upset. All right? Everyone has a bad day occasionally."

But she didn't usually cry about it. Welcome to the world of pregnant women. Last week she had wept over a TV toilet-tissue commercial.

"Listen," she said to them, her voice spiraling upward. "If you had an ex-husband who was sleeping in your basement, you'd cry, too! Whoever heard of such a thing?" Having delivered what was clearly an exit line, she tossed her head and did a fast waddle up the stairs to her bedroom.

John and Alice looked at each other.

"Did any of that make sense?" Alice asked after a moment.

"I'm not sure. Did she mean she's crying because I'm sleeping in the basement instead of with her? Or did she mean she's crying because I'm here in the first place?"

"I have no idea."

"Maybe I should talk to her."

"It's up to you of course, but..."

"Bad idea?"

Alice nodded. They heard doors slamming upstairs. Half an hour later Penny came back down the stairs. This time she was wearing a voluminous orange robe and she had cold cream on her face. Her hair was piled on top of her head.

She stopped at the bottom of the stairs, her expression furious. "Okay, John, you've got me feeling guilty as hell about the kids. I don't think it will change a damned thing, but I agree to your stupid reassessment!"

John rose to his feet. "I appreciate that."

"Just don't push, okay?" She glared at him.

"I won't. I promise."

"And don't be charming!"

"Whatever you want. No charm."

"Don't patronize me!" She placed her fists where her waist used to be and scowled. "I have to know this. Are you just being amiable like we agreed, or do you still feel something toward me?"

"Of course I still care about you. You're the mother of my children. We were married—happily, I thought—for a lot of years. Maybe I don't love you like—"

"If you laugh, John Martin, I'll never forgive you!"

"I swear, I'm not laughing," he said. But his voice sounded peculiar.

She narrowed her eyes. "You have that funny look like you're trying not to laugh!"

"Maybe it's the cold cream, but you look—" Hastily he spread his hands. "I'm not laughing."

"Okay. That's all I wanted to say." Turning, she took hold of the banister, then glared back over her shoulder.

"Honestly, I'm not laughing."

"This reassessment is a waste of time, it's too late. You have to understand that."

"I'm sure you're right. I just think we should be very certain about what we're doing."

She looked at him. Her face was shiny with cold cream; the orange robe fell around her like the folds of a parachute. She looked vulnerable and adorable. And she would have flown into a fury if he had said so.

"Okay, as long as you understand how it is. We care about each other, but we don't love each other. If it wasn't for our children we would be one hundred percent sure of the divorce. Before we go our separate ways, we're going to take one last hard look."

"That's how I see it."

"All right. Good night."

When he heard her bedroom door slam, he returned to the sofa and grinned at Alice. "No doubt about it...the woman's crazy about me."

Alice laughed then clapped a hand over her mouth and shot a look toward the staircase. "You're both crazy."

Chapter Four

Each morning, John ticked items off the list from the day before and compiled a list for the current day. Since the list of things he actually had to do was shockingly brief he added such things as: fix breakfast—a task he had relegated to himself—phone office, go to the post office—there was no mail delivery in Alice's subdivision—read trade journals, pick kids up from school, check closing market quotes, stop by grocery if needed.

Dull stuff, he thought, as he drove to the post office one afternoon to mail his comments on Emil Blackman's client report. Not that Emil had solicited his comments, he thought sourly. Out of sight, out of mind had never been truer. Every time he phoned in, his office pretended to have forgotten his name, made a joke out of reminding him that he was on vacation.

He mailed his comments, then paused before the bulletin board mounted near the post office door. The Optimist Club announced it would host a pancake supper on Saturday night to benefit the Syshell family whose home had burned. Miss Applesham's subject for the Wednesday Garden Club was edible mountain plants. The Sax Act, a rock and roll group, was opening at the Holiday Lounge. Mike at Peak Five offered free Labrador puppies to anyone who would give them a good home.

Surprising himself, he wondered idly who was organizing the pancake supper, not that he would have recognized anyone's name. Organizing a pancake supper sounded kind of fun, figuring the ingredients, stirring up vats of batter. It reminded him of college.

"Good Lord," he muttered when he realized what he was thinking. Talk about small-town boredom. To the best of his memory, he had never attended a pancake supper in his life, let alone organized one. Yet for a minute there...

"How do, John," Wes Pierce called when he stepped outside. "Have yourself a seat. The show's about to start."

"What show?" It was absurd to feel flattered that this old man had invited him to share a bench. But Penny insisted Wes Pierce didn't invite just anybody to sit on his bench. Thrusting his hands into his pockets, he hesitated, wondering what had prompted the invitation.

"Jim Anderson hired that Ute Indian fella to do a snow dance."

"You're kidding!"

Sure enough, when he turned in the direction of Wes's nod, John saw a man in full feathered regalia sitting cross-legged in the center of the town square. Despite the frigid temperature, he was bare chested. For all the notice he took of the cold he might have been sitting in the heart of Los Angeles. He wore a feathered headdress, doeskin britches, and moccasins. At the moment, he appeared to be in a trance, sitting before a long feathered pipe resting in a pipe stand.

After conceding he didn't have anything pressing to do, John decided he could spare a minute or two. He sat beside Wes Pierce on the bench and pushed his driving cap back on his hair.

"Do you people really think that guy can make snow?"

Wes Pierce shifted to look at him. "Who knows? Can you say for sure that he can't?" When John smiled and shrugged, Wes turned back to the Indian. "God knows we need something. The ski areas have already delayed opening twice. What little snow we're getting isn't sticking and the machine-made snow just isn't the same as the real thing."

As they watched, the Indian reverently lifted the pipe from the stand and raised it toward the cold blue sky. After pushing himself to his feet, he offered the pipe to the four directions. No one in the crowd understood what this meant, but everyone murmured approval. A round of applause erupted when he returned the pipe to its stand and picked up a drum. Beating his palm against the drum in a slow commanding cadence, the Indian dipped his feathered headdress and began to sing and dance in a circle, which narrowed into a series of intricate patterns too complex to follow.

"He's loud," Wes Pierce noted with approval. "You got to be loud or it isn't any good." With the snow dance satisfactorily under way, he turned his full attention to John. "Now then, son. How's the romance coming? You making any progress?"

John couldn't believe it. This noisy old man wanted details of his personal life. Anger stiffened his response. "I'd say that isn't any of your business."

"Not good, huh?" Wes shook his head and made a clucking noise. "Too bad. First thing you have to do, you have to get yourself out of the basement." He raised a hand to stop John's outburst. "I know, I know. Penny's mighty pregnant. But that doesn't mean you can't cuddle. Women like to cuddle. You aren't going to get anywhere with this romance while you're still in the basement, take my word for it. Now if you ask me—"

John stood abruptly. "I'm not asking you, Mr. Pierce. I don't appreciate this kind of interference. Not from you, not from anyone."

"Prickly fella, aren't you?" Wes Pierce narrowed his eyes and pushed back his baseball cap to look up at John.

"No offense, but when I want your advice, I'll ask for it. Okay?"

"Sounds to me like you could use a bit of advice, son. How long you been here? Two weeks? And you're still sleeping in a bunk bed? That doesn't sound like much progress to me. It's time to get on with it."

Exasperated, John stepped away, feeling the indignation tensing his shoulders. "Look, Wes. Let's make a deal. You don't help me. I won't help you. Agreed? We'll both live and let live."

"Stubborn and prideful. Just like a city boy." Shaking his head, Wes looked at the ground before he lifted his head. "Son, I'd say there wasn't much hope for you except I noticed this time you didn't lock your car when you went inside. I guess that's progress of a sort."

"What?" Horrified, he spun to look at his Porsche. As far as he could tell no one had broken into it.

Wes smiled at his expression. "It's not likely someone is going to steal it during the five minutes you're inside, and with me sitting here watching." Removing his baseball cap, he ran his fingers through a thatch of iron-gray hair. "This isn't by way of helping out, you understand, but I heard you were looking for coffee beans. Auntie Maud's carries coffee beans. Down by the pond." After waving to someone in the crowd watching the snow dance, he settled back on his bench and spoke without looking up. "If I were you, I'd hang up that tweed cap and get me a good pair of Levi's at the store up in Leadville, and while I was at it, I'd get me a fleece-lined jean jacket so I wouldn't look like a dumb tourist."

For an instant John was too flabbergasted to do anything but stare. Then he turned on his heel, clamped his lips together and strode toward the Porsche. He couldn't believe he'd been so careless as to leave it unlocked while he was inside the post office. A quick check confirmed nothing was missing. All his tapes were accounted for. His camera was still on the seat.

After looking toward Wes Pierce's bench, he swore, then slapped the car in gear. Since he still had a hour before he was scheduled to pick up Amy from Brownie Scouts, he cruised Main, seething over the encounter with Wes Pierce. Was there anyone in this damned town who didn't know every intimate detail of his life? Down to the sleeping arrangements at Alice Sage's house?

Did they also know that he ached for Penny every night? And hated himself for it? Did they know that his emotions were in a conflicting mess? That he was afraid he would lose his children just as he was finding them again?

What he needed was a cup of coffee. With a grimace of annoyance he found himself parked in front of Auntie Maud's, debating if he should go inside. When he recognized he was stubbornly resisting solely because Wes Pierce had made the suggestion, he got out of the car, locked it and opened the glass door to Auntie Maud's.

The shop was patterned along the lines of an old-fashioned general store. A pot-bellied stove glowed on the back wall. He inhaled the salty tang from the pickle barrels and the sweet aroma from a row of tobacco jars. A glass case filled with penny candy—now selling for a dime—occupied the space near the door. There were shelves of various dry goods, racks of parkas and ski clothing. The jars of coffee beans were behind the cash register.

"Can I help you?"

"I thought this was a restaurant," he said, feeling foolish. "I was looking for a cup of coffee."

"Got some right here." The smiling woman behind the counter poured coffee into a paper cup from a thermos she kept under the counter.

"I didn't mean . . . Well, thank you," he said, accepting the paper cup. "How much do I owe you?"

"No charge. Compliments of Auntie Maud's." The woman's gaze flicked to his driving cap. "You're Alice Sage's son-in-law, aren't you?"

Finally he understood. It was his driving cap. That's how they were recognizing him. Maybe that's what Wes Pierce had been trying to tell him. Before the woman behind the counter could advise him on his love life, he inquired about the coffee.

"You're drinking plain ole Folger's. I carry the beans for bulk buyers, but for personal use I just buy a can at City Market. Less trouble."

Though the selection was limited, he bought a pound of French Roast and a pound of vanilla-flavored beans, then he selected a couple of sticks of penny candy for the kids. Deliberately he kept the conversation focused firmly on coffee.

"Aspen Springs could use a good coffee shop," the woman agreed. Her name was Jennifer Woodly. "Art Friedy was talking about putting in a coffee place last year, but then he and Jean moved to Phoenix because their little boy had asthma so bad. So nothing came of it, but—"

"Thank you very much," he interrupted, making a show of consulting his watch. "I have to run."

"Right. Brownies should be letting out any time now."

It wasn't until he was parked in front of the Scout leader's house that he realized Jennifer Woodly had guessed where he was going.

"Dammit," he muttered. He didn't know how Penny and Alice tolerated the whole damn town's knowing their every move. First thing tomorrow, he would buy a pair of jeans, a jean jacket, and a baseball cap or a ski cap. Maybe if he looked like a local, people wouldn't notice him.

One thing was certain. The easiest job in Aspen Springs had to belong to the sheriff. Tracking down a suspect's moves would be as simple as following a string.

"Hi, Daddy!" Amy's braids fell forward as she rushed up to the car window. Penny had tied the ends with little bows to match Amy's Brownie uniform. "I got a new badge!"

Leaning, he opened the door for her and made a production of inspecting the new badge. "Not bad. What did you have to do to earn this?"

He listened carefully as Amy explained in excruciating detail exactly how she had earned the badge. Her excitement and expression were like nectar for the spirit. How many small wonderful events had he missed in the past because he had been too busy? Looking at his daughter, he realized how quickly she was growing. One day the golden braids would be swept into prom curls. Her figure would blossom and her legs lengthen. She would start talking about boys and college and a career and a home of her own.

He hoped to God he would be there to see the changes as they occurred, to share in her triumphs and disappointments. The very real possibility that he wouldn't be turned his expression grim.

"YOU LOOK TIRED," Dr. Adler said, raising a silvery eyebrow. "Are you getting enough rest?"

"I haven't been sleeping well," Penny admitted, swinging her legs over the side of the examining table.

"Are you sleeping on your side? One leg straight, the other bent?"

"If I don't know the routine by now, I never will," she answered, smiling.

"So what's the problem?" Dr. Adler asked, leaning back against the sink. "Are you worrying about John? Work? The kids?"

"All of the above." She touched her fingertips to her forehead and sighed. "It seems everyone wants to tell me how I should run my life."

"What do you want to do?"

"I don't know," she said, looking at him between her fingers. Doctor William Adler was a handsome man approaching sixty. Silvery white hair and mustache, a tall quiet bearing. Thirty-two years ago, he had delivered her. "John couldn't have come at a worse time. We're approaching record crowds at Santa's Village and it's only going to get worse. I just don't need any distractions right now."

"How are the kids coping?"

"Better than I am." Amy and Flash had swiftly adjusted to having John back in their lives. They adored sharing their basement quarters with him. She heard them in the mornings laughing and shouting; heard them romping together when she arrived home early enough in the evenings. At times she had an uncomfortable feeling that she was becoming an outsider. The family had subtly shifted into a different configuration.

"They seem to think everything is solved and John is here to stay. Alice is no better. Everything she says indicates she assumes John and I will get back together." Tilting her head, she stared at the ceiling. "I'm feeling pressured on all fronts. Pressured to make a decision I thought was already made. Pressured to compromise. Pressured to give in. Pressured at work. Pressured at home."

"We can remove one of those pressures. I'd like you to stop working about the third week in December."

Her head snapped down and she stared. "Not possible. I can't. That's going to be our busiest time at the Village. Lydie would kill me if I took a leave then. Allenby would go into cardiac arrest. I'd be letting everyone down." Sliding from the table, she reached for her coat. "Is it dangerous for me to continue working?"

"No," Dr. Adler said slowly. "You're healthy, the baby's healthy. I suppose you could continue working right up to the moment John drives you to the hospital. But if you can manage it, I'd advise you to consider taking a leave of absence a couple of weeks before your due date. The rest will do you good."

"Maybe after Christmas," she said to appease him. More likely she would continue to work up to the moment baby Whosit started knocking at the door. The week between Christmas and New Year's was traditionally the Village's busiest week.

Alice stood when Penny emerged from the examining room and smiled at Dr. Adler. "Well, Bill, does she get a clean bill of health?"

"Clean as a new whistle. This girl should have ten children. She makes it look easy," he said, smiling. "You look especially nice today, Alice."

Penny looked up from the counter where she was writing a check. Alice did look especially nice. Her hair was softly curled, and her makeup had been applied with special care. She wore a jersey dress the same energetic color as her eyes. But there was something peculiar about her today. She seemed to have developed a tic in her left eye, which made it look as if she were winking. And she was making strange gestures with her hands, until she saw Penny was watching. Then she brought her hands up to her face and studied her fingernails.

"Alice, are you feeling all right?" Penny asked as they walked to the car.

"Never better. Why?"

"You've been acting a little strange lately."

"Good heavens! I can't think what you mean."

"You seem distracted, like your mind is a thousand miles away. Remember last week when you put your car keys in the freezer? And a few minutes ago, you were winking like crazy. If I didn't know better, I'd swear you were flirting with Dr. Adler," she teased.

"Take my arm. I don't want you to fall."

"For heaven's sake, the pavement is dry as a desert. I'm not going to fall."

"Your exercise class is tonight, isn't it?"

"You're changing the subject, but yes. Why?"

"Oh, nothing. Just that John mentioned he would like to go with you..."

"What?" She stopped in her tracks. "I begged him to go with me when I was pregnant with Amy. Asked him when I was pregnant with Flash. He was always working. Now he wants to go?"

"That's what he said."

Her eyes narrowed. "Did you suggest it?"

"Haven't you noticed John's been reading your pregnancy books?"

She hadn't. "I don't think John has read anything except the *Wall Street Journal* in years. As far as I know, the only thing he knows about pregnancy is how women get that way. This has to indicate a new level of boredom."

"Or a new high of interest."

They slid into the car and Penny switched on the ignition. "I'm not being fair," she said with a sigh. "John's always been interested in my pregnancies. He just didn't have time to pursue it. But he insisted on being in the delivery room when Amy and Flash were born. And he was wonderful." She bit her lip.

"He's trying, Penny."

Another sigh compressed her chest. "I know," she whispered.

"I DON'T KNOW if it's a good idea to have dinner with you," she said, intending the comment as a mild tease. "Look what happened to me the last time we did this."

Immediately she regretted the reference, as memories assailed her. She remembered soft candlelight and a twinkling view of Los Angeles. Remembered long looks over the candle's flame, a brush of fingertips that set her skin on fire. Then the mad dash back to her hotel room and the urgency of their lovemaking. Their hunger had surprised them both. It seemed they could not get enough of one another. A rush of crimson stained her cheeks as the images flashed through her memory.

"It was a beautiful night," John said in a low voice, guessing what she was thinking. "You were so lovely. You wore a green silk dress, remember?"

She remembered, but she was astonished that he did. "Good heavens," she murmured, staring at him. "Is it possible I was married to a romantic all those years and didn't know it?"

A groan accompanied his smile. "Ouch. I'm wounded. Do you mean to say you've forgotten the notes I used to leave you?"

Whenever he departed for work before she did, he'd left a note on the counter by the coffeepot where she would find it first thing when she came downstairs for her morning coffee. Usually the notes were brief, a quick "I love you," followed by what time he expected to be home that evening. Maybe a request to pick up the cleaning or a reminder that they were having dinner out. Sometimes the notes apologized for an argument, sometimes they gave rave reviews of the night before. But always they ended with "I love you." During all the years of their marriage, he had never once forgotten to leave her a note.

The first morning she'd awakened in Aspen Springs without a note had devastated her. She had stared at the spot in front of the coffeepot where the note should have been, then her knees had collapsed. She'd sat at the kitchen table, buried her head in her hands and wept.

Clearing her throat now, she poked at her pizza. "Odd, but I never thought of the notes as romantic. I considered them a thoughtful gesture. In retrospect, you're right. It was romantic." It seemed so obvious now. Now that she had no notes and no romance in her life.

The waiter appeared with coffee and removed the pizza tray.

"Penny, everyone in this crazy town wants to know if I'm making progress with you." Reaching across the checkered tablecloth, he took her hand in his. "Where do things stand? Is it time to have another serious talk?"

She hesitated. "No matter what happens between us, you're going to stay until the baby is born, aren't you?"

"Of course." One eyebrow tilted in surprise. "I was there for Amy's and Flash's births. I don't want to miss this one."

Her instinct was to ask him to reconsider. But in some secret part of her heart she wasn't sure if that was really what she wanted. The thought of going through labor and delivery alone overwhelmed her.

"Penny?" Lowering his head, he tried to see her face. "Have you been thinking about things? About us?"

"It isn't that I don't care about you, John," she whispered.

"Thank God. I was worried that—"

"But loving someone isn't enough." She raised her head and met his eyes. "Maybe love solves everything in the storybooks, but in real life it doesn't work that way."

"It's a good starting place."

"We've shared a lot of ups and downs. You're the father of my children. And I'll always love you for that, but . . ."

"I love you for the same reasons, Penny, and there's nothing wrong with those reasons. Maybe neither of us is sure right now exactly what they're feeling. But love based on habit and history isn't such a bad thing. It's a start."

"John, we grew apart. We're not the same people we were back when. You and I want very different things out of life. Loving each other isn't going to change our personal goals or make our differences easier to live with." Dropping her head, she pulled her hand from his and twisted her wedding ring on her finger. "Look. You have a right to live wherever you please and work until you collapse, if that's what you want to do. I have that right, too. But I've reached the conclusion that neither of us has the right to inflict our wants and needs on the other."

"Surely two people who care about each other can find a compromise..."

The tenderness in his gaze wounded her. "We tried. And we failed. There's no compromise on this issue. All there can be is surrender. One of us gives up entirely. And that's not fair to either of us."

"The stakes are high, Penny. If we proceed with the divorce, I lose my children. I can't stand the thought of losing Amy and Flash."

They stared at each other across the table. "Every time you say something like that," Penny whispered, "I feel so guilty I want to cry. That isn't fair, John. We're both to blame for things going wrong."

"I'm not blaming you for anything. Please believe that. But the truth is the stakes are higher for me than for you. If we proceed with the divorce, you lose a husband. I lose a wife and my children. Penny, I can't stand the thought of losing Amy and Flash."

"I don't know what to say. I...I'm sorry it has to be that way."

"Well," he said after a lengthy silence. "At least you've admitted you still care about me."

"Please John. Remember what I said. Love isn't enough. Love isn't going to dissolve our obstacles or make them easier to bear. That's the tragedy of this whole mess." The ever present tears that seemed to plague her lately stung her eyelids. "I think we're going to be one of those couples who love each other, but who can't live together."

"I hope not. That sounds terrible," he said quietly.

She drew a breath and swallowed the tight lump in her throat. "We're going to be late for class." Pressing her hands on the table edge, she struggled up from her seat and blinked at her watch. "Are you sure you want to do this?"

Smiling, he helped her on with her coat. "I can't imagine you doing a workout. Jogging, yes. One, two, three, kick— no."

"You can say that again," she said, making herself return his smile. "I am definitely a runner. I run to work, run around Santa's Village, run here, run there." A sigh accompanied her smile. "Running has become my sport."

The exercise class was held in a meeting room above Dr. Adler's clinic. Nearly everyone had arrived when Penny began introducing John to the other prospective parents.

"You're just the man I've been hoping to meet," Dan Driver said, shaking John's hand. "I'm the President of the Optimists Club. We're hosting a pancake supper Saturday. The reason I've been eager to meet you is that I have it on good authority—your daughter to my daughter—that you're quite the cook. Is that true?"

"Not since college," John said. Immediately he liked Dan Driver. Driver reminded him of a Viking, tall and golden, fierce-looking until he smiled. "Actually, I'm a banker."

"Dammit, just my luck." Driver groaned. "We're short-handed in the kitchen for Saturday and I was hoping to coerce you into lending a hand. No one else is a cook, either. God knows what those pancakes are going to taste like."

"Actually... I'd be glad to help out," he heard himself say.

He turned his head in time to see Penny's look of astonishment. It was no greater than his own. He could not believe what he had just done. As if Dan Driver suspected he was about to withdraw the impulsive offer, Driver backed away toward his wife.

"Great! I'll call you tomorrow with the details."

"I can't believe I did that," John marveled as he followed Penny to the exercise mat and helped her sit down.

"I can't, either. You must be bored out of your mind."

"You're right about that."

Except he wasn't. Not exactly. At first he had thought he was bored. Bored with Aspen Springs and a pace a snail would consider too slow. But he had thought about it carefully last night when he couldn't sleep, and he realized it wasn't the town or the pace he found boring as much as the inactivity. When he examined that realization, he had to admit the fault did not lie with Aspen Springs as much as with himself. His constant phone calls to his office and creating make-work projects to fill the day were forcing him to realize that Penny was probably right about his being a workaholic. He needed something constructive to do.

"Good evening, class. Everyone feeling okay?" Greta Ecklund, the instructor, bustled into the room and tossed her coat on a table. "Doing your exercises at home?"

"Are you?" John whispered, looking down at Penny. She lay on her back on the mat, her reddish-gold hair spread around her head like a halo.

She gazed up at him. "Yes. Alice helps me."

"Okay, class. You know the drill. Let's hop to a few knee thrusts."

Doing as the other fathers-to-be did, John moved forward on the mat to kneel in front of Penny's feet as she pulled her legs up. "What am I supposed to do?"

"Place your hands on the outsides of my knees. When I push my knees apart, you're supposed to provide a little resistance."

If she hadn't been eight months pregnant, her position on the mat would have been intensely sexual. She was lying back, her knees drawn up, her eyes closed and her lips parted. He stared at her soft expression, at the graceful arch of her throat, and thought she was the most beautiful woman he had ever seen.

When he placed his hands against her knees, it was a caress, not the resistance she had requested.

Her knees flopped apart easily and she lifted her head to glare at him. The moment she saw his expression, her own expression altered. For a moment their eyes held, then she lowered her head and closed her lashes. "Let's try it again," she murmured in a throaty voice.

He could feel the warmth of her skin beneath her sweat pants as he pressed his hands firmly to her knees. Tiny beads of sweat appeared on Penny's temples as they continued the exercise. He felt sweat appear on his own brow, but not for the same reason.

"Okay, class. Good. Now we're going to practise breathing and working with labor discomfort. Fathers, pay attention, please. Some women enjoy stroking during the phase before delivery. They find it calming and relaxing. Other women can't bear to be touched. Right now there is no way to predict which your wife will prefer. So we're going to practice stroking so you'll know how to do it."

"Oh boy," Penny groaned. "I forgot about this part."

"This is the part I think I'm going to like," John whispered back, smiling down at her. Her face was moist from exercising, the way it usually was after lovemaking. Her fingers trembled slightly until she laced them together over her stomach.

"All right, ladies. Begin your breathing routine. Gentlemen, we're going to start at her shoulders and work our way down."

Watching what the other fathers did, John leaned over
Penny and gently massaged her shoulder, feeling the tension beneath his fingertips. "Is that too hard?" he asked
her. It was an old joke between them.

"It's never too hard," she whispered, smiling beneath
closed lashes. "Feels good."

When he felt the tension relax in her shoulder, he stroked
her arm. Because he felt an urgency to touch her skin, he
opened the cuff at her wrist and slid his hand up the inside
of her sleeve—and drew a breath at the remembered soft
touch of her. Penny opened her eyes and gave him a drowsy
look midway between pleasure and a frown.

Next, still following the other fathers' lead, he ran his
hand from her throat to her thigh, barely touching her,
tracing the curving outline of her body with his palm.

She drew a breath, almost a gasp, and opened her eyes.

"That's right," Greta Ecklund said above them, star-
tling them. "Make love to her. Gently, softly." She grinned.
"I can see how you two got pregnant. Keep breathing,
Penny. Slow, even. Do the count."

When Greta moved on to the next couple, John placed his
hands on Penny's thighs and stroked down to her calves. He
wasn't certain if she was trembling or if the tremble was in
his own fingers. Moving to her feet, he slipped off her can-
vas shoes and gently worked her foot between his hands. He
placed that foot against his stomach and took the other.
Penny made a small sound and he looked up to see her bite
her lip and turn her head.

Reappearing, Greta Ecklund knelt beside John and gestured him up between Penny's legs. She took his hands and
placed them gently but firmly on Penny's stomach. "Move
with the contractions. In and down. Stroke her, relax her."

"Oh, my God," he gasped, his eyes widening. "The baby
moved!" He blinked at Greta, then turned his astonishment to Penny. "It moved! Did you feel that?"

She laughed and threw out her hands. "This baby has a dozen fists and feet. You bet I felt it."

"What does it feel like from your side?" he asked, his hands on her rounded stomach. He had forgotten the stroking in the wonder of the tiny thrust against his palm. He could have remained like this, frozen, his hands on her taut flesh all night, waiting for the next sign of a miracle.

"It feels like ... I can't explain it ... like a tiny spinning pinwheel, maybe. Or maybe, less romantically, like gas." She smiled up at him, enjoying his wonder. "Too bad we can't trade places."

"It did it again!" His dark eyes widened. "Good Lord, Penny." He stared at her. "We're going to have a baby!"

"One of us is," she said, smiling. "And she needs to breathe."

After class they drove home in comfortable silence, enclosed within the dark warmth of the car. Underlying the comfort and silence was a deep awareness of each other. In other circumstances, the intense awareness would have expressed itself sexually. Now the sexual electricity transmuted to tenderness and a deeply shared sense of intimacy that extended beyond any need for words. It was the nicest moment they had shared since John's arrival, and he treasured it.

When he opened the door to help her out of the car, he regretted the end of the drive.

"It's getting frosty," she said. Lifting her chin from the collar of her coat, she looked at him, then slipped past and hurried toward the porch.

"Well, I'll be damned." Tonight was made for marvels. A swirl of snowflakes danced out of the black sky and eddied through the light shining from the yard pole. "The Indian did it!"

Alice was waiting when they came up the stairs. She had changed into a pair of designer jeans and a creamy sweater, which struck Penny as peculiar. Usually by this time of night, Alice was wearing her robe and slippers. "Shhh," Alice said, placing a finger across her lips. "The kids are finally asleep, I think. They wanted to wait up for you. Anyone ready for a drink or some coffee?"

Penny hesitated, then glanced at John and shook her head. "Thanks, but I'll pass. I think I'll turn in early."

He felt the same. He didn't want anything to interfere with the warmth he was feeling right now, he wanted to hold it close as long as he could. Taking her hands, he looked down into her face, her soft blue eyes.

"Thank you for tonight," he said, meaning it. They had shared something very special.

Then, wonder of wonders, she raised her arms and embraced him wordlessly. That is, she tried to. Her fingertips reached his shoulders, the curve of her stomach pressed against his abdomen.

"That's about as close as I can get," she said, smiling. "Thank you, John. It was a nice evening."

She could have gotten closer for a better hug, she thought as she undressed and creamed her face. But it would have meant leaning forward at an awkward angle and pushing out her fanny. Not a pretty sight from Alice's interested viewpoint.

It had probably been a mistake to hug John at all. But the moment had felt right. It would have been wrong not to end the evening with an embrace.

Once in bed, she touched the empty pillow next to hers and tried not to think of his hands stroking, caressing her. Not easy for a woman who had not been kissed in eight months.

God, she missed him. The situation was impossible.

AFTER SAYING GOOD-NIGHT to Alice, John descended the stairs into the hushed basement. First he looked in on Amy and pulled up her blankets against the cold night. Light from the doorway gleamed on her braids and turned them the color of spun gold. The faint scent of Ivory soap lingered on her cheek when he bent to kiss her.

"Did you and Mommy have a good time?" she whispered as her arms stole around his neck.

"The best. What are you doing still awake?"

"We wanted to see if the snow dance worked."

He tucked her in, smoothed back her bangs. "Sure did. It's snowing now."

"I knew the dance would work," she murmured drowsily. "I love you, Daddy."

"I love you, too," he whispered.

When he entered the room he shared with Flash, he stood beside the bed for a moment looking down at his son's freckled cheeks, the tousled gold hair so like Penny's. *My cup runneth over*, he thought, feeling his throat tighten.

Then he raised his eyes to the top bunk and a rueful smile touched his lips. As long as he was sleeping in a bunk bed, his cup didn't quite runneth over, after all.

After stripping off his clothes, he climbed the rungs at the end of the bed, pulled back the covers, then, shivering, he crawled inside.

Then he swore and leapt out of bed as if he had been shot.

Jumping to the floor, he grabbed his pants and stepped into them, then flipped on the light and stared at his son who was trying hard to feign sleep.

"Okay, Flash. I know you're awake. What's going on here?" Anger firmed his voice. He tossed back the blankets on the top bunk and ran a hand over the sheets. "Flash? I want an explanation."

His bed was wet from the pillow to the center. Thoroughly wet. Soaking wet and cold.

"Gee, Daddy, what's wrong? I don't know anything about any water." Sitting up, Flash blinked at him.

Amy appeared in the doorway, rubbing her eyes with an exaggerated movement. "What's all the noise?"

He looked at them. Innocence in flannel. "All right. What happened here. Why is my bed soaked?"

"Soaked?" They both looked at his bunk with dumb-struck expressions, which he didn't believe for a minute. "We don't know how it happened, Daddy."

"That bed didn't get soaked by itself."

Flash looked at Amy. Amy looked at Flash. Then they said in unison. "I guess you'll have to sleep with Mommy."

Now he understood. A breath of air rushed from his lungs and his anger vanished as quickly as it had come. He didn't know whether to give in to the laugh building in his chest or the sorrow constricting his throat.

"Listen, fellas," he said finally, sitting on the edge of Flash's bed. He opened his arm for Amy. "I understand what you're trying to do, and I love you for it." The warmth of their small bodies pressed against his sides, and he wondered how he could ever have let them go. "I know you're trying to help, but this is something Mommy and I have to work out alone."

"You aren't going to sleep with Mommy?" Amy's voice was heavy with disappointment.

"No, I'll take the sofa tonight." He pressed her close. "Sleeping with Mommy is a decision she and I will have to make together. Understand?" He looked at each of them, knowing they didn't, couldn't understand.

"I'm sorry," Flash said.

"Me, too."

"It's okay. All's forgiven." Standing, he tucked Flash's covers beneath his chin. "Just no more water in my bed. Don't do it again, all right?"

"Okay." Flash kissed him. "Did all the ice cubes melt?"

"Ice cubes? Good grief."

After tucking Amy in, he found the extra blankets on the closet shelf and headed for the lumpy-looking basement sofa. He had believed nothing could be worse than being banished to a bunk bed at the North Pole.

He had been wrong. A wet bunk bed was worse. And the sofa was almost as bad.

Because he couldn't find a comfortable spot, he kept waking through the night. Sometime around three in the morning, he could have sworn he heard a car in the driveway followed by a bump on the side of the house. Sitting up in the darkness, he waited, straining to hear. When nothing further happened and he heard only the silence of a deep snowy night, he lay down again and thought about Penny sleeping in a dry warm bed upstairs. Alone. For one crazy instant he thought about . . .

No. Patience was the key here. Lifting himself up on an elbow, he dug one of Flash's toy cars out of the cushions and dropped it on the floor, then sought a comfortable position. If there was one, he didn't find it.

Chapter Five

Dear Santa,
Please bring me a million bucks then I'll buy my own toys and it won't be so heavy for you to carry. I also want a savings account and a machine gun that makes noise.

Be good,
Winston B. Tarkington II

Smiling, Penny placed the letter in the pile she was setting aside to be printed in the Village newsletter.

Dear Santa,
If you're real then you already know what I want for Christmas. You also know who this is from.

That one went into the undecided pile.

Dear Santa,
Please bring me a six-pack of valium and a quart of aspirin.

Desperately,
Dennis's mother

Penny laughed out loud. Every mother had "valium days" as Lydie called them. Days when she looked at her kids and wished someone had told her that adorable little babies grew into occasional Excedrin headaches. Deciding that she wasn't stalwart enough to shatter illusions, Penny placed the letter from Dennis's mother in the Do Not Print file.

Dear Santa,
My name is Jimmy Asquith and I live at 347 Lariat Loop Drive in the second house. I am eight and a half and I have two sisters. Please bring me lots of good stuff. How is Rudolph? You don't have to bring my sisters any stuff. Ha. Ha. I want a rocket racer and a space-ship the most.
Say hi to Rudolph and Frosty.

                                    Jimmy Asquith

This one also went to the print pile.

Dear Santa,
If you can please bring me a warm coat and some shoes for Billy and pills for mama and if you can please bring us a daddy because we need one awful bad we don't mind if you can't come this year either that's okay but it would be nice if you did and if you wanted to leave us some tuna or Spam that would be nice too but I like soup better I hope that doesn't make you mad.

                                    Love,
                                    Mary Sealy

The last was the kind of letter that wrenched her heart. She never got used to them; they were always a shock. After reaching her secretary on the intercom, she asked Helen to add Mary Sealy's name to the list of people they would try to locate. Usually it wasn't difficult, for the elf at the admissions booth asked everyone to sign in with an address. But occasionally a letter like Mary Sealy's came through and they couldn't track her down. Penny hoped they would find Mary Sealy and that Mary's mother would allow Santa's Village to give the Sealy family a merry Christmas.

"Hi," Lydie said, poking her head in the door. "Ready for the walk-around?"

"Yes." Penny looked up and dropped her fingers from her temple.

"Doing the Santa letters?" Lydie asked with sympathy.

"Some of them rip your heart out." After rolling her chair back, Penny placed her palms on her desk and hoisted herself up.

Lydie stared. "Am I imagining it or are you swelling up by the minute? I swear you look twice as big as you did last week! That's an awning you're wearing, isn't it?"

"Fashions from Seaworld," Penny said, smiling. "We whales are into wool and plaid this season." She pressed a hand to the small of her back and suppressed a groan. "Let me dash into the bathroom, then I'll be ready."

"I can make the rounds alone if your back is aching."

"And let you score points with Allenby? Not a chance. Just give me a minute." Logic told her she didn't need to go to the bathroom; she had been there five minutes earlier. But at this stage, she never knew if the sense of urgency was real or a false alarm. The situation did nothing for her confidence.

"And you keep saying you don't want the promotion," Lydie said when Penny emerged and slipped into her coat. "If that's true, then I'm the Church Lady."

"You, the Church Lady?" Penny grinned. "Not likely. But I'm too tired and pregnant to argue."

They passed through the administration offices and stepped out onto Main Street. It was still snowing, creating a Christmas idyll. The Village resembled a scene on a Victorian Christmas card. Penny frowned at the cobbled streets. "One of us needs to speak to the snow-removal supervisor. We don't need any icy patches."

Lydie tightened a scarf around her throat. "Someone should find that crazy Indian and make him do a dance to stop this. It's snowed thirteen inches in the last four days. Enough is enough."

"The ski people are ecstatic."

They paused in front of the sled runs and listened to the whoops of laughter darting down the hill. Bright parkas flashed over the new snow.

"Did I see Amy and Flash and your ex here earlier today?" Lydia asked as they turned toward the ice-skating rink.

"John brought the kids over for the works. Sledding, skating, games and lunch with Daddy."

"How's that going?" When she realized her attempt to sound casual had failed, Lydie laughed. "Okay, it's none of my business. But I want to know."

Penny ducked her head and watched for ice patches. "I don't know, Lydie. I'm so confused I can't think anymore."

"Have you talked to your attorney?"

"If you're asking if I've stopped the divorce proceedings, no, I haven't."

"Maybe you haven't noticed, kiddo, but it looks like John is here to stay. Next Thursday is Thanksgiving. He's been here three weeks."

"Thanksgiving already?" Where did the time go? Now that she thought about it she remembered noticing crayoned Pilgrims and turkeys clamped to the refrigerator door.

It seemed only yesterday the door had been plastered with pumpkins and witches.

They stepped inside the North Pole and inspected the lines of eager children waiting to climb onto Santa's lap and whisper secrets in his ear.

"Kurt has started drinking again," Lydie mentioned quietly.

"Oh, no," Penny groaned. Narrowing her eyes, she stared at Santa, looking for signs of anything out of the ordinary.

"He seems okay today. But last night he smelled heavily of bourbon and mouthwash." Lydie shrugged. "Much as I hate it, I thing we're going to have to start looking for a new Santa."

"Has Allenby talked to him?"

"A hundred times. As you know, Kurt's the greatest Santa a kid could wish for. He's terrific from January to Thanksgiving. Then he starts drinking. He's one of those people who gets depressed about the real Christmas."

"This is the first time I've ever understood getting depressed at Christmas," Penny said, making a face. "I don't know how I'm going to find time for it."

"Speaking of which, a huge shipment of toys came in this morning for the Toy Factory. Allenby wants everybody to work late tonight. We've got to inventory the stuff and get it on the shelves."

"Tonight?" Penny stopped at the door. "John's helping out at the Optimist's pancake supper. We were all going to go."

"Tell them to bring you a doggie bag. If we get out of here before ten o'clock, I'll be amazed."

IT WAS A QUARTER TO ELEVEN when Penny got home. The car slid in the driveway and plowed into the snowdrift that had formed across the front of the garage. Common sense demanded she put the car in reverse and rock it out of the drift so she wouldn't be stuck the next day. But she was too exhausted to make the effort.

"I'm home," she called as she hung her cap and coat on the entry-hall pegs, speaking softly so she wouldn't disturb Amy and Flash. But they were still awake.

Amy ran to the stairs as Penny gripped the banister and pulled herself up. "Mommy, Mommy! You should have seen Daddy!"

Flash caught her free hand. His dark eyes sparkled up at her. "Daddy tossed the pancakes in the air! One of them stuck on the ceiling!"

"Lulu Henner ate so many pancakes, she threw up! You should have been there, Mommy. It was great!"

"I wish I could have been." John and Alice were drinking coffee in the kitchen. Amy and Flash climbed on their chairs in front of milk and cookies as Penny took a cup from the hook and poured a coffee. With a sigh, she sat down and pressed her aching back against the wooden rungs of the chair. Summoning a smile, she looked at John. "I gather the pancake supper was a success?"

"It was terrific."

She wouldn't have known it from his expression.

"John was the hit of the evening," Alice said quickly. "I didn't know how talented your husband is. He flipped pancakes behind his back, over his shoulder. Put on quite a show. How much did the Optimists raise, John?"

"About eighteen hundred dollars."

Alice beamed. "Gladys Syshell was in tears. She hugged everyone, especially John, and said the money would help tide them over until their house can be rebuilt."

"I'm glad it was a success," Penny said uncertainly. She didn't understand why John looked so glum. "It's way past the kids' bedtime, isn't it?"

"They wanted to see their mother," he said, meeting her eyes. "I thought it would be nice if you tucked them in for a change. None of us realized you would be this late."

His voice was carefully neutral, but the implied criticism stung. "I'm sorry, but this is the busiest time of year at the Village. If I could have gotten home earlier I would have."

"Exactly when was the last time you were home in time to tuck the kids in?" John's voice remained even, but she saw the accusation in his steady gaze.

"Oh, wait a minute." Leaning forward, she narrowed her eyes and clenched her fists. "Don't talk to me about not being there. You wrote the book on the subject." He flinched, then his mouth tightened. "I'm doing the best I can, okay? This is a temporary situation. I don't like it, either, but there's not much I can do about it right now."

Her feet hurt, her back hurt, she had to go to the bathroom, and pain throbbed behind her temples. She didn't need a case of the guilts. But of course that was what she was feeling. And she had felt it long before John said anything. But surely he didn't think she preferred this killer schedule. Did he imagine she enjoyed bending over boxes, marking prices, arranging displays? Didn't he realize she would far rather have been with her family at the pancake supper?

"There are people here who need you, too," John said sharply.

"That's not fair!"

"Please don't fight," Amy begged. Tears welled in her large blue eyes. Flash lowered his glass, leaving a milk mustache behind. He looked at them with a stricken expression.

Oh, Lord. Fresh barbs of guilt pierced Penny's heart. Reaching, she smoothed Flash's hair and drew Amy to her side.

"We're not fighting," she lied. "Look, fellas, I'm sorry I've been gone so much lately," she murmured against the top of Amy's head. "Things will slow down soon, then we'll see more of each other."

"It's okay," Amy said, laying her head against Penny's stomach. "Daddy's a real good tucker-inner. We don't mind."

Flash nodded solemnly, his dark eyes large above the mustache.

Their loyalty constricted Penny's throat. Ignoring her aching back and pounding head, she stood and took her children's hands. "Come on, you two. Let's brush teeth and put on jammies, and I'll read you a story before you to go to sleep."

"Great!"

Ignoring the silence from John and Alice, she led the children downstairs. And she tried to ignore the hurt when Flash or Amy told her she wasn't reading the story right. Daddy growled in this place, or Daddy tickled them in that place, and Daddy made faces and funny voices. After turning off the lights, she paused, listening to the warm silence. She would be very glad when the December push ended and life returned to normal.

When she emerged upstairs it was after midnight. Alice had tactfully called it a night and had gone to bed, but John was waiting.

"Can we talk a minute?" he asked.

Marching past him, she entered the kitchen and poured a glass of juice, then leveled a steady look over the counter top. "I don't want this to happen again, John. Please don't start an argument in front of the kids."

"I apologize. I was wrong to bring it up in front of Amy and Flash. But the point is valid." Taking one of the counter stools, he sat down and folded his arms. Choosing his words, he continued, "Believe it or not, I understand your position. As you pointed out, I've been there."

Biting her lower lip, she turned toward the dark window.

"Since I've been in Aspen Springs, our positions have reversed. We've been given an opportunity to see each other's perspective. What I'm starting to see is that everything you used to say about my hours was right on target. What I don't understand is why you're putting yourself through this. Wasn't the whole point of moving here to slow down? To spend more time with the kids?"

"What are you suggesting, John? That a woman's place is in the home?"

"Come on, Penny, you know better than that. I've never objected to your working."

"Really?" Her gaze narrowed. "You could fool me. It seems you don't miss an opportunity to make some remark about me rushing off to work or getting home late. If you're not objecting to my job, then what exactly are you trying to say?"

His eyes darkened. "It seems to me this particular job makes excessive demands on your time that doesn't fit your original goals, not as you explained them to me."

"What I can't seem to make you understand is the present situation is temporary." She thrust a hand through her hair and wondered if it would appear she was dodging the argument if she dashed to the bathroom. "The demands on my time will slow abruptly after the first of the year."

"Really? I doubt that. Especially if you win the promotion Alice says you're hoping for."

"I hope Alice also told you I don't plan to accept the promotion if it's offered. I've kept my name in the running solely to discover if I could have had the promotion if I wanted it."

It was obvious he didn't fully believe her, but he chose not to pursue the issue. "There's something I'd like you to think about, Penny." Standing, he moved toward the basement stairs. "If you're going to continue this pace and this life-style, it's a waste to do it here. Come home to Los Angeles and let's do it together. Emil would love to have you back at Blackman Brothers."

"The present pace is *not* going to continue!" she called to the top of his head as he disappeared down the stairs. "This is only *temporary*!"

There was no way to know if he heard. With the children and her mother in the house, the argument had been conducted in whispers.

Tense with frustration, Penny stomped up the stairs and into her bedroom. She was beginning to understand why divorced women got a mad gleam in their eyes when they talked about their ex-husbands. Some men heard only what they wanted to hear.

IT AMUSED JOHN TO REALIZE what he had said to Penny was true. They had switched traditional roles. Every morning she rushed off to work, while he called his office, then worked through a list of domestic chores to keep himself from going bananas. On the days Alice worked at the library, he cleaned up the breakfast mess, made the beds—except Penny's—tossed some laundry into the washing machine and ran the vacuum if the carpet looked as if it needed going over. He picked the kids up from school, supervised their homework, made them clean up their supper plates, monitored their TV watching. Gradually he had taken over the household errands. He took in the cleaning, did the shopping.

Now, as he pushed his grocery cart up and down the aisles of City Market shopping for Thanksgiving dinner, he admitted he enjoyed taking an active role in family life, but he also felt a little itchy. He craved the stimulation of a good old hostile takeover. Or did he? Was that really true?

Frowning, he wondered if he was genuinely missing Blackman Brothers, or if his restlessness stemmed solely from a lack of challenging activity.

Reaching for a bag of prepared stuffing, he examined the label, then replaced the bag on the shelf. He would make the stuffing from scratch.

Actually, he wasn't entirely inactive. He was keeping up with his client list, checking in every day. Staying current with the news and the markets. Reading the journals. He made the daily post office run. But it wasn't enough. He missed working.

At odds with this realization was an uncomfortable suspicion that he had reached a crossroad in his career. After this vacation he would return to the same frenzied pace, the same unrelenting emphasis on the bottom line, the same cynical attitudes. Dog eat dog. Oddly, he hadn't looked at it that way before. Maybe it was time to consider shifting departments.

"Hi, John. Heard you were a smash at the pancake supper."

Looking up from the cranberry bin, he discovered Jennifer Woodly smiling at him from the lettuce display.

"It was fun." He was glad he'd purchased jeans and had hung up his driving cap. Sneaking a look behind him, he noticed several tourist types, flocking into Aspen Springs to take advantage of the new snow. The man behind him, speaking in a heavy Oklahoma accent, wore wool plaid slacks and a driving cap very like John's. Absurdly, he felt a bit superior. He was a quasi-local, whereas the Oklahoman was a tourist.

Jennifer Woodly sidled up to him and spoke from the corner of her mouth. "I know we're all dependent on the tourist trade, but will you look at the coat that guy's wife is wearing?"

John snuck a look behind him, pretending to examine a bin of oranges. The gorgeous woman on the Oklahoman's arm was wearing a calf-length black mink.

"If she wears a coat like that to the grocery store, what do you suppose she wears when she's dressing up to go out?" Jennifer giggled into her hand and nudged John with her shoulder. "Oh, I almost forgot. I ordered the Parisian Cinnamon coffee beans you wanted. They'll be here tomorrow, in time for Thanksgiving. By the way, the crust on my pumpkin pie doesn't brown properly. Any suggestions?"

"Brush the edges with egg white," he said, pleased she had asked his opinion. After double-checking his list, he pushed his cart to the checkout line and found himself parked behind Susan Galloway, who lived on the road below Alice's house.

"Glad I ran into you," Susan said as she placed her grocery items in front of the cashier. "I was going to call today and thank you for picking the boys up from school yesterday."

"It wasn't any trouble. They're nice kids."

She glanced at his cart. "Are you doing the Thanksgiving cooking?"

Smiling, he lifted his hands in innocence. "I'm not a cook, honest. I've done more cooking in the past two weeks than in the past ten years. In real life I'm a banker."

Susan Galloway laughed. "Not in the eyes of this town. Gladys Syshell is spreading the word far and wide that you are the best cook ever seen in these parts. You're one of us now, a dyed-in-the-wool local."

His stock had risen a hundredfold since the pancake supper. Even without his driving cap, people recognized him and insisted on stopping him for a word. The good news was, only a few wanted to discuss his love life; most just thanked him for helping the Syshells. The thanks embarrassed him, but it was better than discussing the sleeping arrangements at Alice's house.

As he loaded the groceries into the Porsche and drove to the post office, he thought how pleasant it was to run into people he knew at the grocery store. The thought brought him up short. First, that he knew enough people in Aspen Springs with whom to exchange greetings, and second, that he found the experience enjoyable.

Worse, he glumly acknowledged he was forming a relationship of sorts with Wes Pierce. When he emerged from the post office, he did so slowly, waiting for Wes to invite him to sit a spell.

Wes eyed him up and down, approving the jeans and fleece-lined jacket. "Looks too spanking new, but better." He nodded at the bench beside him. "If you wash those jeans in bleach a few times, you won't look like such a dude. That's not helping out, mind you, just a comment."

Grinning, John crossed an ankle over his knee and leaned back against the bench, looking out at the snowy square. "Good. I believe we agreed not to interfere, that is, help each other. I'm holding up my end of the deal."

"Heard you put on some razzle-dazzle at the pancake supper. I would have been there, but the missus forgot about it and fixed her famous sauerbraten. Sorry I missed your performance. Heard it was something to see."

"It wasn't that big a thing."

"Yes, it was, son. Nobody expected you to agree to help out. Especially me. Wouldn't have blamed you if you'd taken a pass." He slid a look toward John. "It said a lot that you showed up."

Uncomfortable, John glanced toward the Porsche. He had tied the trunk down over the groceries. What was a wonderful car in the city was wildly impractical in the mountains. One more point in favor of big-city living.

"So. How's the romance coming?"

Though he was glad to change the subject, exasperation brought a frown to John's brow. "I thought we agreed my personal life is strictly my business."

"You agreed. I didn't. I got my reasons for being interested."

One eyebrow lifted. "Really? Mind sharing those reasons?"

"Yep, I do. At this point it doesn't concern you except at the edges."

Straightening, John stared. "Let me understand this. You want to know the intimate details of my personal life, and you have some reason for thinking it's your business to know, but I'm not permitted to learn that reason?"

Wes Pierce grinned. "That's about the size of it, son."

"Does that sound fair to you?"

"Didn't say it was fair. Didn't even say I agreed with it. All I'm saying is this town has its reasons for being interested in what happens between you and Penny."

"The whole town?"

"If you don't mind my saying so, you being the prickly sort, some of us think you're losing ground." Tilting his head, Wes pursed his lips in a speculative gesture. "Maybe you should rethink your tactics, son. Penny was in here yesterday and she did not look like a happy camper. She didn't have that romancy glow, if you take my meaning."

"I don't believe this!" What he didn't believe was his own stupidity in thinking he could sit five minutes with Wes Pierce without getting hot under the collar. "Look, I don't give a damn why this town thinks my business is their business. But you can tell anyone who asks that what goes on between my wife and myself is none of their damned concern!"

"Now that's where you're wrong. But I can understand why you don't see it. And right now you're not supposed to. That's the point."

Because he didn't think he could say another word without losing his temper, John stood up, strode to the Porsche and spun it out of the post office lot.

No one knew better than he that everything came with a price tag. The price tag for knowing enough people with whom to exchange a friendly greeting in the grocery was also knowing people like Wes Pierce, who seemed to believe they had some kind of crazy right to know other people's personal business.

Leaning forward, he patted the dashboard. "Hang in there, old girl. We'll be going home in a month or so."

A month or so. He groaned aloud. A couple of more weeks and everyone in Aspen Springs would know his shoe size and which side of the bed he slept on.

A goldfish had more privacy than the residents of a small town.

ANXIETY GRABBED PENNY when she awoke and saw the bedside clock. Good Lord, she had overslept badly. Throwing back the blankets, she pressed her hands to her stomach and heaved herself sideways. Then she remembered.

It was Thanksgiving. She had the day off. Dropping back to the pillows, she released a blissful sigh and stretched languorously.

"You're awake, too?" she murmured, smiling at a series of small thrusts against her nightgown. Placing her hands against the rising swell of her stomach, she stroked the flannel. Whether or not the motion was soothing to little Whosit, she didn't know, but she liked to think it was.

Each pregnancy was different from the last. With Amy, she had been consumed with every tiny detail. She had read everything she could get her hands on about pregnancy, had poured over books of names, had been unable to talk or think about anything except her impending motherhood.

She had started wearing maternity clothes in the third month, before she even had much of a tummy.

When Amy was born, she had fussed like any first-time mother. She had scrubbed walls with disinfectant, given away the cat, sterilized the entire condominium, made John put on a boiled smock before he held the baby.

This lasted until she discovered Amy cheerfully eating a dust bunny Penny's eagle eye had missed. When Amy didn't immediately require emergency treatment, she had wondered if she was overdoing things a bit. Then one day she had tiptoed into the nursery toward the end of Amy's nap and found that her daughter had discovered the contents of her diaper along with an artistic bent. The diaper contents were painted on the crib headboard and on Amy herself. At that point, Penny decided babies were sturdier creatures than she had realized.

She was more relaxed with Flash. She had stopped sterilizing visitors before the end of the first week. The boiled smock had vanished and she made no effort to replace it. Flash ate dust bunnies on a regular basis and thrived.

She peered at her stomach and smiled. "Poor baby. By the time we get to you, I'll be borrowing other people's dust bunnies for your midmorning snack."

Most likely her more relaxed attitude toward this pregnancy was the natural outcome of having been through it before. Not to mention the really lousy timing.

Although she had started by not wanting this baby, she had reconciled herself to the idea. For the most part, anyway. Having a baby at this time in her life was going to complicate things enormously.

It already had. If she hadn't been pregnant, John would have spent a week with the kids, then he would have been on his way back to Los Angeles. He wouldn't be camped in the basement, pressuring for unconditional surrender, and running her emotions through a shredder.

Plus, if she hadn't been pregnant, the possibility of a promotion might have looked different. Certainly, she would have felt more prepared for the hectic schedule between now and the first of the year.

"Poor baby," she said again, stroking her stomach gently. "You're getting shortchanged in this deal."

Unlike her other pregnancies, she hadn't devoted a lot of hours thinking about the new baby. There just hadn't been time. Not with the upheaval of moving to Colorado, filing for divorce, finding and settling into a new job, and all the attendant et ceteras. By this time with Amy and Flash, she had chosen names, had fantasized what they would look like. But this baby didn't seem real. The difference lay in seeing oneself as pregnant or seeing oneself as a mother-to-be. Penny saw herself as pregnant. She couldn't see past that point.

But she definitely saw herself as pregnant, she thought, as she rummaged through her closet seeking something attractive to wear. The rose tent or the green parachute—which was it to be? The striped awning or the plaid sofa cover? Sighing, she eyed a row of belts. Oh, to wear a belt again. Something at the waist that was not elastic. After a spasm of indecision, she chose a pair of cream-colored slacks and a matching sweater that cupped under her tummy.

"That is ghastly," she pronounced, staring at herself in the mirror. "You look like Tweedledum." With emphasis on the dumb. Why hadn't she behaved herself that night in Los Angeles last March?

Because she loved him.

But love wasn't enough. Once she would have argued with anyone who claimed love wasn't enough. Now she knew the truth of it. And the truth hurt.

After a moment she opened her eyes, pulled her hair back and tied it with a green ribbon, threw an emerald-colored scarf around her shoulders, then followed the wonderful aroma wafting from the kitchen.

"Sorry I'm late. I overslept," she said guiltily when she saw preparations for the feast were under way.

"Exactly what we wanted you to do," Alice answered cheerfully, pouring her a cup of coffee. "We sent Amy in to turn off your alarm. Thought you could use a sleep-in day."

"What can I do to help?"

"Not a thing, madam," John said. Throwing open the oven door with a flourish, he allowed her a peek. "The turkey is stuffed and roasting, the pies are coming along nicely. That wonderful smell is the giblets, slow cooking for gravy."

"Good coffee," she murmured after praising the rich warm scents filling the kitchen.

"Freshly ground." His smile removed any hint of the ongoing coffee-beans-versus-can argument.

"Daddy's doing all the cooking, Mommy," Amy said proudly.

"So what am I?" Alice demanded, hands on her apron-clad hips. "Chopped liver?"

The kids giggled as Alice winked at Penny.

"Actually they're mostly right. John has taken over."

"Good heavens," Penny blinked and smiled. "Send a guy to one pancake supper and he goes berserk."

Laughing, John nodded. Putting on a show for the kids, he did some fancy work over the chopping block, cutting apples for a Waldorf salad. Amy and Flash watched in awed fascination.

"To tell the truth, I'm enjoying this." Scooping the apples into a bowl, he squirted lemon juice over the pieces. "I'd forgotten why I wanted to go into the restaurant business all those years ago. Part of the reason is because I like to cook."

"Hey, you get no argument from me," Penny said, smiling over her coffee cup. "I just wish you'd displayed some of this creative cookery a few years earlier. When I think of all the dinner parties I slaved over, when you make it look so easy.''

Pleased by the compliment, he looked up and grinned.

"Mommy, you look like a snowman," Flash observed. "Can I touch your tummy?"

A snowman. No more all-white ensembles. "Sure, honey. Come say hello to Whosit." Both kids placed their palms against her sweater.

Alice wiped her hands on her apron. "If we have everything under control here, I think I'll set the table. Where did I put the place cards? Penny, do you think I should put Dr. Adler next to Winnie Greene, or should I put Winnie next to John?"

John groaned. "You've been worrying about this since dawn."

"You have?" Penny asked, surprised. Alice wasn't usually the type of woman to come unglued over something as inconsequential as place cards.

"I vote for Dr. Adler," John said. "If you put Winnie Greene next to me, she'll spend an hour telling me how to woo my wife."

"Your—" Penny bit her tongue. She had been about to say *your ex-wife.* But she looked at the children and changed her mind. The mood was close and warm; she didn't want to spoil it with technicalities. And then, she realized, that technically they were still husband and wife. "You're probably right," she amended. "Put Winnie at my end of the table."

"Good idea," Alice agreed. But she continued to look flustered and uncertain.

When everyone arrived and the time came to be seated, however, Penny discovered Winnie had been placed at the head of the table and her own card was next to John's.

She and John exchanged a glance, then they both looked at Amy and Flash who were begging Dr. Adler to make quarters appear out their ears. Both children steadfastly avoided their parent's lifted eyebrows.

"It's Thanksgiving," John whispered in her ear as he seated her. "What the heck."

After a moment Penny capitulated. Every holiday had its special memories. This would go down as the Thanksgiving dinner that Winnie Greene presided in the hostess's chair. Winnie looked a bit startled, then flattered. Then she gazed fondly at John and Penny and gave them a knowing wink.

"Do you get the feeling this whole town is in collusion about you and me?" she asked when John had carved a perfect bird and filled the plates. She knew she wasn't imagining it. Winnie, Dr. Adler and Alice continued to glance at her and John with encouraging little nods.

"You've noticed, too?" He seemed genuinely surprised. "I assumed I was the only one getting advice."

"I can't stop at a traffic light without someone pulling up next to me wanting to know how you and I are getting along." Frowning, she stared at her plate. It looked like a photo from a gourmet magazine.

"What do you tell them?"

Lifting her head in the sudden hush, Penny leveled a mock glare at the table. "You're all shameless, do you know that?"

"Yes, yes, dear, we know," Winnie said, leaning forward. "But what do you tell them?"

"I don't answer," Penny said, smiling sweetly.

Dr. Adler laughed. "And right you are." He lifted his wineglass. "I'd like to propose a toast to the cooks, John and Alice. And to a lovely table and a wonderful dinner. Thank you all for sharing this holiday with friends. And to Winnie and Penny whose beauty and grace compliment the event."

"What about us?" Flash demanded.

"And to Flash and Amy whose suspected creativity is to be commended."

"What does that mean?" Flash asked, his freckles twisting into a frown.

Penny managed a weak smile in the burst of general laughter. "It means your handiwork with the place cards."

Flash's dark eyes swung toward Amy and they both giggled, then applied themselves to their heaping plates.

"Everyone is right, John," Penny said. "Your dinner is wonderful."

His eyes, filled with warmth and pride, held hers for a long moment. "Thank you."

When she finally looked away, Penny thought of what Lydie had said about spending holidays alone. Listening to John's deep laughter and the flow of conversation, she could not imagine this dinner without him. It would have been dismal.

As if Alice had guessed her thoughts, she looked down the table at Penny and raised her wineglass in a silent toast. Penny wasn't entirely sure what they were toasting, but it was a nice moment of accord. Then Alice turned to Dr. Adler and the moment passed.

Looking about the table at her friends and family, Penny decided she had a lot to be thankful for. Then tears brimmed on her lashes as she thought ahead to next Thanksgiving. It was going to be so hard facing the holidays alone.

"What are you thinking?" John asked, pouring more wine into her glass.

"I was thinking how complex the human mind is. How we can want something and reject it at the same time."

Lifting her head, she looked at him, so handsome, so relaxed. His tan had begun to fade making his eyes seem especially dark and seductive.

She had to talk to him very soon and tell him she had done all the reassessment possible and had made her final decision. But not today.

Chapter Six

When the phone rang, Penny dismissed the snow-removal supervisor, Frank Spats, and reached for the receiver. Lydie's voice erupted in her ear.

"We've got a problem. King size."

"What's happened?" Frowning, Penny stared at the loudspeaker mounted near the ceiling of her office. "Rudolph the Red-Nosed Reindeer" was playing for the millionth time. The melody set her teeth on edge. She had begun hearing it in her dreams. "Come on Dasher and Dancer and Prancer and Vixen, Comet and Cupid and . . ."

"Kurt Pausch is dead drunk in his dressing room. It looks like he didn't go home last night—he's still wearing his Santa suit." A sniff of distaste sounded over the phone wire. "Need I mention the suit is a little the worse for wear?"

"Did you phone the evening-shift Santa? What's his name? George Hanson."

"I called George immediately, but his wife said he's in Denver for the day. Then I called everyone on our emergency list. No luck. And that, my fat pregnant friend, is the problem. We don't have a Santa and I can't find one."

Penny covered her eyes with her hand. "We've got five busloads of kids coming up from Denver today. Plus the usual crowd."

Lydie groaned. "That's right. The Police Association is bringing up a new group of underprivileged kids. They're more disadvantaged than they know. They don't even get a Santa."

"Lydie, we can't let that happen. There must be someone we can grab on short notice." Eyeing the loudspeaker, she considered hurling the bowl of ornaments at it. Who could think with "Rudolph the Red-Nosed Reindeer" playing cheerily in the background?

"I've hit a wall, Penny. I even called your doctor. But your mother said he'd just left for the hospital in Vail. One of his patients went into labor."

"My mother? You must be mistaken. What would Alice be doing at Dr. Adler's? She's at the library this morning."

"It sounded like Alice. Never mind that, what are we going to do? If you've got any magic rabbits in your hat, Ms. Martin, now is the time to pull one out."

Penny couldn't think of a soul. "Wait a minute." No, it would be asking to much. "I could try John. He'd planned to go skiing this morning..." She darted a glance at the wall clock. Hands shaped like Christmas trees edged toward eight o'clock. "I could try him. Maybe he hasn't left yet."

"Call him! Fast." Lydie hung up.

Biting her lip, Penny looked at the telephone and hesitated. Then she thought of the busloads of kids the Police Association were bringing to Santa's Village. This might be the only Christmas treat those kids would have. They deserved a Santa.

She dialed home and listened to the phone ring and ring, her heart sinking. Who else could they ask?

"Hello," John said after the sixth ring. "You just caught me. I was in the garage when I heard the telephone. What's up?"

She came at it the long way. She told him about Kurt Pausch getting depressed at Christmas, about his drinking problem and how he was now passed out in Santa's dressing room. She informed him of the busloads of underprivileged kids. She explained that Lydie had called every replacement Santa they could think of and they had drawn a blank.

"Penny, is this leading where I think it is? You want me to play Santa?"

"I know it's an imposition. I know you planned to ski today. But I don't know where else to turn. If you'd lend us a hand, John, we'd really appreciate it."

A silence stretched over the phone pressed to her ear. Then he laughed and her shoulders relaxed.

"Why not? How soon do you need me?"

"An hour ago. The park opens in thirty minutes. How quickly can you get here?"

"I'm on my way. Oh, would you phone Alice at the library and ask her to pick the kids up from school? I assume I'll be ho-ho-hoing all day."

"I'm afraid so—the shift ends at five. I'll phone Alice right now." She drew a breath. "John? Thank you."

Keeping the phone to her ear, she disconnected then dialed the library. "May I speak to Alice Sage, please?"

"I'm sorry, Mrs. Sage isn't here. Can I help you?"

Penny frowned. Alice had left at the usual time this morning, dressed for work. "This is her daughter—"

"Oh, Penny. I didn't recognize your voice. Do you want to leave a message for Alice?"

"I thought she would be there. Well, when she comes in, would you tell her..."

After hanging up, she considered the telephone for a moment, wondering where Alice was and if she should be worried. Then Allenby stuck his head in her office door and asked about yesterday's gate receipts; then Helen relayed a message concerning a contretemps among the kitchen staff at Mrs. Claus's Kitchen. Twenty minutes later the elf at the gate phoned to inform her that John had arrived.

"Tell him to meet me at the North Pole."

When she arrived, Lydie was showing John the baskets of lollipops and candy canes beside Santa's throne. "You get a coffee and pottie break once in the morning and once in the afternoon. An hour for lunch, but Allenby prefers you eat in your dressing room. He doesn't want any of the kids seeing Santa wolfing down an ordinary cheeseburger."

It annoyed Penny to realize that Lydie was flirting with John. It also aggravated her that Lydie had a waist and wore a soft clinging jersey dress that showed it off.

"This way," she said crisply, beckoning John toward the dressing room. A row of Santa suits hung in the closet along with the requisite padding and false beards. Penny stared at the figure sprawled across the cot against the wall, then swung her gaze to Lydie. "You just left him here?"

Lydie shrugged. "I didn't know what to do with him."

Kurt Pausch opened one bleary eye and looked at John. "You the replacement Santa?" John nodded. "Don't let the little buggers bite you."

"They bite?"

"They spit, too." His eyelids sank, then rose with difficulty. "They're just showing off, that's all. Or they're scared. Or mad about something. 'Fraid they won't get what they want. Or maybe they're 'fraid they will."

As they watched, Kurt gave them a dreamy smile. Then his eyes closed and his head fell backward. A moist snore rattled his chest.

"Yo-ho-ho and a bottle of rum," Penny murmured. A sad expression crossed her features. "I'll check the records and find out where Kurt lives. Lydie, will you scare up somebody to drive him home?"

"Will do." Lydie had seated herself at the makeup table and showed no sign of leaving any time soon. Smiling at

John through a sweep of dark lashes, she crossed one ny-lon-clad leg over the other.

A flash of jealously tightened Penny's lips and she stepped closer to John. The feeling surprised and irritated her. For the first time it occurred to her that after the divorce John would probably date other women. The thought brought an unpleasant taste to her mouth.

"I think you should get moving on it immediately," she said to Lydie. "Hopefully we can get Kurt out of here before the park opens. Too late," she added, glancing at her watch. "Well, do what you can to make sure none of the kids sees Santa being carried out to a car."

"If anyone sees, I'll tell them he was run over by a reindeer."

When John laughed, Penny glared at him. "After you," she said to Lydie, opening the door. With a last look at John, Lydie sighed and stepped outside. Penny's glare intensified. "Hurry up, will you?" she snapped at John.

"Is something wrong?" He glanced at her over the beard he was holding to his chin. Even with a flowing beard, he looked heartachingly handsome.

"You aren't here to flirt with the staff. You're here for the kids. The North Pole was supposed to open fifteen minutes ago!"

"Flirt with the staff? What are you talking about?"

"You know perfectly well what I'm talking about, John Martin!" Lifting her nose in the air, she did an about-face, then sailed, stomach first, out the door and slammed it behind her.

But not before she heard him say, "Well, I'll be damned," then laugh.

Crimson burned on her cheeks. She hoped one of the little buggers bit him.

IAN ALLENBY STOOD beside her at the entrance to the North Pole, his hands clasped behind his back. They examined the lines of children peering past each other to stare wide-eyed at Santa while they waited their turn.

"Your husband is a natural," Allenby commented, pleased. "I don't suppose..."

Penny smiled. "No. John's just filling in for today. I believe Lydie has found someone to replace Kurt through January. The new Santa will arrive this afternoon to observe the evening shift."

They watched John cuddle a three-year-old for the photographer. The flash popped, then he reached into the basket beside him and presented the little girl with a bright candy cane as he whispered something in her ear. The tiny girl smiled, then wrapped her arms around John's neck in a quick shy hug. The photographer gave the girl's mother a Polaroid print just as a little boy ran up the steps and hurled himself into John's padded lap.

After checking the animated figures, Ian Allenby took Penny's arm and turned her toward the street outside. He helped her into one of the horse-drawn sleighs and asked the driver to take them to the administration building.

"Are you sure we can count on you to be here until the first of the year?" he asked, lifting an eyebrow in the direction of the coat buttons straining over her stomach.

Dr. Adler's voice echoed in her ear, but she pushed it aside. "Absolutely. But after the first..." She smiled and shrugged.

"How long do you anticipate being absent?"

It was a loaded question. Village policy offered six weeks maternity leave. Therefore, the question Allenby was really asking addressed attitude and commitment.

"Barring anything unforeseen, I plan to return to work a month after the baby is born."

He nodded. "Penny, Santa's Village has been very pleased with your performance. I believe you know that." Turning his head, he automatically checked the hot-chestnut carts, the flow of people passing in and out of the shops. "What problems do you foresee regarding meshing your work schedule with the demands of an infant?"

Another loaded question. Penny drew a breath and held the frosty air for a moment. "I don't anticipate any difficulties. I believe I mentioned I live with my mother, and she's willing to care for the baby until I get settled in my own place and hire a nursemaid."

"If you're chosen as my replacement, your hours will increase."

"I'm aware of that." It was a bridge she would cross later.

He cleared his throat with an uncomfortable sound. "I dislike prying into people's personal lives, however I think you'll understand when I say it doesn't make sense from the company's standpoint to hire and train someone who may be planning to move out of the area. For that reason, much as I hate to ask, I feel I must inquire as to the status of your marriage. Are you planning to return with your husband to Los Angeles?"

"No," she said very quietly after a brief hesitation. "I am not." She plucked at the button pulling across her stomach.

"I didn't hear?"

"No," she said in a firmer voice. "My home is in Aspen Springs. My children attend school here. This is where I plan to live and stay."

"Future promotions could require relocation," Allenby said as he helped her to the cobbled street. After glancing toward a leaden sky, he looked at her again. "You're aware of that, naturally."

Another problem to be faced later. "Of course."

"Well, then." He opened the heavy glass door leading into the administration building and followed her inside. Before he turned down the corridor to his office, he asked her to thank John for filling in as Santa.

"I will."

Once inside her own office, she leaned back from her desk, chewed on a pencil and tried to assess the conversation. Did it mean the powers that be were edging toward a decision?

Helen buzzed on the intercom and told her that Mrs. Johnson, the head seamstress, needed to see her immediately.

"Tell her I'm on my way."

Rising, she glanced around her office, at the candy-cane wallpaper, her overflowing desk. Her gaze lingered on the photos of Amy and Flash positioned beside the basket of ornaments.

All questions regarding the possible promotion were moot. Nothing for her to waste time thinking about. For a moment Penny felt ashamed for having forgotten even for a moment. "I don't want the promotion. I won't accept it if it's offered," she said aloud. And she meant it, she really did.

When she arrived at the costume department, she found John bent over at the waist and Mrs. Johnson kneeling behind him, patching a tear in the seat of of his Santa suit.

"There's justice, after all," Penny remarked, grinning. "One of them bit you on the butt?"

He turned his head to look at her and smiled. "Nothing that dramatic. The kids have been wonderful."

"What then? Did Lydie grab you?" An acid edge appeared in her voice.

Before he answered, Mrs. Johnson spoke around a mouthful of pins. "That's why I called you, Mrs. Martin. Apparently there's a nail coming up on the Santa throne.

Maintenance should have a look at it. Don't want some child gouging his leg or getting scratched. Never mind your husband's, uh, behind.''

"You couldn't pound down a loose nail?" she asked John.

One eyebrow lifted and he looked at her curiously. "I offered to take care of it, but Jim—he's the photographer—"

"I know."

"—said the union wouldn't approve. He said you've got a union guy around here dressed like an elf who does minor repairs.''

She absolutely was not being fair and she knew it. Which made her angrier. "It still seems to me you could have given it a whack," she snapped, hating herself. It wasn't like her to be so unreasonable.

"Penny—"

"Never mind, I'll phone the union elf." The sooner she got out of the tailoring department the better. She knew she was behaving badly, but seemed unable to stop herself. And there was no way she was going to admit her snappishness had anything to do with jealousy. It was just too ridiculous.

John caught up with her in the corridor. "Wait a minute." He cupped her shoulders between his hands. "Honey, what's wrong? Why are you so upset?"

"Please, John. I've asked you not to call me honey."

"You weren't this testy the last time you were pregnant."

Her eyes narrowed. "Why does everyone insist I'm being unreasonable because I'm pregnant? You, Lydie, my secretary, even Alice, has made some remark."

He grinned. "Well, then, why are you being so unreasonable?"

"Dammit, I am *not* being unreasonable!" Yes, she was. She bit her lips and stepped back from the warmth of his hands. "I'm sorry," she murmured, pushing a hand through her hair. "I guess I am a little out of sorts today. Allenby talked to me about the promotion. No, he didn't offer it," she added when she saw John's expression. "And Alice isn't where she's supposed to be. So I'm worrying if she received the message to pick up Amy and Flash. I have a dozen phone memos on my desk that I don't have time to return. It looks like a late night again tonight, and . . . well, you get the picture."

"How late do you think you'll be? I'd like to talk to you."

He looked so damned appealing, standing there in the chunky Santa suit, his eyes like melted chocolate above the white beard. Penny swallowed and took another step backward.

"We both look pregnant," she said, trying for a smile to ease the moment. Then she made a show of glancing at her watch. "I don't think I'll make it home before ten," she said. "And I already know I'm not going to feel up to a serious talk. But soon, John. We'll talk soon."

"I don't have anything serious in mind," he said, leaning against the candy-cane wallpaper. "I'd like to discuss Christmas. Our Christmas."

"Oh. Well, that shouldn't take too long."

"Okay, it's a date."

She wished he hadn't phrased it that way. But it was her fault. He didn't know yet what she had decided. She definitely had to find the right time for a serious talk. No matter how much she dreaded it.

PENNY'S MOOD had not improved by the time she arrived home. As she hung her coat and cap in the entryway, she promised herself that she would apologize to Lydie first thing in the morning. She had been sulky through dinner, rebuffing Lydie's attempts at conversation. Whether Lydie had actually flirted with John or whether Penny had only imagined it, the implications of being bothered by either circumstance made her head ache. The bottom line was that she had behaved unfairly toward Lydie. It didn't help her feeling of guilt that Lydie seemed to understand.

"You look tired, dear," Alice said, glancing up from her knitting. A fire crackled in the fireplace, and the news was ending on TV.

"I am," she said as John offered a cup of hot mulled wine. After casting a suspicious eye over the furniture, all of which was wickedly soft, she lowered herself onto the raised hearth and let the fire warm her back.

John switched off the TV, then sat on the sofa where he could see her. "Alice and I have been talking. If you agree, we'd like to make this a real old-fashioned Christmas for the kids."

"I like the idea so far," Penny said with false brightness, too fatigued to feel genuine enthusiasm. "What are you planning?" And how much time would it require?

Excitement sparkled in John's eyes. "For starters, I was thinking we could cut our own tree this year. And instead of buying gifts for friends, we could give them a basket of homemade cookies."

Penny blinked, her mind racing. Cutting a tree would require the better part of an afternoon. Baking Christmas cookies was an all-day project.

"John, our resident cook, has volunteered for the cookie patrol," Alice offered, reading her daughter's thoughts.

John leaned forward, speaking earnestly. "The thing that struck me while I was playing Santa is how commercial Christmas has become. How would you feel if we agreed that everyone has to give each other at least one homemade gift?"

"Is that what this flurry of knitting is all about?" Penny asked, nodding toward the yarn in Alice's lap, stalling while she marshaled her energy. "By the way, where were you today?"

"I was at the library, of course."

"You weren't there when I phoned. I was worried about you."

Alice waved a knitting needle. "Nothing to be worried about. I'm a big girl, for heaven's sake. I had breakfast with a friend, then ran a couple of errands before I went in."

"What do you think, Penny? The kids could string popcorn and cranberries for the tree—"

"Popcorn and cranberries is probably not a good idea," Alice interrupted. "I'm old enough to remember how hard that is. How about a modification? Paper chains and strings of macaroni."

"Great! Well, Penny?"

"I love the idea," she conceded slowly. It sounded wonderful. Exactly the sort of Christmas she had imagined they would have in Aspen Springs. Except . . . there just were not enough hours in the day to do all the things she wanted to do.

"Good. It's settled then." Leaning back, John smiled broadly. "I'll get the tree permit tomorrow."

Penny sighed. "Great," she said finally, mustering a smile. "The kids will love it."

THERE JUST WEREN'T enough hours in the day.

After tightening the belt of her bathrobe, Penny frowned and leaned against the freezer. She adjusted the beam of the flashlight to shine on the carton of ice cream she was struggling to open. Good. By sheer luck she had managed to locate the lemon custard. Midnight cravings were a pain in the neck, but what was a pregnant lady to do?

For a moment she considered turning on the garage light so that she could see what she was doing, then rejected the idea. If one of the Galloways couldn't sleep, either he or she might look up the hill and notice the light and wonder if something was wrong. All she needed to cap another long day was to have Bill Galloway pounding at the door and waking everyone at three in the morning.

Leaning against the freezer, she spooned a bite of lemon custard into her mouth and held it on her tongue, savoring the flavor, feeling foolish to be shivering in the garage at three in the morning for the sake of some ice cream, of all things. It was so cold she could see her breath between bites.

After swallowing another spoonful of lemon custard, she tightened the collar of her bathrobe around her throat and swept a glance over the darkened shapes filling the third bay of the big garage. The furniture she had brought with her from Los Angeles, covered now with sheets and moving pads, waited for the time she found her own house. The sight of her broken household was too sad to bear thinking about, so she turned her gaze to the hood ornament on her car and ate another gazillion calories of lemon custard.

Where was she going to find the time to do everything she was committed to do? A sigh lifted the ice-cream carton propped against her stomach. She loved Christmas. At least she used to, back in the days before listening to "Rudolph the Red-Nosed Reindeer" had become a teeth-grinding experience. Before the thought of making homemade gifts caused her eyes to glaze over and her throat to tighten in panic. Where would she find the time? Or the creative energy? Whenever she tried to think of something she could make for Amy and Flash, her mind went blank.

Covering her eyes with one hand, she drew a long breath. Something had to go. She could not continue at this pace and hope to enjoy the holidays. But what? She didn't immediately see which responsibility she could set aside.

A sweep of headlights flashed across the garage windows just then, curved over the wall and across Penny's startled face, then cut to blackness.

For an instant she froze. Then she set the ice-cream carton on the lid of the freezer and hurried between her car and

John's toward the garage windows. Holding her breath, she peered outside.

She saw nothing unusual. The only car in the driveway was Alice's, parked in the usual place beneath the yard light. Frowning, Penny pressed her cheek to the frosty glass, straining to see beyond Alice's car.

When the bump sounded against the house, she jumped, even though she realized she had been half expecting the noise.

The bump was faint enough that Penny could almost persuade herself that she had imagined it. But the sweep of headlights had been very real. And they proved she was not imagining someone in the driveway even though the car had seemingly vanished.

Maybe the driver had not.

This frightening, confused thought raised the hair on the back of her neck, and she quickly backed away from the row of garage windows. Responding instinctively, she rushed inside the house and headed down the basement stairs. Not pausing to question that she automatically turned to John, she tiptoed into Flash's bedroom then reached to the upper bunk and shook John awake.

"John," she whispered urgently when he rose on an elbow and blinked at her. "Someone's in the yard! I heard a car and saw headlights."

Instantly, he threw back the blankets and swung his legs over the edge of the bunk before he dropped to the floor beside her. A flash of nakedness skimmed her gaze before she hastily averted her eyes. But she felt her cheeks burning in the darkness. It wasn't that she had forgotten he slept naked; she had forgotten she wasn't supposed to look at or appreciate what a wonderful body he had. Gradually she was deciphering the etiquette for divorced partners, and staring at one's naked soon-to-be ex-husband was probably not the accepted thing. Judging by her response, it was definitely not a wise move.

Outside Flash's bedroom, she pushed aside any thoughts of firm naked bodies and leaned to John's ear. Speaking in a low voice, she told him what had happened.

But her thoughts were not focused as sharply as they should have been. Aside from the electric jolt of seeing him naked, she felt a growing embarrassment that she had come to him at all. They were estranged; she should have handled the problem herself instead of responding to habit and running to John. She didn't like the underlying thought that she still needed him.

A frown drew his brow as he listened. "I know what you're describing. I heard the same noises a couple of weeks ago." His lips pressed together and he glanced toward the basement stairs. "Do you have a flashlight?"

She pushed it into his hands, then followed him up the staircase. "All I could see from the garage window was Alice's car. It's her turn to park outside."

"Wait here."

Cupping her hands around her face, she leaned to the window beside the door and watched the flashlight bob over the snow toward Alice's car. He circled Alice's Subaru, then disappeared around the corner of the garage.

When he returned inside, John shook his head. "I've been all around the house and there's no one there," he said, hanging up his coat. "I can't tell if any of the tracks are fresh or left from yesterday. You're sure you saw headlights?"

"Positive." They stared at one another. "The only way headlights would sweep the garage is if a car were actually in the driveway. It couldn't have just vanished." She thought a moment. "Maybe it doused its lights and drove away while I was downstairs waking you."

"Obviously that's what must have happened. Maybe one of your neighbors has a drinking problem, came home late and turned into the wrong driveway."

"Why not just back out and go on home? Why the mystery? And, John, this isn't the first time this has happened."

"Maybe the person has a persistent drinking problem and persistently turns into the wrong driveway. He cuts the lights because he doesn't want to wake anyone, or maybe because he's embarrassed about making a mistake and doesn't want to be identified."

He didn't sound entirely satisfied with this explanation and neither was she, but nothing else sprang to mind. "Maybe," she said doubtfully.

"You know," John said, looking at her, "it just occurred to me—why were you in the garage at three-thirty in the morning?"

She gave him a sheepish shrug. "The freezer is in the garage. I wanted some lemon custard ice cream."

He didn't smile as she expected him to. Instead, he raised a hand still cold from the night air and touched her cheek. "Couldn't sleep?" he asked softly.

"I've had a lot on my mind." His touch paralyzed her. Then a rush of heat warmed her cheeks and she stepped back away from his hand. Dammit, it was over between them. She wasn't supposed to react like this.

"Want to talk about it?"

"Now?" she asked, surprised.

"Why not? I have an idea neither of us is going to go back to sleep. Come on. I'll put on a pot of decaf. It'll be like old times."

Silently she followed him upstairs, seated herself at the kitchen counter and watched as he made coffee. There had been a time early in their marriage when sleep hadn't seemed to matter much. Too excited by work or by each other, too wound up to sleep, they had raided the fridge at two or three in the morning, laughing and whispering in the darkness like teenagers. She pressed her lips together and looked away from him, feeling an ache deep inside. So much of her personal history revolved around John.

"Come sit beside me on the sofa," he suggested when the coffee finished perking. "I'll help you up later."

"I'd better stay where I am," she said in a low voice. And she stopped him when he moved to turn on a table lamp. This was as good a time as any for the serious talk she had been avoiding. And it would be easier to say what she had to say in the darkness. She didn't want to see his expression.

"You've made up your mind," he said quietly when the silence between them had grown uncomfortable.

The pain of what was coming clamped her body like a vice.

Chapter Seven

"I've thought about everything, done the reassessment you asked, and I've realized nothing has changed. I won't go back to Los Angeles, John. It isn't what I want for myself or the children. I think . . . a divorce is the right thing."

Because she couldn't bear his awful silence, she continued talking, speaking above the vice that had tightened by a notch around her chest. "I didn't reach this decision lightly or without difficulty. I've given it careful thought." That was the understatement of her life. She had scarcely been able to think of anything else. And the pain of the decision was with her always. A long sigh collapsed her shoulders and she lowered her head to look unseeing into her coffee cup. "I'm sorry, John."

"I thought we agreed we care about each other. I thought we were getting to know one another again. Putting things back right."

Sudden tears blurred the darkness. "As I mentioned earlier, loving isn't enough. I wish it was, John, but it isn't. And the John Martin you are now isn't the same John Martin who lives and works in L.A. This John Martin is on vacation. More relaxed than I've seen him in years." She shook her head. "You're right. These weeks have been more easygoing than any we've experienced in years. And maybe we're seeing different sides of each other. But once you return to Los Angeles and work, the regular routine..."

"Is that why you won't return to Los Angeles? You resent my job?"

"Look, John. If I had to describe you in one word, the word I would choose is ambitious. And you're a workaholic. I don't resent Blackman Brothers. If it wasn't Blackman Brothers, it would be something else equally as demanding." She spread her hands. "Another rat race. Another treadmill. Whatever job you have, you'll throw yourself into it one hundred percent. Don't you think I've noticed how hard it is for you to relax? You can't. At least not for long. People pay thousands of dollars to vacation in Aspen Springs, but all you've done since you arrived is look for something to do. How many times have you skied? Twice? Three times? Sure, you've taken the kids sledding and snowmobiling on the weekends. But during the week, you're phoning your office a couple of times a day, doing work you receive through the mail, reading mounds of reports and journals. And the rest of the time... Can you honestly tell me you aren't going crazy with boredom?"

"You're being unreasonable, Penny. I didn't quit Blackman Brothers, I took a vacation. I have to keep up with what's going on or I'll be lost when I return." Leaning forward, he placed his elbows on his knees and looked at her across the dark room. "As for being a workaholic, I admit it. I've never fought you on that point. What I've objected to is your opinion that being a workaholic is negative. I saw it as a positive, as an extra source of fuel, maybe, that would get us where we wanted faster. What you need to understand is that I've taken a hard look at my work habits since coming here. Frankly, my reassessment was prompted by watching you."

"What is that supposed to mean?" she asked sharply.

"You are as much a workaholic as I am."

"That is utterly ridiculous!"

"Observing you these past weeks has given me an opportunity to see myself more clearly. And every objection you ever voiced was valid. The workaholic surrenders the best of his personal life and causes inconvenience and frustration to those around him."

Penny leaned forward angrily. "Are you accusing me of sacrificing my personal life and disrupting the lives of those around me?"

"Yes. Exactly as I did all the years we were married. The point I want to make is that I've finally seen the light. I'm not ready to retire as you seem to want me to—"

"Which you think is an irresponsible attitude on my part!"

"Frankly, I do. I'm thirty-five, Penny, too young to be put out to pasture. I'll continue to work because work is satisfying to me. But I won't continue at the same pace as before. I won't do that to myself anymore, or to the people I love. You have my word on that."

"Your word is several years too late!" She was practically sputtering. Drawing a deep breath, she held it until she felt her blood pressure return to normal. "I know you believe that now, John, but that's not how it will work out. Something drives you. From one point of view, that's a wonderful quality. From my point of view it means never seeing you, never spending as much time alone with you as I'd like. It means taking second or third place in your life."

"Penny—"

"I know exactly what would happen. You'd have all the best intentions in the world. At first you would work nine to five. Then it would be one night a week, then two. Then an occasional weekend. Very soon everything would be just like it was. We'd be seeing each other at parties, or late at night, and talking on the telephone instead of in person. We'd be right back trying to convince ourselves that spending a lot of time with our children isn't as important as making that time 'quality' time. Well, quality time is a lie designed to ease a parent's guilt, John. Ask any kid. Ask any wife. Children and wives need more than an hour or two a week, even if that hour or two is utterly fantastic!"

"Penny, will you just listen for a minute? I—"

"The difference is that my situation is temporary. It's not a habit or a way of life. With you, it is."

"Was. Not is. Something happened to me after you left. I woke up and realized I had sacrificed everything important in my life." After a pause, he continued, "One night I came home early and the condo was too silent, too empty without you and the kids. I had to get out of there, so I decided to call someone and meet for a drink. But there was no one to call. I was surrounded by millions of people and there was no one I really wanted to see or be with. It wasn't a drink I wanted, I wanted you and Flash and Amy."

"On your terms," Penny said sharply. "When you had a night off."

"I understand that now. And I intend to change it." He looked at her, his face a pale blur in the darkness. "I know no career is going to consume my life ever again. It's been a tough lesson to learn and I've hurt a lot of people. But now I know what's important and what I want. I want you and my family. I don't want my kids growing up with 'steps,' as Flash puts it. I don't want you working a murderous schedule because you're worried about money. I've enjoyed the kids tremendously these past few weeks, and I've learned how much I missed by not being there all those years. I don't want to miss anything else, especially our new baby."

Sudden tears wet her lashes. She heard his sincerity, knew he believed what he was telling her. But she also knew John. And she couldn't believe he could change that much. Tigers didn't change their stripes.

"Is it possible you're mistaking loneliness for something else?" she asked, trying to put her doubts in a tactful manner.

"Of course I'm lonely. Aren't you, Penny? I don't like sleeping in the North Pole while you're sleeping a million miles away. I miss lying in bed with the lights out, sharing the day's events. I miss waking up and finding you smiling at me. I even miss trying to shave over your head while you're putting on your makeup. I hate it that we're so carefully polite with each other, that we don't really talk. You're afraid to tell me what you're feeling because I might misconstrue what you're saying and think you're making some kind of commitment. I'm afraid to tell you what I'm feeling because you might think I'm pressuring you. And on we go. But I don't want you back because I'm lonely, if that's what you're thinking. I want you back because I love you and because I believe in us. I think you do, too."

"Not anymore." They were the hardest two words she had ever spoken. "There's too much water under the bridge."

"Come on, Penny." Now she heard anger enter his voice. "Are you so afraid of loving that you won't look at the truth? For instance, you're sitting here raking me over the coals for being ambitious, for being a workaholic, but what about you?"

"I've explained it over and over again. My present work situation is temporary."

"If you believe that, Penny, you're deceiving yourself, and that isn't like you. The day I played Santa, I had a look around the Village. And I kept my ears open. Other employees aren't killing themselves, working till they're exhausted." He stared. "Did you know the supervisory staff resents the pace you and Lydie Severin are setting? The two of you are competing so hard for Allenby's position that you're establishing expectations of perfection that no one can meet. You're both asking too much of your employees and yourselves so you can look good.''

Penny gasped. "That's not true!"

"It is true. You're driving yourself and your staff beyond what's reasonable. Everyone around you sees it. Why can't you?''

"Because that's not what's happening," she snapped. "I have responsibilities, I have—''

"Look, I'm the first person to understand what you're doing. And I certainly don't fault you for having ambition and wanting to move up the ladder.''

"I do not want that promotion! I just—''

"I know. You just want to know if you can win it." He lifted his head and looked at her, but the darkness was too thick to read his expression. "We've heard that one before, haven't we? Only it was me speaking the words. Me involved in the self-deception.''

"You are so wrong, John.''

"If I'm wrong, then show me. Take yourself out of the running. Take a hard look at your priorities, Penny. Is this what you wanted to do when you moved to Aspen Springs? Work yourself into exhaustion? Ambition isn't a bad thing. It's a quality we share. But it's something that's a problem for both of us. If we work together on it, maybe we can find a solution we can live with. But first, you have to admit ambition is driving you, too.''

White-faced, she slid from the counter stool and pulled the collar of her bathrobe to her throat. "Somehow you've managed to shift this conversation to make me the bad guy.''

"I'm not trying to make anyone a bad guy. I'm trying to point out how easy it is to fall into the trap. And under different circumstances there would be nothing wrong with that. But it isn't what we decided we want right now. Not for either of us. We decided we wanted a slower pace and more time with our kids."

"There's nothing like a recent convert when it comes to preaching, is there?" she said sharply. Then she added in a defensive tone, "Besides, I am spending time with the kids. It's—"

"Quality time?"

Crimson flooded her cheeks and she was glad he couldn't see her expression in the darkness.

"Penny, you were right about quality time. First, there's never enough quality time, and second, it isn't really quality. I suspect you're doing what I used to do. Thinking about inventory and gate receipts while you're reading bedtime stories, for instance. Were you really watching the Disney feature last Sunday, or were you worrying about replacement Santas and removing the snow from the Village ice rink?"

The crimson intensified in her cheeks. "I know what you're doing, John," she said finally, her voice tight. "The best defense is offense, right?"

He was silent for a moment. "Maybe that's part of it," he finally admitted. "I don't think it's fair for you to give up on us. Especially not when you're doing what you're accusing me of."

"Maybe that's how you see it, but that's not how it is."

"I think you're fooling yourself. It looks to me like we're both at a career crossroads. Me, willing to gear down. You, preparing to gear up."

"I didn't tear up my life and the lives of our children to move here and fall into the same old trap. You have it wrong." She moved toward the upper staircase feeling like an angry basketball in motion. It was difficult to effect dignity when her stomach preceded her. "It's time we ended this discussion."

"Penny—"

"No, John. All we're doing is rehashing an old argument." She drew a breath. "You're welcome to stay until the baby is born. I...I'll be glad to have you with me. Then we'll go our separate ways." She drew another tight breath and blinked at the tears scalding her eyelids. "I'm sorry it has to end like this. I know you are, too. But that's how it is. We'll make a nice Christmas for Amy and Flash, then you and I are finished. And that's final, John." Before either of them could say another word, she hurried up the staircase and away from him.

THERE WAS NO POINT returning to the bunk bed. Sleep would be impossible tonight. Instead, John seated himself at the kitchen table, drinking the rest of the decaf, thinking and watching the sky lighten toward a gray cloudy dawn.

After silently reviewing the conversation, he reached the same conclusion. Penny was deceiving herself. He didn't blame her. No one understood what she was doing any better than he. He had played the same scene often enough in the past. Eventually the promotion would be offered or it wouldn't, then she would have to confront what was going on inside.

Because he knew her and because he believed in her, he trusted she would not flinch from the confrontation. In the end, her basic values would assert themselves and the deception would fall away. What she did then would measure the depth of her commitment to the ideal that Aspen Springs represented.

Whatever happened, it would happen here. Not in Los Angeles. Penny was not coming home. He had recognized the conviction in her tone.

He drank his coffee and thought about that.

Actually he should have anticipated her decision. Aspen Springs had always been the dream.

It was a quiet group who gathered for the breakfast he prepared. Penny looked as if she hadn't slept; her eyes were pale and red-rimmed. A fresh pot of Hawaiian ground coffee beans was not enough to prevent Alice's yawns. Even the kids seemed subdued this morning.

"Your shirt is buttoned wrong," Amy said to Flash, her tone ripe with an older sister's scorn. It was a provoking statement and she knew it, though her heart didn't seem to be in it.

"Is not," Flash replied, gulping his milk.

"Is too."

"Amy, your braids need redoing," Alice said. But she didn't volunteer for the task. Instead, she turned sleepy eyes to the window. "Overcast but not snowing," she announced to no one in particular.

"Good. Maybe my flight won't be too bumpy," John said.

Penny's head jerked up from her coffee cup. "What flight?"

He cleared his throat and turned to pour more coffee. "I'm returning to Los Angeles. My flight leaves Denver at noon."

They stared at him. Tears welled in Flash's eyes; Amy's lower lip trembled and her shoulders sagged.

"Hey, guys. It's just for a couple of days."

"When did you . . . ?"

He looked at Penny and thought how lovely she was even with faint circles bruising her eyes. He had never known another woman with that particular shade of reddish-gold hair or eyes as blue as the Mediterranean. How had they ever been so foolish as to let things reach this point?

"I called early this morning for a flight. The reservation desks are open twenty-four hours a day."

"You are coming back, aren't you?" Alice asked, looking wide awake now. A frown deepened the lines between her eyes.

"Something has come up that has to be taken care of in person," he replied, adding sugar to his coffee. "It shouldn't take too long. I'll be back Friday night in time for the town's tree-lighting ceremony." He smiled at Amy and Flash. "And guess what we're going to do Saturday afternoon? We're going to find the perfect Christmas tree!"

They fell on him with hugs and kisses before they ran for their coats and caps and schoolbooks. Alice discreetly found something to do upstairs. Standing, Penny moved around the counter and placed her fingertips on his sleeve.

"John, are you leaving because..."

Briefly he touched her cheek, then let his hand drop. "I think we need a little time apart." His gaze swept the rounded swell of her stomach beneath a wool smock. "I'll be back in a couple of days. You said I'm welcome to stay until the baby comes, and I plan to take you up on that."

"I didn't intend to drive you away."

"You haven't." A humorless smile brushed his mouth. "This is a damned peculiar conversation for two soon-to-be-divorced people to be having, isn't it? Seems like you should be glad I'm leaving."

She frowned and her hands moved. He thought he saw a struggle ensuing behind her eyes, then she shrugged and gave him a helpless smile. "This whole mess is confusing, isn't it?"

"Yes," he said, watching her walk away from him.

HIS EYES BEGAN TO STING the minute he stepped off the airplane, which impressed him as odd, for he didn't usually notice Los Angeles's infamous smog. Six weeks of crisp clean mountain air had apparently stripped away his immunity.

After renting a sedan at the Hertz counter, he found his way out of the rental-car parking lot and turned left onto the highway. If he was lucky the Santa Monica Freeway wouldn't be too crowded and he'd have a straight shot to Harbor and Wilshire.

Maneuvering skillfully through the heavy traffic whizzing along the freeway, he started to relax, enjoying the warm temperature, the green plantings, and the feeling of being home. No one in the next lane was going to roll down a window and shout advice or questions about his relationship with his wife. Anonymity was the name of the game here. A man became anonymous the minute he stepped outside his usual perimeters. He became just another face in the crowd.

John frowned. He had never thought of it in those terms before—losing one's identity. But of course it was true. The people driving the cars enclosing his had no meaningful identity, not to him. He didn't care about them; they didn't care about him. He would never see them again.

The same could be said about the people he sat near in the Grand Avenue Bar, or at Perino's, one of his favorite restaurants. If by chance he made an ass of himself, he didn't have to suffer jokes about it the following day from people who had been sitting at the next table. They were strangers. Los Angeles, like any huge metropolis, was populated by strangers, by people who brushed the periphery of one's life, then moved on, having left no appreciable effect.

Frowning, he gripped the steering wheel and edged into the ramp lane. The man driving the car he cut in front of shouted out his window and made a rude gesture. The fast lane had its minor disadvantages, John thought with a mirthless smile.

Somehow it didn't surprise him when Jason, the doorman at the Blackman building, gazed at him without a flicker of recognition. The blank look lasted only a moment, then Jason's face broke into a grin. It was Christmas, after all, a time when doormen were remembered. "Mr. Martin, nice to see you," he said, beaming. "You've been gone a few days, haven't you?"

"Six weeks."

"Has it been that long?" Jason shook his head, unsure how to proceed. From his expression, it was a fair guess he assumed John no longer worked at Blackman Brothers.

John pressed an envelope into Jason's gloved hand. "Merry Christmas," he said, feeling foolish. Outside the air-conditioned lobby, it was a balmy seventy-seven degrees. Despite the plastic holly garlands draping the lobby and the plastic tree near the bank of elevators, the humid heat made Christmas seem impossibly distant.

"Thank you, Mr. Martin." Jason lifted his cap and smiled broadly as he escorted John to the elevators.

The first thing he saw when he stepped onto the twenty-second floor was the bowl of ornaments decorating Marla Simpson's receptionist desk. It reminded him of Santa's Village. Except Marla wasn't wearing winter wool; she was dressed in crisp lime-colored linen.

She blinked when she saw him, then grinned and flipped through a bowl of paper slips, withdrawing one. "We have an office pool betting on how soon you'd return." Her smile widened. "Walt Hanson in corporate finance wins." She waved the slip of paper. "He predicted you'd be back before Christmas."

John smiled. "Don't pay off yet. This is merely a visit. Is Emil in?"

Emil Blackman shook his hand when he was shown into the senior partner's plush office. "John! I wish I could say this is a surprise, but it really isn't." He smiled broadly. "In fact I understand there's an office pool..."

Emil continued speaking, but John wasn't listening. Instead, he studied the office he had coveted as long as he could remember. The mauve carpet was thick and rich; the furnishings were upholstered in buttery soft leather. There was a scattering of polished glass tables. Museum-quality paintings adorned the cherry-wood walls. A spectacular view of the bay opened behind Emil's oversize desk. In recognition of the holidays, Emil's secretary had installed and decorated a small artificial tree on top of a side table. A few gifts wrapped in distinctive Rodeo Drive paper lay beneath the branches.

John's office was down the corridor, a smaller, less lavish version of Emil's. Briefly he closed his eyes.

This is what he had sacrificed his wife and children to gain. A thick carpet, company paintings, a great view, and his name on the door in discreet gold letters. For this he had traded warmth and love. A smiling face on the pillow next to his. Small arms and sticky kisses.

"Emil," he said, interrupting. "We have to talk."

AFTER LEAVING Blackman Brothers, he drove to the condo he and Penny had bought almost eight years earlier. During the drive, he rolled down the car window, letting the warm breeze rush over his face. Palm trees and oleander lined the freeway. The day was humid and overcast. People in the cars flashing past him were in summer pastels.

In Aspen Springs Amy's scout troop would be ice-skating on the pond today. The ski slopes would be crowded. The temperature would hover at a chilly twenty-eight degrees. Wes Pierce would be sitting on his bench in front of the post office warming his face in the steam from a thermos of hot chocolate.

A person had to be crazy to trade palm trees and sunny beaches for freezing weather and snowdrifts.

In the lobby, he distributed Christmas envelopes to the doorman, the maintenance super and the head of housekeeping. He left envelopes for the paperboy and the maid service with the doorman, then rode the elevator to the eighth floor.

With half the furniture in Colorado, his living room looked spartan. The condo smelled dusty and hot, unused. After throwing apart the curtains, he opened the balcony doors to let the California light and air in to the rooms. Stepping onto the balcony, John glanced at his watch, then leaned on the railing and looked down to the swimming pool below.

Amy and Flash would be home from school by now, telling Alice about their day, doing their homework under her supervision. He wondered if Amy had done well on her math test, if Flash had had a good time at Billy Galloway's birthday party.

Turning back inside, he walked down the corridor to their rooms, standing for a moment in the doorways. Penny had taken the kids' furniture to Aspen Springs, and their rooms were empty. Idly he noticed the walls needed a coat of paint. A box of outgrown clothing sat forgotten in Flash's closet; Amy had left her swim fins behind.

Because he found the silence oppressive, he returned to the living room and snapped on the TV, tuning to CNN. When the national weather came on, he carried a cold beer into the living room and listened as America was informed that a cold front was sweeping toward the Rockies from Canada.

When the forecast ended, he finished his beer and slowly walked through the condo, seeing Penny in every room. He remembered the night of her thirtieth birthday, the day they had brought Flash home from the hospital, the afternoon Amy swallowed the bottle cap, the night they had celebrated a quarter-of-a-million-dollar commission.

Suddenly the silent condominium on Moss Morency Drive seemed the loneliest place on God's earth.

"DO YOU THINK Daddy misses us?" Flash asked for the hundredth time, looking up from the strips of paper he was coloring with fat crayon stubs.

"I'm sure he is," Penny said in an expressionless voice. After checking to make sure Flash wasn't also coloring the tablecloth, she added, "Right now Daddy's probably having dinner with friends."

A woman friend? It wasn't any of her business, she reminded herself with a frown. But they probably should have talked about it. She should have mentioned he was free to date if he wanted to. The thought made her feel lightheaded. He didn't need her permission, for heaven's sake. The divorce papers could be considered an official invitation to the dating game.

Amy brushed white paste over the ends of Flash's crayoned strips and pressed them together, adding to the growing paper chain that twisted across the kitchen floor.

"Do you think Daddy will call us?" she asked.

"Tonight?" Penny asked, glancing at the stove clock. "He probably won't get home until after you're in bed. But I know he's thinking about you."

Ha. Like hell he was. Right now, John was probably calling for more champagne, leaning across a candlelit table to gaze deeply into the eyes of his dinner date. And the longer Penny thought about John taking some bimbo out to dinner, the angrier she became. He could at least have waited until the divorce was final before he started acting like some romance-crazed teenager, hitting on every available woman who crossed his path.

She could just see it. He had probably taken the bimbo to the Spice Shack and was sitting with her in Penny's favorite booth. Mario would have given the bimbo a fresh daisy at the door, raising his thick eyebrows when he saw John was not with Penny.

The bimbo would slide into Penny's place in Penny's booth. She would be wearing something low cut in black silk or satin, and she was probably braless, because that's how bimbos were; it was in the bimbo rule book. You could not be a bimbo unless you had big breasts and went braless. And it was a given that bimbos turned up their noses at panty hose. They wore only black garter belts and smoke-colored stockings—rule number two. And every man alive knew it.

The bimbo would be raven-haired and look like a young Joan Collins—Penny was certain. Her eyelashes would be as long as the tines on a garden rake, as sultry as a Johnny Mathis recording at midnight. Her fingernails would be perfectly manicured, painted crimson and made for scratching a man's naked back. Her seductive voice would purr as she uttered inanities that would bore any intelligent man to tears. Except she would be wearing a perfume so provocative it wiped out a man's intelligence quicker than an erase key on a computer board.

John didn't have a chance. The bimbo would have him wrapped around her crimson-lacquered finger before the salad was served.

"Penny?" Alice looked up from the macaroni she was stringing on a needle and frowned. "Are you all right? You have the most peculiar look on your face—"

"How could he!" Penny flared, her cheeks as red as the bimbo's lips and nails. "The divorce isn't even final and . . . and it's Christmas!"

Amy and Flash looked up at her.

"It just isn't fair!" Slapping a bag of unopened macaroni on the kitchen counter, Penny scowled at it. "I'm home for dinner for the first time in weeks, and is he here to notice? No! He's in California having dinner with some painted bimbo who has a waist!" She placed her hands on her swollen stomach in the vicinity of the hips she used to have. "Well, I'll tell you this. He's not the only one who's free to date!"

They stared at her.

"Alice? You asked what I wanted for Christmas? I want a black lace garter belt and a pair of smoke-colored stockings!"

"Really?"

But who in the world was going to ask an eight-and-half-month pregnant woman for a date? And if, by some miracle, such a crazy man appeared, would she really want to to go out with him? She didn't remember how to date. What did strangers talk about? What if he tried to kiss her good night? The idea of kissing anyone other than John made her shudder. Ugh.

And where would they go? Dancing? Right. Skiing? Oh, sure. In her condition about the only choice was a movie, and then only if her date agreed to pull her out of the seat afterward.

Then there was the problem of how her date would introduce her to his friends. "This is Penny Martin, my date. I didn't do that to her. Ha, ha." Or, "Yes, she's pregnant, but she's still a sexy exciting woman." Wink, wink.

Oh, God.

"I don't want to date," she said, spreading her hands. Her voice sounded suspiciously like a wail. "It just wouldn't work out and I don't want to, anyway."

When she saw Alice, Amy and Flash staring at her as if she had lost her mind, she burst into tears, spun and did a fast waddle out of the room.

"What's a bimbo?" Flash asked Alice, his dark eyes wide.

"What's a garter belt?"

"Why is Mommy crying?"

Alice sighed, frowning after her daughter. "Well, kids. Your mother has a rich fantasy life, you see. And generally that's a good thing." Lifting a piece of macaroni, she sighted through it, then pushed it over the needle. "And she's pregnant. Being pregnant messes up a woman's metabolism." Amy and Flash looked at each other, then back at her. "Metabolism? Well, never mind. We have to be understanding during this difficult time for your mother, okay? Now, how are you progressing on that paper chain?"

Penny swept back into the kitchen. Her eyes were a bit red and her hands weren't as steady as she'd have liked as she dumped the bag of macaroni into a bowl. "The paper chain looks very nice," she said, her voice artificially bright. "Now who's going to help me string this macaroni?"

"Mommy, what's a bimbo?"

"Ask your father," she said grimly, squinting at the needle and string.

THE DAYS PASSED in a busy blur, then suddenly, it seemed, it was Friday. The tree-lighting ceremony was almost finished by the time Penny arrived at the pond. Before dashing out of her car, she cut the headlights, then paused to catch her breath and peer through the windshield at the group gathered on the ice.

Mayor Windell had already pressed the official lighting switch. A thirty-foot Christmas tree lit the center of the frozen pond with brightly colored twinkling lights. Skaters flashed across the ice, cutting through the light from the torches and the red and green shadows cast by the Christmas tree. Myrna Gordon led the carol singing.

As Penny stepped out of the car and drew on her gloves and pulled her cap over her ears, she spotted her family standing near the front of the group. Dr. Adler and Alice shared a song sheet; Flash and Amy were pressed against John. Penny imagined she could hear his clear baritone rising above the other voices.

Biting her lips and holding her arms out for balance, she placed each boot carefully in the snow and made her way down to the pond.

She was late again, and slightly embarrassed by how glad she was to see John. In the back of her mind she had half expected to receive a phone call telling her he had changed his plans and would be remaining in Los Angeles for the holidays. Also, she was angry with herself for being so consumed by curiosity. What had he done in Los Angeles? Who had he seen? Where had he gone?

A flush of pink heated her cold cheeks as she remembered how her imagination had run away with her a few nights before.

The idiotic part of it was that she hadn't felt particularly jealous when they were married. She had been secure enough in herself and in their marriage that even when John worked late, as he usually did, it had never occurred to her to question it. Her imagination had not soared into overdrive and tormented her with jealousy-provoking suspicions. So why was she behaving so badly now? It didn't make any sense.

When he saw her, John's face lit with a smile of genuine pleasure, and her heart turned over in her chest. Knowing she would regret it later, she moved into the arm he opened for her and stood close to him, bending her cap over the song sheet.

" 'Joy to the world, the lord is come . . .' "

When she had regained her equilibrium, Penny smiled and waved at Alice and Dr. Adler. Colored Christmas lights blinked across the faces of Alice and John and her children as they sang. Amy, her cheeks tinted from the cold, looked radiant in her joy of the moment; Flash gripped John's hand and happily sang off-key in a loud boyish soprano. Alice had moved to link arms with Dr. Adler and sang in a clear bright voice, harmonizing with the doctor.

Silvery breath rose in front of the carolers. The exuberant swish of skates sounded on the ice.

Suddenly Penny remembered Christmases past, standing in this same spot, her hair braided like Amy's, her small hand clasped in Alice's. Even then she had sensed that some day she would be standing here with a family of her own, gazing in joy and wonder at the bright star blazing atop the tree while carolers filled the night with song.

Myrna Gordon's strong vibrant voice rose above the others.

"'Oh holy night, the stars are brightly shining...'"

Penny's throat closed and the bright Christmas lights shimmered behind a moist film. It was so beautiful. The star shining from atop the tree, the frosty night, Myrna's joyful voice soaring, and John's arm warm around her shoulders. The faces of her children. The tension falling away like snow melting down a window pane.

This was Christmas. This was what it was intended to be. Joy and fellowship and family. Voices raised in celebration. This was the way she had remembered Christmas all those years when she was so far from home. This is what she had wanted for her children.

And for John.

Chapter Eight

"'Hi ho, hi ho, it's off to work we go,'" John sang. After glancing back to grin at the kids, he adjusted a small ax on the shoulder of his parka and led the march from Penny's car to the area flagged by the forest service.

Other families had also driven up the mountain to search for the perfect Christmas tree. Voices called across the snowy mountainside, shouting greetings, calling Merry Christmas.

"Watch out for the stubs," John called over his shoulder to Flash.

Stumps of trees stuck out from the carpet of snow, evidence of the previous year's Christmas harvest. Flash manfully maneuvered his sled around them, happily singing "'Hi ho, hi ho,'" at the top of his voice whenever John did.

Penny and Amy brought up the rear, calling and waving to friends, trying to keep up with Flash and John.

"What do you think, sport?" John stepped back in the snow to squint at a perfectly shaped spruce.

"It isn't big enough, Daddy," Flash protested. Amy agreed.

"I believe you're right. We need a big one. How are you holding up?" he asked Penny. To her surprise, he seemed to be in his element, thoroughly enjoying the outing.

"Fine," she lied, pausing to catch her breath. Women as pregnant as she was had no business hauling themselves through a snowy pine forest. Granted, the slope was gentle, but she was so bulky and awkward that even flat land presented a problem.

"I wish you'd agree to wait in the car."

"I know you're thinking of my welfare, and I appreciate it, but I've dreamed about cutting our own tree for years. How much it would mean to the kids. And I want to be part of it, okay? Will you please stop fussing over me? Just let me do this at my own pace and I'll be fine."

"Okay," he said, raising his gloves in surrender. "But if—"

"John!"

"Just don't be stubborn, all right? If it gets to be too much, I'll take you back to the car."

Maybe it was a dumb idea to insist on sharing the experience, but she was determined to see it through. And, she thought grimly, she was determined to enjoy it.

The sky was a brilliant cobalt blue, and winter sunlight cast a sparkle of diamonds across the snow. If the cold hadn't been so intense, it would have been a fabulous day. But it seemed to Penny that she inhaled icy needles with each breath. As no one else appeared to notice the cold, Penny pulled her cap more firmly over her ears and summoned a cheerful smile. She made a vow not to spoil the outing by focusing on her discomfort or dwelling on how difficult it was to hike through knee-high snow while baby Whosit did somersaults inside her stomach. She told herself for the hundredth time in the past five minutes that she absolutely did not have to go to the bathroom. But she eyed the forest, looking for a wide-based tree just in case.

"Anybody want to rub my tummy for luck?" she joked, trying to take her mind off the cold.

"Our resident Buddha," John said grinning. They all patted her tummy, then John led them deeper into the forest. "Is this the perfect one?" he asked, stopping in front of a snow-tipped pine.

"It doesn't have enough branches," Amy commented doubtfully.

"Right you are. Okay, how about that one? Is that the perfect tree, or am I seeing things?"

Penny struggled after them, hoisting her boots over the drifts or breaking through them. "This is fun," she told herself grimly. Fighting up slopes through knee-high drifts was a great family outing. Everyone should cut their own tree. "Wouldn't have missed it for the world," she muttered.

At this point she could have sworn she had been pregnant, bulky and longing for a nap, most of her adult life. Among other things, she could no longer recall the convenience of bending from the waist. Since she could no longer bend, John had had to push her snow boots on her feet and lace them for her. And as if she wasn't bulky enough, the layers of woolen underwear and heavy clothing made her feel like a cartoon character, one of those with so much padding that his arms stuck straight out at his sides.

Panting from the exertion of climbing through drifts of wind-sculpted snow, she finally caught up to the others, who were waiting for her with expectant faces.

"Look, Mommy! I found the perfect tree!" Grabbing her hand, Flash eagerly pulled her forward.

Penny eyed his sled enviously, wishing pride would allow her to let someone pull her back to the car.

"Looks terrific to me," she enthused, guiltily aware she would have said the same thing if the tree under discussion had been an anemic specimen with only three branches. It seemed as if they had been fighting the deep snow and walking for hours. Days. Everyone's cheeks were bright pink from the cold. Eyes sparkled and silvery vapor puffed in front of each mouth.

"Okay, guys, now that Mommy's given the official approval, here we go." John applied himself with the ax and in a moment the tree was down. Laughing at Flash and Amy's efforts to help, he tied the tree to the sled, then straightened and smiled at Penny. "You know, I've always wanted to do this." Pushing back his cap, he looked at the sky, inhaled the heavy pine scent perfuming the frosty air. "Buying a tree from a lot will never be the same."

This was no time to rhapsodize. Not when one-fourth of the tree-cutting party was freezing, exhausted, and had to go to the bathroom in the worst way. *It's all in your mind,* Penny told herself.

"Wagons ho," she called, leading the long waddle back to the car.

By the time they returned home and Alice had served marshmallow-capped cups of steaming hot chocolate, Penny felt like a truck had rolled over her.

"I'm pooped," she said, dropping onto a stool in front of the counter.

Alice nodded, understanding. "I remember the final month when I was pregnant with you. It seemed to last forever. All I wanted to do was sleep. The least little thing wore me out."

John emerged from the basement carrying the carton of ornaments and Christmas decorations.

"We're going to decorate now?" Penny groaned. Being surrounded by Christmas every day at work had diminished any need for an immediate display of Christmas decorations. Then she saw the excitement lighting the kids' faces and she bit her tongue.

"Look, Grandma Alice!" Amy clasped her hands together and stared at the tree John was fitting into the stand, her eyes shining. "Isn't it the best Christmas tree you ever saw?"

"The very best," Alice agreed, smiling.

"I found it," Flash claimed proudly, crawling under the branches to help John.

Penny watched with a tired smile. She didn't recall John's having so much patience in the past, but he didn't complain as Amy and Flash continually got in his way in their efforts to help. He seemed to be enjoying himself, and he praised the kids when they managed to actually assist, more by accident than anything else.

"Do you need help with the lights?" Penny asked when the tree was secured in the stand. She hoped he would say no. She wasn't sure she had the energy to do anything more than watch.

"I don't think you can get close enough to the tree to do much good," John said, smiling. "Alice? Can you give me a hand?"

"I'll do it," Flash insisted.

"You're too short, sport. Maybe next year."

Sitting at the counter, unreasonably feeling left out, Penny sipped her chocolate and watched the lights wind around the tree, then the strings of macaroni and the paper chains. When she saw the pride in Amy's and Flash's expressions, she realized the macaroni and the paper chains had been a wonderful idea.

"Penny, you look absolutely exhausted," Alice commented, looking up from the box of ornaments she was opening. "Darling, why don't you pop yourself into a nice hot tub? Relax for a while. I'll call you for dinner."

A sudden overwhelming case of the guilts overtook her. She was too pooped, too pregnant to participate in the tree trimming. And she hadn't even thought about offering to help with dinner. The tree reminded her that she hadn't started her Christmas shopping, hadn't give a thought to the homemade gifts she had agreed to. She should have phoned Lydie an hour ago to see how things were going at Santa's Village. She should have paid bills last night. Tomorrow or the next night was Amy's and Flash's Christmas program at school. Vaguely she remembered promising to bring a plate of cookies. Where would she find the time?

"Thanks for the suggestion. I think I'll do that," she said to Alice, sliding from the stool. John and Amy were singing along with the carols playing on the radio and happily selecting silver and red ornaments from the boxes. Flash shouted and laughed and flung handfuls of tinsel at the lower branches.

It didn't seem to Penny as if they would miss her.

Leaving the scent of pine behind her and the familiar sound of carols, she climbed the stairs to her bedroom, entered the bathroom and turned on the water in the tub. For a moment she inspected herself in the mirror tiles, seeing the pink wind burn across her cheeks, the fatigue dulling her eyes. Alice was right. She looked ready to fall over.

Maybe John was also right. Maybe she was keeping too hectic a pace. But it was only temporary, dammit. A frown drew her brows together as she discovered that her bottle of bubble bath was empty. Amy must have borrowed it again. After dropping the empty bottle into the waste can, she added shampoo to the bath water and nodded as bubbles foamed across the surface of the water.

She locked the bathroom door, symbolically shutting out the world, then stepped into the hot water with a sigh of pleasure and carefully lowered herself into the bubbles.

But she couldn't lock away her thoughts.

This was the Christmas she had dreamed of all those years in Los Angeles. She could remember standing on the condo balcony on Christmas Day last year, looking down at people splashing in the swimming pool below, and longing for a good old-fashioned snowy Christmas in Aspen Springs.

She had felt almost a physical craving for the clean cold softness of new snow on her cheeks, for the scent of freshly cut pine. Something in her heart had rejected the sight of Christmas lights wound through palm trees and jacaranda shrubs, had protested Santas dressed in red bermudas and short sleeves. She had yearned for a real Christmas. A Charles Dickens Christmas, with frost lacing the windowpanes and fat snowflakes tumbling out of the sky. With the cinnamon smell of home-baked cookies and the tang of green pine boughs and holly wreaths.

Now that she had what she longed for, but she wasn't enjoying it as she had thought she would.

For one thing, it was difficult to be enthusiastic about all the Christmas trimmings when she was surrounded by them every day at work. For another, it was hard to enjoy much of anything when she felt so tired all the time.

And she felt left out.

It was her own fault, of course, but she felt the sorrow and regret just the same. She was running as fast as she could, but the tree-lighting ceremony had begun without her. Naturally. She couldn't go ice-skating or snowmobiling with John and the kids on weekends because she had to work or catch up around the house. Of course. It was the busiest time of year at Santa's Village. It seemed that all she had done today was struggle to keep up, arriving at one tree, panting and gasping, just as the others were moving on to the next. Now her family was enjoying the warmth and camaraderie of decorating the tree. And she was too pooped to take part. She was a quart low on Christmas spirit.

Christmas was turning into one big headache.

Folding her hands over her stomach, Penny sighed and pushed her toes against the water spigot.

The night she had told John she would not return to Los Angeles, he had said she was afraid of loving. In addition to everything else she had to think and worry about, she had been thinking about that.

She was not afraid of loving; she was afraid of the pain when the loving was no longer enough. She did love him. Covering her face with one sudsy hand, she drew a long breath. She loved him so much it hurt.

The John Martin who had arrived on her doorstep was the John Martin they had both lost sight of. If he could be like this all the time—wonderful with the children, tender and loving toward her. With no distracted frowns, no late nights and weekends at work. And if he could do it here, in Aspen Springs. If, if, if.

She scrubbed her hand across her forehead. It was going to be terrible for Amy and Flash when John returned to Los Angeles. As terrible as leaving him the first time. Maybe worse, because he had spent so much time with them, had genuinely gotten to know them and let them know him.

It would also be terrible for her. Already she felt hints of the renewed pain of missing him.

The new baby would help, she thought, gently tracing her fingertips over her stomach. And she had her job to keep her busy. But still...there were the nights. The long lonely nights.

This line of thinking was taking her nowhere and was only upsetting her. She would wrap herself in a warm robe and join the others.

Because she couldn't bend forward to reach the drain, she opened it with her toes. The water receded around her and she waited until she thought she could push herself up without splashing the floor.

Then she pressed her heels against the bottom of the tub and pushed her hands against the sides. Her heels shot out from under her, and before she could catch herself, she slid awkwardly down the back of the tub until she was lying flat on her back as the last of the water gurgled down the drain.

Feeling foolish, thankful there was no one to see, Penny pushed her feet against the base of the tub. Her shoulders rose up along the back curve, but she immediately slid down flat the moment she moved her feet.

It was the shampoo, she realized. Unlike her usual bubble bath, the shampoo had left a slippery residue. The tub was as slick as oiled porcelain. There was nothing on which to get a grip.

"This is nutty," she muttered, flat on her back on the bottom of the tub. She tried to bend forward to sit up, but it was like trying to fold a beach ball.

Lying flat, she stared up at the heat lamp, wishing she had turned it on. "Now, think about this," she told herself. After a moment, she decided to try a sideways maneuver. She would roll on her side, draw her feet up, then, wedged on her side with something solid to press against, she could pull herself up.

Rolling sideways was a mistake. When she tried to draw her legs up, all that happened was that she slid toward the drain and had less control than she seemed to have on her back. Plus, she saw that she would not fit sideways in the tub.

Now she was beginning to get cold. Doubling her efforts, she slid and slipped around the tub, pushing herself up the back curve, sliding back down. She began to feel frantic.

There was only one thing to do if she ever hoped to get out of this rotten tub, and she hated the thought.

"Help," she whispered, closing her eyes and imagining what she looked like. A naked wet hippo wallowing in a shampoo-slick trap.

"Help!" Would they hear her over the carols on the radio and their voices?

"Help!" she shouted.

John paused beside the tree, an ornament in his hand. "Was that your mother?" he asked Flash.

"I thought I heard something, too," Alice said, glancing up from the pot of chili she was stirring on the stove. "Amy, honey, run upstairs and see if your mother wants something."

When Amy returned, her blue eyes were wide. "Mommy's stuck in the bathtub. She can't get out."

"What?" John stared at her.

"She wants you to come, Daddy."

They all went. John tried the bathroom door. "Penny? The door's locked."

"I know," she answered in an embarrassed voice. "I can't reach it."

"Is there a key?" he asked Alice.

Alice shook her head. "If there is, it disappeared years ago. But I'll search. The bathroom lock is a push button. It works from the bathroom side of the door."

"Penny? Are you all right?"

A silence ensued. "I'm getting cold," she finally called out. "I can't reach the towels." There was another silence while John stared at the door. "Are the kids out there with you?" Penny asked.

"I think I'll have to break down the door."

"Good heavens," Alice murmured. She straightened her shoulders. "Come along, children. Let's . . . let's finish the tinsel, then you can set the table."

"I want to watch Daddy break down the door," Flash begged. His dark eyes sparkled with excitement.

"Me, too! We can, can't we, Daddy? We can stay and watch?" Both children looked at him with awed eyes.

"I don't think your mother would like that."

"Your Daddy's right," Alice interjected hastily, eyeing the door. "Let's go."

The dragged their feet, faces long with disappointment. John studied the door until Alice and the children had gone.

He had seen this done on TV a hundred times. How hard could it be?

"Penny? I'm going to break it down." Actually, it looked pretty sturdy. "Stay out of the way."

"John, I can't get in the way! I'm stuck in the tub."

Moving back a step, he contemplated the door, deciding where he would hit it. "Don't worry, honey. I'm coming to get you."

"Be careful!"

There was enough room to take three running steps. His shoulder hit the door and he bounced back, landing on the floor. Rubbing his shoulder, he swore between his teeth.

"What happened?" Penny called anxiously.

He pushed himself to his feet and narrowed his eyes on the door with a look of grudging respect. It was built to last. But they broke down doors on *Miami Vice*. They did it on *Wiseguy* and the *Equalizer*. Tom Selleck had built a career around breaking down doors. Television made it look easy. According to those guys, there was nothing to it. He rubbed his sore shoulder and stared at the door.

"John? Are you okay?"

"Tom Selleck is a fraud. Did you know that?"

"What?"

"Stay out of the way."

"John, I told you . . ."

This time, knowing what he was up against, he bunched up, imagined he was a tank and hurled himself at the door, hitting it with all his strength. The door hurled him back. Pain ran up his shoulder in a hot pulsing current. Sprawled on the floor, he rubbed his shoulder and cursed through a clenched jaw.

"What the hell is this door made of? Steel?"

"It's solid oak," Penny called from the other side. He groaned. "John? I don't mean to rush you along, but . . . but it's cold . . ."

"Okay. Hold on, I'm coming. I'm going to kick in the lock." His shoulder felt like it was on fire. The lock looked as sturdy as the rest of the door. But by God, he was going to rescue his lady. "Stand back."

"Listen, if you say stand back one more time—"

"Here goes."

The Karate Kid he was not. His heel struck, then slid off the doorknob, and he crashed to the floor, convinced he had sprained his back. For a moment he lay there, staring up at the closed door, swearing mightily. First he was going to get a blowtorch and open that damned door if it was the last thing he ever did. Then he was going to hurl the TV set off the balcony. It wasn't only kids who watched too much television. Then he was going to write an acid letter to Tom Selleck and Don Johnson, telling them exactly what he thought of their door-breaking scenes.

Alice walked into the bedroom and stared down at him. "Are you all right?"

"Do I look all right?" he asked sourly, getting to his feet. Groaning, he placed a hand at the small of his back. "At present it's three for the door, zip for the home team. Do you own a blowtorch?"

"Something better," she said, opening her hand. The key to the bathroom door lay in her palm. "I found it."

"Thank God."

"I'll be downstairs," Alice murmured, discreetly withdrawing as John bent to fit the key into the lock.

Penny looked pitiful. She was laying flat on her back on the bottom of the tub, her knees drawn up, her hair wet on her bare shoulders. She was shivering and her teeth were chattering.

"Penny, honey, I'll have you out of there in a flash," he said, flipping on the heat lamp before he bent over her.

Tears of embarrassment and frustration formed in the corner of her eyes. "I was out of bubble bath, so I put shampoo in the water, but it's so slick! Then, after I drained—"

"I know, darling. Here, let me get you under the arms."

"—the water, it was like the drain was pulling me down too, and—"

The angle was excruciatingly awkward. Once he got his arms around her, he was leaning too far over the tub to exert any upward strength.

"—every time I tried to get out, I kept slipping back down."

When he saw he wasn't going to succeed, he released her. She gasped, then slipped down the back curve of the tub again. She lay on the bottom of the tub, staring up at him.

"Was that supposed to be funny?" she asked in an expressionless voice.

"This is more difficult than I thought. I don't want to risk dropping you or having you fall."

The heat lamp spread a rosy glow over her naked body. If it hadn't been for the goose bumps, she would have been ripely beautiful. Lush and dewy. He hadn't seen her naked in, well, in almost nine months. Exerting massive self-control, he kept his gaze focused on her face, but he could still see her magnificent breasts from the corners of his eyes. He swallowed.

"I know that look, John Martin," she said in an accusing tone, narrowing her lashes. "And believe me, this is not the time! I'm trapped and cold and I need to get out of this tub! Please, do something."

"Okay." He shook his head, shaking free of the hypnotizing sight of her. The rose-tipped breasts, the golden triangle. "Let's try it sideways."

She pointed to her stomach. "I won't fit sideways."

"All right, can you kinda lean sideways then, at least enough so I can get a firm hold under your arms?"

Her breasts were sensational. Her skin glowed. With her golden hair wet on her shoulders, with that radiant skin, she looked like a pregnant Venus. The touch of her reminded him of cool smooth ivory.

When he had his hands under her arms, trying not to think about touching her, he leaned near her face, his eyes lingering on her mouth. "This is what we're going to do. I'll lift you to a sitting position on the edge of the tub, all right? And I'll hold you steady while you swing your legs around to the floor."

"Okay." The trust in her eyes steadied his hold.

"On the count of three."

Penny pushed; he pulled. When he had her sitting on the edge of the tub, he chanced to glance at the mirror tiles on the back side of the tub and caught a quick breath. She was splendid, beautiful. Radiant in impending motherhood. He stared at her image, hypnotized. Reuben would have killed to paint skin tones like hers.

Finally she was standing, shivering, her forehead pressed to his shoulder. "Thank you," she whispered.

Grabbing a towel, he rubbed her body briskly, restoring the warmth to her glorious skin.

He supposed there were men who were turned off by their wife's pregnancy, but he was not one of them. In his opinion, Penny never looked lovelier than when she was pregnant. Something wonderful happened to her skin. It became like satin, creamy and smooth, almost luminous. He wanted to touch her, stroke her, wanted to shape his hands around the firm swell of his child, wanted to cup her heavy breasts in his palms. The feeling was reverential, but it was sexual, too.

"Right now I wish you weren't pregnant," he murmured against her hair, his voice husky. He held her against his warmth while he toweled her back.

"Me, too," she whispered.

Before he could decide if she meant she was weary of being pregnant or if she meant she wanted him, too, she stepped away from him and wrapped herself in the voluminous orange robe.

"I don't know what I would have done if you hadn't been here," she said, bending slightly to wrap her hair in a towel. "Thank you, John."

"Actually, I didn't do much of anything." Now he was beginning to feel the ache in his shoulder. It was going to be sore for days. "Alice found the key. She's the heroine of the day."

They looked at each other across the small space, Penny leaning against the sink, him standing with his hands in his pockets.

Finally Penny dropped her eyes and plucked at her robe. A blush rose on her cheeks. "The chili smells good, doesn't it?" she whispered.

He cleared his throat. The moment passed. "Ready for something to eat?"

"Starving."

When she stepped past him, he caught the scent of shampoo and soap and baby powder and the scent that was uniquely Penny's. After a moment, he sighed and followed her. She tried to open the bedroom door and frowned.

"That's odd," she said. "The door will only open a crack." Placing her eye to the crack, she looked down at the knob. Amy's jump rope had been tied around the handle. By shifting position, Penny could see the other end of the rope tied to the handle of the guest-bathroom door. "You won't believe this! We're tied in."

She banged her fist on the door. "Kids? Amy and Flash? Let us out of here right now!"

John groaned. "Amy's last Brownie badge was for knots."

Carols blasted on the other side of the door. Amy or Flash had turned up the radio until it was loud enough to rock the house. And drown out any cries for help.

John glanced at Penny's bed, then smiled at her. "Right idea, wrong methods."

She gave him a weak smile, then returned to beating on the door.

When Alice finally came to see what was keeping them—and unlocked the door—she found Penny napping in the bed and John sitting in the chair next to her pretending to read.

"I DON'T GET IT," Lydie Severin said, tucking her chin into the scarf wound about her throat. Thick snowflakes swirled out of the evening sky and danced in the light shining beneath the Victorian lamps lining Main Street.

"What don't you get?" Penny asked, as they stepped into the employee cafeteria bringing a blast of cold air with them. At a dozen good-natured protests, they quickly shut the door. Then they hung up their coats, took trays from the rack and started down the cafeteria line.

"When you talk about John, you get a mushy look in your eye. It's like you're still in love with him." Lydie leaned over the glass counter then pointed to the chicken-fried steak. "I'll take the chicken-fried, please. Yet you aren't stopping the divorce."

"I do love him," Penny admitted. She ordered a fruit salad, thinking about the weight she had gained. "But love isn't enough. Unfortunately."

"You're kidding," Lydie commented when they had settled themselves at a table away from the door. She flicked her napkin across her lap. "A job certainly isn't enough. Try snuggling up to a title or a paycheck. Kids aren't enough. They're terrific, sure, but what do you do after they go to bed?"

"Come on, Lydie. You know what I'm saying."

"No, I don't. Hey, look at the sign behind you—Christmas Is Love. In my opinion, *life* is love. That's what it's all about. The whole ball of wax. What else is there that counts for anything?"

"I'm not saying love isn't important. I'm just saying other things are important, too." Penny looked at the fruit salad and decided she wasn't hungry, after all.

"Not a chance. I think you're nuts."

"Come on, Lydie, give me a break. Lately it seems like you're always on my case. I thought you were my friend."

"I am your friend, dummy. I'm trying to understand what you're thinking. You have this terrific guy you love and who loves you. But you say love isn't enough. You'd rather have a job that's wearing you to a frazzle, and raise three, count 'em, three, kids by yourself, not to mention sleeping alone. Does it strike you that possibly there is a flaw in your thinking? That just maybe you're making a bad bargain?"

"Love shouldn't mean one person has to surrender everything that's important."

"Hey, it's not a perfect world. But think about what you just said. Where does it end, Penny? Once you start saying, I'm not the one who's going to give in . . . then what you're doing is placing conditions on love. How do you get off that trip?"

"What are you talking about?" Penny asked, frowning.

"Isn't that what you're doing? Aren't you saying to John that you'll love him if he'll give up his career, move to Aspen Springs and live your life-style?"

"That's what he's saying to *me*. But I don't think either of us should have to give up our ideals."

"Giving each other up is better? Look, suppose John gave in and did it your way. What happens next? What's the next condition? You'll love him if he's home for dinner every night? You'll love him if—'' she spread her hands, searching for words "—he never mentions business after five o'clock or takes a business call at home? If you ask me, this whole thing sounds like a power play.''

"I don't recall asking you," Penny replied coldly. The bright color had intensified in her cheeks.

"Listen Penny, you won't believe this right now, but what I'm going to tell you is true." Lydie pushed her chicken-fried steak to one side. "Three months after your divorce is final, you'll be looking for another man. You'll join the ranks of the single and the recently divorced. And we're all looking for the same thing. Love. We aren't looking for a man who is geographically convenient, or a man who will promise to spend every single weekend at home, or a man who is as wealthy as Midas. We aren't thinking about conditions. We're looking for a man we can love and who will love us in return. Those are the criteria. Look around you. Take a look at Helga." She nodded toward the next table. "What do you think Helga wants from Santa?"

Penny didn't answer.

"Love. That's what Helga wants. It's what we all want. Dear Santa, please bring me someone to love who will love me in return. Penny, love is damned hard to find. You're one of the lucky ones, but you're too confused right now to recognize it."

"Look Lydie, I know you mean well, but I don't want to discuss my personal life. Okay?"

"Suit yourself. I just think you're making a big mistake, that's all."

Penny poked her fruit salad. "And if I pack up and return to Los Angeles, you get the promotion. That wouldn't be influencing your advice, would it?"

"That isn't fair, Penny." Lydie's shoulders straightened and her expression stiffened. "Since you've said you won't take the promotion even if it's offered, I'll get it anyway."

She paused. "Unless you aren't shooting straight with me and you do want the promotion."

Suddenly Penny remembered John saying, "Show me. If you don't want the promotion, then take yourself out of the running."

Frowning, she turned her coffee cup in the saucer. Until now she hadn't taken time to realize that it was possible she was building her ego at the expense of Lydie's. If she did indeed win a promotion that she didn't plan to accept, she would have the ego stroke of knowing she had won. But Lydie would be left with the knowledge that she was second choice.

"If my circumstances were different, I would want the promotion," she admitted slowly, working it out in her mind. Sometimes when she couldn't sleep, she thought about the changes she would make at Santa's Village if things had been different and she could seriously consider accepting the promotion. Even knowing it was a waste of time, she couldn't help thinking about it.

"Then I wish your circumstances were different," Lydie said, looking at her across the table. "I wish this was an honest competition."

"It is honest, but it's just…" There was no point in going over it again. She drew a breath and shifted the topic. "Some of our employees feel we're pushing them too hard because we're both competing so strenuously for Allenby's approval," Penny said quietly. "Some of the staff believe we're asking too much of them and of ourselves."

"Maybe we are," Lydie conceded after a moment. "I blew up at Don Compton yesterday over some little thing that didn't really merit such a strong reaction." After a pause, she added, "I'll be glad when the choice is made and the suspense is over."

Penny noticed that Lydie looked tired, too. "Oh, Lydie, do you really think I've been deceiving you? That I'd change my mind and accept the promotion if Allenby offered me the job?" she asked in a soft voice.

Lydie studied her friend. "Honestly? I don't know, Penny. It's difficult to believe you'd drive yourself this hard if part of you didn't want it."

The observation was distressing. Long after Lydie had departed for the day, Penny thought about their conversation. She was still thinking about it when she turned out the lights in her office and walked through the park to the deserted parking lot.

It was ten o'clock at night, her children were asleep, her back ached, she was hungry enough to wish she had eaten the fruit salad, and she couldn't wait to fall into bed.

"Dear Santa," she said as she scraped snow and ice off her windshield. "Please bring me three extra hours a day. And give the promotion to Lydie. It would make things so much simpler."

Simpler? What could be simpler than saying no? But it wouldn't be simple, because deep down she admitted she wanted the promotion. At least she wanted to know she could have had it if her circumstances had been different.

And, Santa, she added after a moment, if you can manage it, please bring me a solution to John. Because she wanted him, too.

It looked like this would be the year Santa didn't bring anything on her list.

Chapter Nine

A brightly lit Christmas tree occupied one side of the school stage. A manger scene crowded the other. Wes Pierce, dressed as Santa Claus, sat in a rocking chair beside the tree, beaming and ho-hoing and presenting gifts to the kindergartners and first graders, who were dressed in pajamas and holding teddy bears in their arms.

Sitting in the darkened audience, Penny leaned over her stomach when it was Flash's turn to recite his poem. She held her breath and smiled encouragement. Beside her, John and Alice leaned forward, too, silently mouthing the first words of the poem.

Flash gripped his teddy bear and approached the front edge of the stage. He stood there, not speaking and squinting at the audience as the silence lengthened. A whisper prompted from the wings, but Flash ignored it, saying nothing.

Penny raised her hand above the heads in the audience so that Flash could spot his family. A broad smile pleated his freckles, and he leaned forward from the waist and bellowed his poem.

"Santa, Santa, Santa dear/ Here's my wants, I hope you hear/ Bring us peace and bring us health/ Bring Mama rest and Daddy wealth..."

"I coached him," John whispered as the audience chuckled. He gave Penny's hand a proud squeeze.

"...and a train for me!" Flash finished, shouting the words. The Flash Martin school of performing equated loud with excellence. The audience laughed and applauded, then Dr. Adler's granddaughter stepped to the front of the stage to recite the next Christmas poem.

Like a wave passing over the audience, one set of parents strained forward to mouth words as another set leaned back in their seats, beaming with pride and relief.

Penny, John and Alice leaned forward again when Amy, dressed as a shepherdess, followed the Wise Men onto the stage. Possibly there were other speaking parts, but they heard only Amy as she waved her crook over the manger and said to the audience, "Oh, what a beautiful baby!"

"Oh, dear," Penny murmured when Amy's part was over. She gripped John's arm in alarm. "I was supposed to bring a plate of cookies, but I forgot until this minute!"

"Don't worry," John whispered, covering her hand with his. "Alice remembered. I baked cookies this afternoon and she brought some with us. The Martin family honor has not been tarnished." He grinned.

"You baked them?"

In all likelihood, if Penny had remembered the cookies, she would have stopped at Santa's Village Bake Shoppe and bought a bag. An edge of panic sharpened her nerves. There was too much to do and not enough time. She couldn't keep up with it all. There was Amy's Brownie party and Flash's class party; was she supposed to furnish cookies for them? She needed to organize an office party for her staff, and she recalled seeing a couple of holiday invitations in the mail. And when was she going to address cards?

She suppressed a groan at the thought of all the letters she needed to write to enclose with her cards. Maybe this was the year for the Christmas letter, that generic impersonal enclosure she had always professed to dislike. What she hated most about the "Dear Friends" Christmas letter was its relentlessly cheerful tone. No one ever wrote a "Dear Friends" Christmas letter that said: "I'm pregnant and I don't want to be, but I've left my husband anyway and here I am living in a small town in my mother's house and working too many hours to get a promotion I don't plan to accept. I'm exhausted, thirty pounds overweight, confused and upset. But I hope you have a nice Christmas."

Nope, this was not the year to send out a Christmas letter. And now was not the proper time to start making mental lists of all she needed to do tomorrow and everything she had forgotten to do today.

As she forced herself to relax and focus on enjoying the remainder of the Christmas program, Penny gradually realized this was another of those close moments with John that she had begun to love and to dread. She was very aware of his presence beside her. With each breath, she inhaled the expensive spiced scent of the cologne he wore, could sense his genuine pleasure in the shared moment, at watching their children perform. His arm lay across the back of her seat, possessive, near enough that she felt his solid warmth enclosing her.

Suddenly a rush of longing overwhelmed her. She experienced an urgent disconcerting need to rest her head against his shoulder and deepen the emotional sharing to some physical expression. They were as one in their pride in their children; at the moment she longed to close the circle and reach for him.

Swallowing hard, Penny clasped her hands tightly over her stomach. She fixed her eyes on the stage and leaned slightly away from the warmth brushing her shoulders.

The divorce had been her idea; she wanted it. Nothing had changed. They were still entrenched in their positions.

But the divorce was not working out as she had envisioned. Because her job demanded more time and energy than she had anticipated, she was not spending as much time with Flash and Amy as she wanted and as she had planned. She had been in Aspen Springs nearly a year, but she was still living with Alice; she didn't have a home of her own. Consequently she didn't really feel settled. Finally, she hadn't dreamed how much she would miss John. Naively, she had believed that once the decision to divorce was made, the confusion and the ache would end. She had been wrong. That's when it began.

She darted a look at him from the corners of her eyes, wondering what he was thinking right now. Unquestionably, he was the most handsome man in the audience. Intense, golden, a beautiful man. When he noticed she was staring, she quickly looked back at the stage.

What if she agreed to return to Los Angeles? This wasn't the first time she had asked herself that disturbing question, but it was the first time she hadn't shouted a silent *no!* Did this mean her resistance was crumbling?

And actually, was Los Angeles really so terrible? Of course it wasn't. But it wasn't Aspen Springs, either, and something inside her needed a small community. As well, she had to admit Aspen Springs wasn't working out as she had hoped. The pace of her life hadn't slowed; the values she sought to regain seemed to hover just out of reach. And what if Lydie was right? What if—eventually, in a few years—she decided she wanted to date or remarry? What were her chances of finding Mr. Right in a small town like Aspen Springs? Frankly, the opportunities would be slim.

Especially when Mr. Right was sitting beside her now, beaming at the stage. She bit her lip. John was so right in so many, many ways. But so wrong in the areas she considered vitally important.

"You look like you're about to cry," Alice said to her as the lights came up and the stage curtains swished shut for the final time. "Christmas makes me cry, too," she said, dabbing her eyes with the cuff of a Liz Claiborne sweater. "It's so lovely."

"This is what Christmas is all about," John commented, still looking toward the stage. "Children singing carols, demonstrating their faith and their belief in a better and peaceful world."

"Can't argue with that," Dr. Adler agreed, appearing beside them. Smiling, he shook John's hand, then Penny's. "How are you feeling?"

"Tired most of the time. Ready to get this show on the road." Dr. Adler smiled with understanding as Penny smoothed a hand over a festive smock. "This one is going to be an athlete. He danced to every carol."

Dr. Adler chuckled, then linked arms with Alice. "Mrs. Sage, I wonder if I might have a word with you?"

Amy and Flash ran into the audience as Dr. Adler led Alice toward the tables of punch and cookies.

"Did you see me, Mommy?" Amy called, catching Penny's hand.

"I was the loudest, wasn't I?" Flash demanded, looking up at John.

John laughed and swung Flash up on his shoulder. "Absolutely, sport. They could hear you in Denver. I predict the birth of a star. And you," he said to Amy, giving her braid an affectionate tug, "were fabulous. You put those other kids to shame!"

All over the auditorium parents were praising their children. Here and there Penny noticed a family with one of the spouses missing. Next year she would be among them, trying to speak with two voices, trying to make up for John's absence. A shudder constricted her shoulders and she ducked her head.

"Are you cold?" John asked. When she shook her head, he set Flash on his feet and gave both children a hug. "Let's find those cookies, shall we? I'll bet acting makes a guy hungry for cookies." As they passed Wes Pierce dressed in his Santa suit, John grinned and murmured, "Suits you."

"Ho, ho, ho. And what do you want Santa to bring you, son?" Wes asked, clapping John on the back.

"A bit of privacy."

Wes chuckled and patted Penny's arm. "Guess we know what you want," he said, winking at her stomach. "Are we hoping for a boy or a girl?"

"No preference," Penny answered, smiling.

"Looks like the buzzer could go off any day now," Wes noticed.

"Bite your tongue!" Penny said with an exaggerated groan. "I don't have time to have a baby right now. Lydie and Ian Allenby would have a fit if I took off during our busiest season. I've promised to wait until after the first of the year."

"Last I heard, babies don't take much account of their parents' wishes in the matter. They show up when they're darn good and ready and never mind if it's a convenient time for the parents. So what's this little critter's name going to be?"

Penny didn't look at John. "We haven't decided yet."

Wes grinned. "Better start thinking about it. Soon."

John hung behind as Penny caught the children's hands and started toward the refreshment table. He found himself following Wes Pierce backstage, leaning in the doorway as Wes changed out of his Santa suit.

"The scenery was great," Wes said, stripping off his fake beard. "Didn't know you were handy with a hammer."

John shrugged. "I thought you knew everything." But the compliment pleased him. Now that he wasn't phoning Blackman Brothers every day and his mail had all but stopped, he had expected to find time dragging. But it hadn't worked out that way. His morning list was a long as it ever had been, but the emphasis was different. Now it included such items as building stage scenery.

"Tell me something, Wes," he said casually. "You have money. You could live anywhere in the world. Why did you choose Aspen Springs?"

Wes unbuckled his Santa's suit. "Let me ask you a question, son. Do you think you could run for mayor of Los Angeles and have a chance of winning?"

"I doubt it. It would take years and a small fortune to build name recognition, then a vigorous campaign, and the results would still be up in the air." He lifted a curious eyebrow. "Have you ever been mayor?"

Wes nodded. "Served three terms here in Aspen Springs. Every man ought to be mayor at least once in his life just to understand the meaning of the word *aggravation*. My point, son, is that here you can do it. Hell, you could throw your hat into the ring next fall and have as good a chance as anyone of winning. In a town like Aspen Springs, you can make a difference. One man has a chance to change the things he doesn't like, a chance to make life a little better for his community and his family." He stepped into a pair of corduroy pants then looked up at John and grinned. "Take a guy like you. You start out cooking pancakes for a benefit supper, then you move up to building scenery for a school play, and before you know it, you're looking at the potholes thinking maybe you'll sit for a position on the town board, and you can do it. That's what community is all about, John, and it feels good. Helping others, and getting help when it's your turn to need a hand."

John shook his head. He had too much pride to ask anyone for help. It was an admission of failure. "Why Aspen Springs specifically?"

"Why not?" Wes shrugged. "The scenery is spectacular, the people congenial. It's a nice little town. I like it." He snapped off the light and dropped an arm around John's shoulders. "I guess you heard I made a lot of money when Vail was developed. You've made a lot of money, too. But think about that baby in the manger scene we saw tonight and the man he grew up to be. Some day we're all going to be standing before him having a little talk about our lives. I don't think he's going to say: 'Wes Pierce, how much money did you make in your lifetime?' I think he's going to say: 'Wes, how did you treat the people in your life? Did you enjoy the life you were given?'"

"Interesting point of view."

"Sure there are lots of places to live. Good places. But for me, I enjoy life best right here. And every now and again I have a chance to help someone. Keeps life interesting."

"Have you ever asked for help?" John inquired.

Wes's iron-gray brows lifted in surprise. "Sure. Lots of times." He paused in the doorway and looked out at the crowded auditorium. "It's easy to give help, son. Nothing to it and you walk away feeling good about yourself. What's hard is to accept help." He transferred his gaze to John. "But no man is truly part of a community until he's asked for help. Once he's done it, he's never the same. A man doesn't truly understand that humanity is one big family until he draws on that family for help and learns it's there for him. I guess you could say it's a growth step."

"Isn't it also a risk?"

"What isn't? But you have to trust in community and in yourself." He patted John's shoulder and his arm fell away. "And I'd say that's a good bet."

The conversation was hard to shake off, and there were points he wanted to argue, but John placed it on the back burner when he rejoined Penny. "So. What do you think about Scott Eliot Martin?" he asked after accepting a cup of punch and a paper plate of cookies. "I've always liked the name Scott."

"But . . . Eliot? I don't know. What if it's a girl?"

"How about Penelope Anne Martin?"

"I don't like juniors. Two Penelopes is one too many, don't you think?" Pushing back her sleeve, she glanced at her watch. "If we can find Alice, we should think about leaving. I have some inventory forms to review tonight."

A distance appeared in John's gaze. "Let's not rush the kids, okay? This is their night. It's not every day they get to be stars." Turning away from her, he looked toward Flash and Amy who were standing with their friends, basking in the afterglow of their performances.

Penny pressed her lips together. Of course he was right. "Talk about role reversal," she murmured with a sigh, trying to make a joke out of it. In the past it had been she who had to admonish John about not hurrying away from somewhere. John gave her a thin smile but said nothing.

By the time they returned home, it was nearly midnight, and she was too tired to review the inventory forms.

And too confused. All the things she had believed settled still weren't. Least of all her own feelings.

"Mommy," Amy said when Penny tucked her in and leaned to kiss her good night. "The Brownie party is Tuesday after school. You said you'd come."

"I will, honey."

Amy beamed. "You promise?"

"I promise. You were terrific tonight. I was so proud of you!"

Amy's eyes closed. "I knew you'd be there. Flash said you wouldn't, but I knew you would. I love you, Mommy."

Penny stared at her daughter in shock. Did Amy really believe she would have let anything cause her to miss the school program? Apparently, Amy did.

Deeply troubled, she tiptoed from the room.

"GOOD HEAVENS!" Penny gasped, halting at the top of the stairs. She stared toward the kitchen. The air was fragrant with the warm scent of cinnamon and heavy spices, but she had never seen such a mess.

Cooling cookies crowded the counter top; broken pieces covered what empty space remained. Crumbs and splotches of raw dough littered the floor tiles. It seemed that every bowl and every pan Alice owned was dirty and stacked in whatever available space could be found. As Penny walked slowly toward the counter, she noticed that Flash had cookie dough clumped in his hair; cinnamon and melted chocolate stained Amy's new blouse. Both children were painted like Indians, their cheeks artistically streaked with food coloring.

"Hi," John called cheerfully, looking up from the bowl of dough he was kneading. "You're home early. Did you have a good day?"

"Busy," Penny said.

"We're making cookies and cakes," Amy explained. After giving Penny a sticky kiss, she returned to her chair at the table to position red-hot buttons down the fronts of a row of gingerbread men.

"I can see that," Penny said. Frosting dribbled from the front of the stove and down the lower cabinets. As Penny's eyes widened, Alice stepped on a gumdrop and lifted her foot to glare at the bottom of her shoe. "You guys are making a spectacular mess."

"It'll clean up," John said, dismissing the dough zone with admirable unconcern. Opening the oven with a flourish, he removed a golden coffee cake. "The coffee cake and puff pastry are for us. Wait until you taste this!" He placed the coffee cake on a rack above the cutting board. "But not until it cools and is frosted. Okay, Flash, what happened to the white icing?"

"I colored it red, Daddy," Flash explained, waving an empty bottle. "Red frosting is the best."

"Can I eat another chocolate-chip cookie?" Amy asked.

Alice fell into a chair and waved a napkin before her flushed face. She directed a weary smile toward Penny. "We've been at this all day. When it comes to baking, John is indefatigable. The man doesn't know the word quit."

"You have enough cookies and cakes to feed most of China," Penny smiled, inspecting the cellophane-wrapped packages covering the kitchen table.

"Gifts," Alice explained. "Remember? We have a baked gift for everyone we know, have ever known, or will ever know in the future."

John grinned and pushed at a lock of hair with the back of his hand, leaving a streak of flour across his forehead. "It's great, isn't it?"

"Some of this is pretty exotic," Penny noticed after she poured a cup of eggnog. "Linzer Schnitten? Date Lebkuchen? Spitzbuben and nut meringues? I am impressed!" Then she noticed the pans of fudge, and creamy fondant. "Candy, too? And . . . are these homemade croissants?"

An explosion of powdered sugar erupted at the end of the counter, and Amy and Flash doubled over in giggles at the sight of each other. Faces, hair, hands, they were covered with powdered sugar.

"Don't worry about it," John said, placing a hand on Penny's arm. "We have plenty of sugar. They're making frosting. They know how to do it."

"So I see," Penny said, raising an eyebrow. Powdered sugar drifted toward the floor and over the cabinets. The thought of cleaning up this mess staggered her. "You couldn't have made do with a pan of fudge and a few popcorn balls?"

"Nope." After greasing a pan, John began shaping almond crescents onto the surface. "This is too much fun.

Too bad you had to work," he added, without looking at her. "You missed the action—we're about finished. But you can help with the taffy tomorrow."

Penny's eyes widened and her lips formed a circle. Speculating on what two kids could do with warm taffy was enough to buckle her knees, and she sat abruptly at the table across from Alice.

"There's no stopping him," Alice said with a shrug.

Slowly Penny looked about her, examining the devastation wrought on Alice's kitchen. It was spectacular and total. "This time I think it's you who should have a long soak in the tub. I'll clean this up." While releasing a long breath, she wondered what it was going to take to get the dough and powdered sugar out of Amy's braids.

"You don't mind?" Alice asked gratefully. "It doesn't seem fair for you to do the cleaning—"

"I don't mind. Honestly. I want to contribute something to this project."

"In that case, I think I'll escape before you come to your senses and change your mind." Alice wiggled her fingers in a wave and almost ran toward the stairs leading up to the tub.

"Well, that does it for today," John said with satisfaction, removing the last pan of cookies from the oven. He wiped his hands on Alice's ruffled apron. "By the way, I've been meaning to ask you, who supplies the baked goods for the bake shop at Santa's Village?" When she hesitated, he smiled. "I know, you executives would like the customers to think everything is baked in-house. But when I was playing Santa that day, I ducked into the bake shop for a doughnut and noticed they don't have the kitchen facilities to produce the variety and amounts shown in the cases. Your bake shop can do cakes and pies, but not much else. They must be buying the rest—the pastry items."

"You caught us." After telling him the name of the Denver supplier, she tilted her head curiously. "Why do you ask?"

"I just wondered. Why doesn't Santa's Village use a local supplier?"

Penny spread her hands. "We would, but there isn't one."

"That's what I thought." After a glance at the wrecked kitchen, he untied Alice's apron and dropped it across the counter. "It's really nice of you to volunteer for the cleanup," he said, patting Penny's shoulder with a distracted gesture. "Come on, kids. Let's head for the showers."

Her eyebrows shot up as she watched them go, leaving her to a mess that would have done credit to a dozen chimpanzees. Then she smiled. What the heck. Cleaning up was a small price to pay for having all these cellophane-wrapped Christmas gifts. It was one less thing to worry about.

Whistling under her breath, she tied John's discarded apron around her waist and started loading the bowls and pans into the dishwasher. The almond crescent cookies were terrific and she ate half a dozen as she worked, feeling good that she was participating.

Of course, she didn't realize that devastating Alice's kitchen was destined to become a daily occurrence.

JOHN MADE TAFFY Sunday morning. Despite Penny's misgivings, the event was fun, and they finished with a minimum of mess. In the afternoon, while Amy and Flash played with the Galloway kids in the basement and Penny and Alice watched the Bronco game and twisted the lumps of taffy into colored paper wrapping, John made cheesecakes.

"What do you think?" he asked, handing them each a sample at half-time.

"Another cheesecake? How many did you make?" Penny asked, blinking at the plate in her hand.

"This is an Amaretto cheesecake. The others are strawberry and pineapple. Is the Amaretto taste too strong? It seems a little strong to me."

"John, what are we going to do with three cheesecakes?"

"If I eat another piece," Alice moaned, staring at her plate, "I'm going to look like Penny. Each slice must have eight thousand calories in it."

"We'll send one home with the Galloway kids. Alice can take one to the library tomorrow. What do you think? Too much Amaretto?"

"No, it's perfect." Perfect was too mild a word. The cheesecake was fabulous. "By the way, what is this coffee? It's wonderful."

"Kenya roast. Nothing fancy, but if you blend it with the Viennese mint it creates something interesting, don't you think?"

Penny watched him return to the kitchen, then she blinked at Alice. "Does it strike you that something's wrong here? Isn't it John who should be watching the football game and one of us working in the kitchen?"

"I can't believe a daughter of mine would make such a sexist remark. Will you look at that? Elway got sacked again. When is Reeves going to get a decent offensive line?"

"Alice, I'm serious. What's going on here? John is acting like a new bride who's just discovered cookbooks." She stared into the kitchen. He was leaning on the counter, eating a slice of cheesecake and studying a stack of recipe cards.

MONDAY MORNING, after everyone left for school or work, John poured another cup of coffee and studied his notebook. His lists had outgrown the scratch pad he had been using and were now relegated to the back of a notebook containing market studies, financial breakdowns, sample menus, price lists and sales targets. He added Santa's Village to the growing list of sales targets, then leaned back in his chair, chewed the end of his pencil, and studied the winter sunlight glittering atop Buffalo Mountain.

The first possible obstacle had been overcome. When the idea initially occurred to him, he wondered if he could recover his enthusiasm for baking, or if large-scale cookery was a dead passion from his past. It wasn't. Baking satisfied a creative urge that numbers never had. Every morning he bounced out of bed, looking forward to the day and the excitement of a new discovery.

It reminded him of the good old days, except he had never thought of them as the good old days until recently. Those days of building from scratch, of taking risks, of dreaming and planning. The days when he and Penny had squeezed every nickel, had gone trick-or-treating for a splash of scotch because they couldn't afford to buy their own.

He saw now that having success wasn't nearly as exciting as getting it. The early years had been the best of times. The dreams, the excitement, the sheer adventure of stepping into life and shaping it into what one wanted it to be. He was beginning to see how lucky he was to have this chance at a second career, at seizing excitement and challenge all over again.

It was funny how things worked out. He had resigned from Blackman Brothers and moved to Aspen Springs because Penny believed the divorce was inevitable. But he refused to lose his children. Living here, he would be near them and could share their lives. He hadn't expected, however, to find an exciting work opportunity in Aspen Springs. Something he genuinely wanted to do. He had expected to drift awhile, then eventually settle into a dull job, probably with one of the commercial banks.

Yes, he was a lucky man in many respects. He only wished Penny could share in this beginning as she had shared in the dreams of the past. But she had made her feelings clear. No compromise. The divorce would go through.

Soon, he thought, adding it to his lists, he would have to find a place of his own. The thought was wrenching.

To take his mind off living without Penny, he reached for his jean jacket, found his car keys and consulted his list of today's activities. The first stop was the post office. Maybe the restaurant supply catalogue had arrived, or a response to his letter requesting an appointment with Denver's largest supplier of coffee beans.

"Don't you ever get cold sitting out here?" John asked Wes Pierce after discovering the restaurant supply catalog had arrived and the coffee-bean rep would be in Aspen Springs next week to meet with him. Not even the leaden sky, dark with snow-swollen clouds, could diminish his good mood.

"Thermal underwear, that's the secret." Wes nodded an invitation for John to sit for a spell. They leaned against the bench, watching the locals and tourists moving in and out of the shops facing the town square.

"Penny and Alice sent this for you and your wife," John said, placing a cellophane package on the bench between them. Though he didn't admit it, not even to himself, bringing the package to Wes was the real purpose for his visit to the post office today.

"That's right nice of Penny and Alice," Wes said with a smile. "I heard someone up at Alice's place was doing a lot of Christmas baking." When John didn't comment, his smile widened. "Also heard you were nosing around over at the jeep dealer's." He nodded his cap toward John's Porsche. "Thinking about a trade?"

"Maybe."

"The way I see it, a Porsche isn't much good for mountain driving. And a jeep isn't too impressive on a California freeway. So?"

"So?"

Wes laughed. "So, some of us hereabouts figure this means something. You dyed-in-the-wool Yuppies don't trade in a Porsche for no reason.... Are you still sleeping in the North Pole, son?"

John rolled his eyes and stood up. "Is there anything about my life that Aspen Springs doesn't know?"

"Not much, and that's a fact." Tilting his head back, Wes studied the flinty sky. "If I was you—and I'm not helping out, you understand—I'd take a look at the Hathaways' shop over there across the square. Might suit your purpose just fine, and the price is right."

A sigh lifted John's shoulders. "I had this crazy idea that no one but me knew my plans."

Grinning, Wes looked up at him. "Not hard to figure them out, son. I can't recall the last time this town witnessed a genuine market study. What did you think? That no one would notice all those questions and requests for information?" He paused. "If you don't mind my asking, you haven't told Penny about this, have you? Does this mean you two are dumb enough to let that divorce go ahead?"

John made an exasperated sound. "Remember our deal? Live and let live?"

"Just trying to help out, that's all."

"Wes, I don't want any help from anyone, okay? Not now, and not in the future."

Frowning, he remembered Wes's philosophy about accepting help.

"John?" Wes called, stopping him as he was about to open the door of the Porsche. "Thank you for the baked goods." Wes studied him with a thoughtful expression. "Someone said that a lot of cellophane packages just like this one showed up on the doorstep of Reverend Cowper's church. You wouldn't know anything about that, would you? No, I didn't think so. Too bad. Reverend Cowper is awful anxious to know who to thank. A lot of folks are going to be real happy to get these cellophane packages.''

A flush of embarrassed pleasure climbed from John's collar as he backed his car out of the post office parking lot.

As USUAL it was after ten o'clock when Penny arrived home on Monday. The kids were asleep. Alice was dozing in front of the channel-nine news, and John was cleaning the kitchen.

"You know, I'm starting to think you look cute in a ruffled apron," Penny commented as John poured them each a cup of coffee and slid one across the counter to her.

He laughed. "I'm hoping Santa will bring me something more tailored. Maybe a nice masculine tweed with a leather belt." His dark eyes softened. "It's been a long day. How are you feeling?"

"Baby Whosit has been trying out for the Kiddie Olympics today," Penny said, gently rubbing her stomach. She shifted sideways so that she could lean an elbow on the counter top. "What have you been up to, or need I ask?" The kitchen table was hidden beneath stacks of cellophane packages tied with red Christmas ribbon.

"The first batch were mostly mailouts. I sent packages to our friends in L.A. This batch is for Aspen Springs. I have Alice's list, and I'll need yours by the day after tomorrow at the latest."

"It's really thoughtful of you to do all this, John, but *why* are you doing it? Are you that bored?"

He leaned against the kitchen sink, studying her across the counter. "It's not boredom. I like to bake. Always have. I know," he said, smiling and raising a hand, "there hasn't been much evidence of it in recent years. But I haven't had the time before. Now I do and I'm enjoying it. Plus, I have an idea, something I'm working on."

"Do you want to talk about it?"

He hesitated. "I'd love to talk about it. But this isn't the right time," he said glancing at the clock. "I know you're tired. And I still have some things to check out. Besides, I know you have a lot to deal with already."

Penny frowned. "That makes it sound like your idea is something I'll be upset about . . ."

"That's possible," he said after a minute. It had occurred to him that Penny might not welcome having her ex-husband in the same town. She had wanted him here once, but now that she had decided there was no possibility of a reconciliation, she might feel very differently.

"Then you're right to delay telling me," she said after a minute. "Right now I don't think I could cope with one more thing. Not to change the subject, but before you arrived I'd convinced myself I couldn't tell freshly ground coffee beans from canned coffee. But I have to admit, since you've taken over the coffee-making detail the coffee has been especially good. What's this I'm drinking?"

"I'm experimenting with blends. Do you like it?"

"Yes." She tilted her head and returned his look of examination. "You know, there are sides to you I never suspected."

"Is that good?"

"Yes, I think it is. But it's confusing."

"I suppose there are sides to everyone that just need the right time and the right circumstances to emerge."

"Are you suggesting you've noticed sides to me you didn't suspect?"

"Everyone has hidden aspects."

She sensed he was being tactful, guessed if she had asked if her emerging sides were good ones he would have switched the direction of the conversation. The suspicion made her bristle.

"Well, it's late," she said, sliding off the counter stool. "I'll leave you to finish whatever you're doing and take myself off to figure out next week's personnel schedule."

It didn't make sense to wish John was staying at a hotel, she decided as she prepared for bed, because every hotel room was booked through the holidays, he saw more of the kids by staying here, and his visit would end in a couple of weeks. All good reasons for remaining here. But, oh, how she wished he was staying in a hotel. Seeing him every day was doing strange, confusing things to her nervous system. She thought of him first thing in the morning, and she thought about him while she was driving home from work. At odd times during the day, she wondered what he was doing. Considering the circumstances, it struck her that she was thinking about him much more than she should.

It was going to be extremely painful to say goodbye again after the baby was born. She dreaded the moment and felt a little angry about it. She'd thought the worst was behind her and the children; they had made the final break. Now, after John's lengthy stay, they would have to endure the pain and upset again.

Unless...

But love wasn't enough.

This thought ran through her mind long after she had turned her light out. Tossing, then turning, trying to find that elusive comfortable position, she finally decided sleep was impossible. She kept remembering Lydie's speech about love, and love being the only thing that mattered. The conversation continued to disturb her.

What if Lydie was right?

When she heard the noise, she sat bolt upright in bed, straining to hear. What she heard was the stealthy approach of a car, rolling almost, but not quite, soundlessly over the frost-brittle snow in the driveway.

Throwing back the blankets, Penny swung her legs over the bed and pushed her feet into her slippers. As she knew the pattern, she knew there wouldn't be time to run down to the basement and fetch John. But she could wake Alice and prove once and for all that Alice was wrong, that she was not imagining someone in their driveway.

Quickly she duck-walked down the corridor and rapped on Alice's door. There was no answer.

"Alice?" she called, trying the handle to Alice's bedroom door. The door swung open and she peered inside.

The first thing she noticed was how frosty cold it was in Alice's bedroom. And no wonder. Alice's window was open about three inches, the draperies billowing slightly in the frigid night breeze. A tiny red glow beside Alice's bed indicated the electric blanket was on. Penny decided the electric blanket was the only thing that allowed Alice a hope of sleeping in this cold, cold room.

Except Alice was not sleeping in this room, Penny noticed with a jolt. The coverlet was still in place, neatly tucked over the pillows. Immediately her gaze swung to the luminous dial on the bedside clock. It was three o'clock in the morning. And her mother was missing! Kidnap headlines flashed through Penny's mind.

Before she could spin around to run for help, she heard the familiar bump against the side of the house, louder in Alice's room than she had heard it before. Frozen in place, Penny stared at the window.

Mittened fingers appeared in the crack between the sill and the edge of the opened window. A scream stuck in Penny's throat. The trellis was directly beneath the window; obviously someone had climbed the trellis and was now creeping inside. Every instinct shouted at her to get out of here, to run for John and let him handle the intruder while she telephoned the police.

But she couldn't move. It was as if her slippers had taken root in the floor. Helplessly, her throat working, she watched the window slide silently up. A dark-clad figure climbed over the sill, stepped inside, then bent to close the window.

As the figure started to turn, Penny's paralysis thawed. She screamed.

Chapter Ten

"Mother!"

"Oh, dear." With a sheepish smile, Alice pulled the dark ski cap from her head and shook out her springy tumble of white curls.

Penny dropped to the edge of the bed; her mouth fell open. "I . . . I don't understand. You're the person driving into the yard in the middle of the night?"

Her mind raced. No wonder there was no evidence of a stranger's car when she or John had checked outside. The only car in the yard was Alice's. And if Alice was embarking on midnight jaunts, it was also no wonder that she insisted Penny and John take the spaces in the garage.

"I suppose you want an explanation," Alice murmured, dropping her parka on the chair beside the window.

"You suppose . . . I feel like I'm dreaming! If you discovered *your* mother climbing a trellis and sneaking into her bedroom in the middle of the night, wouldn't you want to know why?" Penny stared at her mother, incredulous.

"I guess I knew I'd get caught eventually." Alice bent to peer at Penny. "Darling, why are you still awake? Couldn't you sleep?"

"Alice, for heaven's sake. Here you are, dressed like a ninja, climbing in windows in the middle of the night, and you want to discuss why I can't sleep?'' Penny rubbed her fingertips against her temples.

The door burst open and John rushed into the room.

"I heard a scream. Are you all right? Is anyone hurt?" The kids were behind him, their sleepy eyes wide.

"Oh, dear," Alice repeated. "This is all my fault."

"We're fine." Penny brushed back her hair and released a sigh as Amy and Flash jumped on the bed beside her.

"It's freezing in here," Amy said, pulling down Alice's coverlet. She and Flash climbed under the blankets.

"You know the sounds we've heard in the middle of the night?" Penny asked John. "It was Alice coming home from God knows where. And...and you won't believe this, but I discovered her climbing up the trellis and through the bedroom window."

They all stared at Alice, watching a furious blush heat her cheeks.

"Wow! Grandma Alice climbed in the window?" Flash's shout was loud with admiration. "Cool!"

"That's neat, Grandma Alice. Can we watch you do it?"

John blinked at Alice's trim black slacks and sweater. "I don't get it," he said slowly. "Why didn't you come in the door?"

"Well," Alice said, rolling a pointed glance toward Amy and Flash, "it's very late. Perhaps we should wait until morning—"

"Oh, no," Penny said, shaking her head. "I want to hear about this right now. Kids, the excitement is over, back to bed you go." She lifted Flash out of Alice's blankets and set him on his feet. "Come on, Amy."

"Aw, we always miss the good stuff."

"Give Mommy and Grandma Alice a kiss," John said, "then I'll tuck you in. Don't start without me," he called over his shoulder as he led the children into the corridor.

Penny and Alice looked at each other, then Alice smiled. A hint of pride twinkled in her eyes. "You really didn't guess?"

"It never entered my mind that it was you. Not once. In fact—"

"No," Alice interrupted, anticipating what Penny was about to say. "I didn't lie about it. If you'll remember, I always tried to change the subject." Walking toward the door, she gestured to Penny to follow. "It's cold in here. I could use a cup of hot decaf, couldn't you?"

John appeared in the kitchen as Alice was pouring three cups of coffee. He grinned as he slid onto one of the counter stools and raised his cup in a salute. "Alice, I have to say there is more to you than meets the eye."

"You sound like you know what this is all about," Penny said, turning to look at him.

"I think I've guessed."

"Oh?"

Smiling, he looked at Alice and raised an eyebrow. "I think it's possible that Alice is having an affair."

"What?" Penny spun on the stool to stare. Alice's cheeks flamed bright crimson. "Mother? You're suggesting my mother is having an affair?" She studied the color on Alice's face and her mouth formed a tiny circle.

"You needn't look so astonished, dear," Alice said in a mild voice. "One has to keep up with the times."

Penny swallowed and pressed the collar of her robe to her throat. "It's true then? You're having an affair?" She couldn't believe it. After glancing at her coffee, she pushed it away. "Forget this, I need a drink. John, is there any wine?"

No one ever quite viewed their parents as sexual creatures, Penny thought. Naturally it could be assumed one's parents had done "it" however many times it required to produce the number of children they had, but beyond that... Few people ever thought about their parents' jumping into bed for fun. Certainly one seldom thought of one's mother—a grandmother, for heaven's sake—as being hot to trot.

"I mean I just..." Penny spread her hands. "I never thought about..."

"Well, I wouldn't exactly call it 'hot to trot,'", Alice said after Penny explained some of her difficulty in accepting what she was hearing. "It's more like giving a long-term affection a chance to blossom into something more." She sucked in her cheeks and contemplated the kitchen ceiling. "On second thought, maybe it is being a bit hot to trot." She smiled. "The younger generations don't have a corner on the market, you know. Just because my hair is white doesn't mean I'm too old to love or be loved."

"I didn't mean that," Penny murmured hastily, her cheeks burning. "I just... I meant..."

"I know what you meant," Alice said, leaning to pat her hand. "It's a shock, that's all. You're accustomed to thinking of me as being alone."

"I've been very shortsighted. But I don't remember there being anyone else since Daddy died."

"For a long time there wasn't." Alice took a seat at the kitchen table. "Frankly life was pretty lonely."

"You never said a word," Penny whispered. "I feel terrible that I didn't realize..."

John spoke into the silence. "Alice, I love the idea of your climbing the trellis and crawling in the window. I wish I had been there to see it. But why didn't you just use the door?"

"Then you and Penny would have known."

"Would that have been so terrible?" Penny asked. "All these months... why didn't you just tell me?" The minute the question left her lips, she guessed the answer.

"The timing seemed wrong," Alice explained gently. "Your life was falling apart. You were devastated, talking to a lawyer about a divorce... It didn't seem right to parade my happiness when you were so dreadfully unhappy. Bill and I decided to delay any announcement until you were feeling better and were more settled about your future.''

"Bill . . . Do you mean Dr. Adler?''

Alice's face lifted in a glorious smile and she nodded confirmation. Then she laughed at John's expression. "You look like one of those cartoon characters with a light bulb flashing over his head. What on earth are you thinking?''

"Now I understand why everyone in Aspen Springs is so eager to push Penny and me together. It's because of you and Bill Adler, isn't it?''

"I'm afraid there aren't many secrets in a small town.''

"Everyone figures the quickest way to get you and Dr. Adler together is to get Penny and me together.''

"Oh, Mother. Didn't you think I could handle the idea of you remarrying?''

"I knew you could handle it, darling. I just didn't want you to have to. Not yet. I believed it would be hard for you to be happy for me when your own situation is so up in the air.''

"I haven't jumped to a conclusion, have I?'' Penny asked uncomfortably. "I mean you are planning to marry Dr. Adler, aren't you? Or is this just...'' She couldn't say it.

Alice smiled. "I think it's fair to say Bill intends to make an honest woman of me.'' Now that the cat was out of the bag, she seemed to be enjoying the conversation. "Although there's a lot to be said in favor of an affair.''

"Well ladies, I have an idea the two of you have a lot to discuss.'' Standing, John finished his cup of decaf, then yawned, pressed Penny's arm and started toward the basement stairs. "I'll see you in a couple of hours.''

"Tell me honestly, Penny,'' Alice said, after John had left. "Are you upset?''

"I'm more upset that you didn't tell me than I am about anything else."

"I didn't know how you would feel about my seeing someone. I know it's been a lot of years since your father died, but still, I didn't know if you would accept the idea of someone taking your father's place."

"I think the world of Bill Adler," Penny said honestly. "And I . . . I'm glad for you." She summoned a smile. "So. Let's have another cup of coffee while you tell me everything. When did you start dating and when is the wedding and will you live here or move to Bill's house? I want to know all."

It was as if a dam had burst. Face glowing, Alice spoke until pink streaks spread across the mountain peaks. Penny heard Alice's happiness and was genuinely glad. She felt guilty to realize that Alice had been right. Watching and listening to her mother's happiness and her plans for the future underscored the chaos and uncertainty in her own life. Alice was beginning a satisfying new relationship; Penny was ending one.

"Will you have a problem with Bill being on twenty-four-hour call?" she asked when Alice paused to cover a yawn. "Babies aren't always born between nine and five."

"No relationship is perfect," Alice answered with a sleepy smile. "When balanced against everything else, I think I can cope with a telephone ringing in the middle of the night."

Before they went upstairs to prepare for work, they embraced each other tightly.

Alice brushed a lock of Penny's hair back behind her ear. "I hope things work out for you and John," she said softly. "He's a good man, Penny. And he loves you."

"There are just too many problems. Maybe you can cope with a man who's at the beck and call of everyone except you, but I don't seem to be able to." A sad smile touched her lips. "Particularly if I have to do it in Los Angeles."

"You always were a stubborn child," Alice said, shaking her head.

"I don't remember that it hurt this much."

"It doesn't have to, Penny. I know you love John."

Penny bit her lip. "Love isn't enough."

"Good heavens," Alice said, her eyebrows rising. "If love isn't enough, then what is?"

The words rang in her ears while she performed a quickie set of exercises before she dressed for work.

Amy ran into her room, ready for school, and jumped on Penny's bed. "Don't forget, Mommy. The party is after school. Don't worry about the fudge, we're making that. And Daddy is going to drop by a plate of cookies."

"What party, honey?" Rolling from her side onto her back, Penny fought to catch her breath. Right now, she would rather have crawled through a blizzard than face a day at Santa's Village. What she wanted was to climb into bed and sleep for twenty-four hours.

Dismay pinched Amy's face. "The Brownie party, remember? You promised you would come."

Oh, Lord. She had forgotten. If she recalled correctly, her schedule was jammed today. After a minute, she rolled back onto her side and looked up at Amy's face leaning over the side of the bed.

"Honey, is this party really important to you?" Of course it was. At age eight every party was important.

Amy hid her face beneath the ends of her braids. "You promised," she whispered, fighting tears. "You said you would come!"

"I know, honey. And I would if I could." Sitting up, Penny stretched out a hand, but Amy drew back. "Sometimes things don't work out like we plan . . ."

But Amy was gone, slamming the bedroom door behind her.

Some Christmas this was turning out to be. What had happened to the joy? To the magic?

What had happened to the love?

Sighing, pulling herself to her feet, Penny went into the bathroom to put on her makeup. But it wasn't her face she saw in the mirror. It was Amy's, filled with the pain of disappointment.

BAKING SATISFIED a creative need John had almost forgotten he possessed. There had been a time not too long ago when he had begun each morning with knots tying his stomach as he reviewed the day ahead. No more. Now he awoke eager for the day, his thoughts filled with variations of this recipe or that blend.

Maybe this was what magazine writers meant by male midlife crisis, this sudden shift of ambitions and priorities. But what he was doing felt right. He felt as if he were awakening from a long period of slumber. On some unrecognized level he had been marking time, waiting for this period in his life, accumulating the wherewithal to pursue dreams he had believed long dead.

Now the dreams had resurfaced with renewed vigor. And to his surprise, he found himself in the perfect place to achieve them.

The real-estate agent unlocked the door to the Hathaways' gift shop and followed John inside.

"It's been vacant for quite a while, as you can see," Lon Thompson said, waving a hand around the dusty interior. "But the size seems right for what you have in mind. The location is good, and the traffic statistics support the town-square exposure."

Slowly John walked the perimeters of the shop imagining how it would be. He could place the pastry cases just there, and a coffee bar would be perfect across the back wall. There was floor space for a dozen four-tops, plus wall space for shelves to display tinned bakery goods and pre-packaged coffee blends. Plenty of kitchen space.

Thrusting his hands into his pockets, he returned to the center of the room to stand in a bar of sunlight falling through the front windows. The tall sunny windows begged for hanging plants. Already he could imagine the fragrance of freshly brewed coffee filling the room, and the yeasty scent of bread hot from the oven. The chatter of customer's voices rising from the tables. The cases would overflow with cakes and pies and cookies the size of saucers. He would sell them by the item or by the slice. Eat here or take home.

During the past weeks of thorough research, he had concluded there was a strong potential market; a quality pastry and coffee shop could be successful. The demand existed. The challenge of launching a new business, a new career, stimulated his competitive nature, stirred his business acumen.

"Do you want to discuss this with Penny before you commit to anything?" Lon Thompson asked as they stepped outside and he bent to lock the empty shop.

John hesitated. He had been waiting for the right moment to discuss his plans with Penny, the changes he had made in his life and the changes he intended to make. But the right moment never seemed to arrive. They saw each other in passing or in the company of Alice and the kids. He suspected Penny preferred it that way.

Moreover, he couldn't guess how she would respond to learning he planned to make a life in Aspen Springs. He suspected she would believe he was doing this for her, when in truth he really wasn't. Somewhere deep inside he had begun to accept defeat. He and Penny weren't going to be able to put things back together. It wasn't what she wanted.

But being in Aspen Springs was what he wanted. The realization still had the power to amuse and astonish him. At some point during the past weeks, Aspen Springs had seduced him with its charm, pace and, yes, its people. There was opportunity here. And most important, his children were here.

"No," he said finally. "I'm ready to make an offer now."

Lon Thompson's face brightened. "Excellent. I don't think you'll regret this decision, John." He walked toward his car. "If you'll follow me back to the office, we'll draw up a contract."

Knowing Aspen Springs, the news would be all over town before supper. That part of small-town living he doubted he would ever like. Frowning, John eased the Porsche onto Main Street. He had to find a private moment with Penny. He preferred that she learn about this from him.

PENNY WAS NOT HAVING a good day.

First, she arrived late to work, sliding into the staff meeting with a look of guilt and frustration, trying to hide her yawns behind her note pad. Second, no one had shoveled the snow off the ice rink because she had forgotten to leave instructions for the crew. Ian Allenby was not happy to discover the rink would open late. Third, she had let the letters to Santa pile up unread, and the editor of the Village newspaper was calling every fifteen minutes pleading for copy. Fourth, her mind kept straying back to that incredible moment when she realized it was Alice sneaking in the window. And finally, Baby Whosit was kicking up a storm, dancing to the Christmas music blaring over her office speaker. She leaned over her desk and closed her eyes.

"We wish you a merry Christmas," kick, kick, punch. "We wish you a merry Christmas," punch, punch, somersault. "And a happy new year." Deep bow, back flip, double kick to mommy's bladder.

Stroking a hand over her stomach, Penny stifled a yawn, sighed, then lifted the top Santa letter and tried to concentrate.

Dear Santa,
Please make Stinky Bolen look at me in science class. He should want to marry me. I also want a kitty, a white fluffy one and a Barbie doll and twirling lessons. And world peace.

Love,
Jeanne Ann

Stinky Bolen—the hunk of tomorrow? Penny smiled. The mating dance began at a younger age every year. She wondered how old Jeanne Ann was. Amy's age? She placed the letter in her undecided pile.

Dear Santa,
I want a color TV for my room and a VCR. Don't bring me any clothes. I want a bionic arm and a cape that makes me invisible. Don't tell Bruce Evans about the invisible cape. And don't give an invisible cape to anybody else. I also want a Nintendo and all A's from Miss Gladden. I'll leave you a glass of milk and cookies so don't eat too much at Bruce Evans's house. Is your beard real?
See you next year.

Your friend,
Al Frye

She wouldn't mind having an invisible cape herself, Penny thought, her mind drifting. Leaning back from her desk, she tapped a pencil eraser against her teeth and studied the snow floating past the window. She kept thinking about what Alice had said.

If love isn't enough, then what is? What indeed?

Was a promise of next time enough for Amy? Did a promise soothe the hurt of knowing her friends' mothers would be at the Brownie party but her own mother wouldn't? Was a quick kiss on the way out the door enough for Flash? Or did he wish she was there to pick him up after school? How much was enough?

Was John satisfied with a terrific challenging job and a view of the ocean? Was that enough for him?

Were midnight trysts enough for Alice?

And what of herself? What was enough for Penny Martin?

A stimulating job in a town she loved? Which she pursued at the expense of the people who loved her?

Guilt deepened the furrow across her brow and she bit down on the pencil eraser.

"Face it," she whispered. "No one's happy. Your mother is sneaking in and out of windows. Your children are becoming strangers and you're disappointing them. You're divorcing the best man you ever knew. You're three years pregnant and running yourself ragged to win a promotion you don't want and won't accept. You're so exhausted, you'll probably sleep through your baby's delivery and miss the whole event. You don't have time for any of the things you used to think were important. And this is the worst Christmas you've ever had."

All because of some stupid idea that love wasn't enough.

If love wasn't enough, then what was? Alice was right. What on earth could be more important than love?

This job? With stunning clarity Penny suddenly comprehended that she had not changed her life-style. She had merely changed location. Ambition in Aspen Springs was still ambition. And she was as much a victim to ambition as John had ever been, she saw that now. She could promise herself from now until judgment day that her schedule was only temporary, but in her heart she knew it was not.

True, the pace at Santa's Village would slow somewhat after the holidays, but her responsibilities were never going to be nine to five. Management positions didn't work that way. There would still be nights when she had to close, weekends that required her presence. The conflicts between her personal and professional life were not going to magically disappear.

That type of conflict was exactly what she had hoped to escape by moving to Aspen Springs. Instead, she had thoughtlessly recreated the same situation she had objected to in Los Angeles. Except she had put herself in the lead role instead of John. And Flash and Amy were relegated to minor supporting roles, a situation she had never wanted.

"Oh, you really fixed things, didn't you?" she muttered, flinging down her pencil. Leaning forward, she buried her face in her hands. "How could you be so dumb?" She had made a mess of every area of her life.

After a moment she realized she was staring down at the next letter in her Santa pile.

Dear Santa,
Please make Mommy and Daddy love each other again. Don't send Daddy back to Los Angeles. And please let Mommy be home more. That's all we want. And a baby sister. Please, please.
                                   Amy and Flash Martin

Penny stared at the smeared page. The word *sister* had been crossed out and *brotter* printed beside it. *Brotter* had been crossed out also and *sister* reinserted. The writing was unmistakably Amy's.

"Oh, God," Penny groaned, rubbing at her eyes.

When she regained her composure, she stood and adjusted her skirt and smock. Then, lips pressed together, she walked down the candy-cane corridor to Ian Allenby's office, feeling her spirits rise with each step. Oddly her decision was not impulsive although she understood it would appear that way. For the moment she understood what she was about to do, she also understood she had been planning it in the back of her mind for at least a week.

"Ian," she said, after knocking at his door. "Can we talk a minute."

"Come in. Sit down."

Show me, John had said. *If you honestly don't want the promotion, take your name out of the running.* But she wasn't doing this for John. Or for Lydie. She was doing it for herself. And it felt good. It felt very, very good.

"You are withdrawing yourself as a candidate for the promotion?" Ian Allenby repeated, his eyebrows rising toward his hairline.

"Yes." She drew a long breath. "My plans have changed. After the baby is born, I . . . I'll be returning to Los Angeles." If John still wanted her. Please God, let him still want her.

A weight shifted near her heart and lifted.

"I'm sorry to hear that," Allenby said, staring at her. "You had a future with Santa's Village."

"I appreciate your saying so, Ian." As the weight floated off her heart, it pulled up the corners of her mouth. Her smile stretched from one pearl earring to the other, a silly happy smile that felt wonderful. "May I ask a favor?"

"Early leave?" he guessed, eyeing her stomach.

"Don't tell Lydie I withdrew my candidacy. Would you do that, Ian? Please?" When he said nothing, she hurried on. "I know this sounds arrogant and I honestly don't mean it that way. But I want Lydie to believe she was first choice. Not the only choice."

Ian Allenby's fingertips touched an envelope lying on his desk blotter. "As a matter of fact, the corporation's decision arrived this morning." His eyebrow lifted. "Do you want to know who they chose?"

She hesitated, then straightened her shoulders. "No. If Lydie was the corporation's choice, I'll feel like a fool for saying these things. If I was the choice, I'll feel . . . well, I'd prefer not to know." It didn't matter anymore. She drew a breath. "What's important is that Lydie has the promotion." As she reached for the door latch, she asked, "When will you tell her?"

"There's no reason to delay," Ian said, reaching for his desk phone. As Penny left his office, she heard him say, "Miss Evans, please ask Mrs. Severin to come to my office immediately."

For a moment, Penny stood in the corridor, looking at the red-and-green candy-cane wallpaper. A prick of moisture stung her eyes. But the dampness behind her lashes was not from regret, but from happiness.

"What's up?" Lydie asked, walking toward her. "Why does Allenby want to see us?"

"Not us, you." Penny pressed Lydie's arm. "Stop by my office when you're finished with Allenby, will you?"

When Lydie returned to Penny's office, she looked stunned. "Did Allenby tell you?" she asked, dropping into the chair facing Penny's desk.

"Congratulations." Smiling, Penny poured champagne into two paper cups.

"You are magic," Lydie marveled. "Where did you find a split of champagne in a children's park?"

"Ah. My secret. To the new manager of Santa's Village!" Penny raised her bubbling paper cup. "You deserve it."

"You're really being terrific about this, Penny," Lydie said uncomfortably. "Look, are you sure you're okay with the way this worked out?"

"Don't I look okay?"

Lydie narrowed her gaze above the cup of champagne. "As a matter of fact, you look better than you've looked in several days. Which doesn't make sense. Didn't you tell me you didn't sleep last night?"

"I feel great! Lydie, I'm so glad you got the promotion."

"Thank you. I was absolutely certain they would chose you."

"Now—" Penny grinned "—I hate to tell you this, but your first problem on your new job is me."

"I knew it," Lydie groaned. "No one is this good a sport."

"I'm quitting. I'm not coming back to work after the baby is born."

"Oh, Penny. Please don't take it like—"

"No, no. It isn't sour grapes. Lydie, this is good news. The champagne is a celebration for both of us. I'm going back to Los Angeles. If John will have me."

"That *is* good news!" Jumping up, Lydie ran around the desk to embrace her. "I'll bet John is delighted!"

"I haven't told him yet. Things have been so hectic." She spread her hands and smiled. "I thought I'd tell him Christmas Eve after everyone else is in bed."

"Very romantic," Lydie said, beaming approval.

"There's more." Penny glanced at the clock. "I'm leaving early today."

Lydie straightened in her chair and frowned. "Quitting I can handle. You being terrific about losing the promotion I can handle. Your leaving early I can't handle. Penny, we're buried. They're shorthanded in the toy shop, Helga is having a nervous breakdown, the new Santa is having an affair with one of the chestnut vendors, two cases of broken nut-crackers have to be packed for shipment, there's no heat in the ice rink and the movie projector is broken again. I need you.''

She didn't waver. "I'm sorry, I really am. But I'm leaving here in twenty minutes. It's important, Lydie."

"What could possibly be more important than the items I've listed?" Lydie raked a hand through her hair and leaned forward.

"A party."

"Tell me you're kidding!"

"Nope." Taking the Santa letter from Amy and Flash off her desk, she folded it into her pocket. "This party is the event of the season. I'll hate myself if I miss it." She grinned. "I understand there will be homemade fudge and gallons of Kool-Aid. And a rousing game of musical chairs."

"The Brownie Scout party. I saw it on your calendar."

"Right. And tomorrow is Flash's class party. Another season spectacular I can't miss." She smiled in Lydie's direction, but the smile was directed inward. "You were right, Lydie. Christmas is love. I don't plan to lose sight of that ever again."

"Well," Lydie said after a minute. She leaned back in her chair. "I guess we'll manage somehow. We always do."

"No one is indispensable." For a time Penny had forgotten that. She wouldn't again.

"MOMMY! YOU CAME!"

Amy bounded across the hall and flung her arms around Penny, tears shining in her eyes.

Penny hugged her tightly, moisture glistening on her own lashes. Kneeling, she smoothed back Amy's bangs. "I told them I had to have some time off. I couldn't miss my daughter's party. It was too important."

"I helped hang the crepe paper."

"It looks terrific!"

For the first time in months she didn't think of Santa's Village once. Although she was too heavily pregnant for musical chairs, she took second prize in Pin the Tail on the Donkey, and she and Amy won first prize in the mother-daughter charades.

"Thank you for coming to my party, Mommy," Amy said sleepily when Penny tucked her into bed that night. "I love you."

"I love you, too, honey."

When she thought how close Amy had come to sitting out the mother-daughter charades, Penny felt a tightness in her throat. It would never happen again, she promised, looking down at her sleeping daughter.

But life didn't make things easy.

Her earlier elation at quitting her position at Santa's Village had begun to fade. She didn't regret the decision, and she knew she wouldn't regret it in the future. But at the same time she felt a little bereft, as if she had lost something important.

She had let her job responsibilities get out of hand, she recognized now. She had let ambition and pride in a job well done run away with her, which was exactly what she had accused John of doing. And that was wrong.

Yet she also knew she would miss working. She would miss the contact with people, the decision making, the sense of accomplishment at the end of the day.

A sigh dropped her shoulders as she tiptoed from Amy's bedroom. She knew she couldn't have it both ways.

Suddenly she wished there really was a Santa Claus.

Chapter Eleven

The next few days were unbelievably hectic. On a constant run, Penny attended Flash's class party, arranged a small dinner party for Alice and Dr. Adler, scribbled her Christmas cards, rushed through her duties at Santa's Village, swept through the shops in a frenzy of last-minute shopping, and attended two holiday parties.

"You look dead on your feet," Susan Galloway noticed, pausing beside Penny with a tray of fancy canapés.

"Thanks. You look terrific, too."

Susan laughed. "Sorry. I guess I could have phrased that better. Seriously, how are you feeling?"

"Like a very large tennis ball that's lost its bounce. I must be the only mother-to-be in Aspen Springs who is looking forward to a new baby as a period of rest." They smiled at each other.

"Before I dash off to play hostess, tell me what you think of John's new venture. I'm dying to know."

"His baking binge?" Penny smiled. She supposed everyone in town knew by now that John had gone berserk in Alice's kitchen and was turning out bakery delicacies as if he had a mission to bury the valley in cookies, cakes and pies. She had no idea what happened to all the pans and sheets of baked goods, although Alice hinted that Reverend Cowper had come into a baked windfall and it would be a happier Christmas for his parishioners because of it. It was both amusing and a little worrisome that John seemed obsessed with making the Great American Cookie.

She saw him across Susan's living room talking to Lon Thompson, the realtor, and Dan Driver, president of the Optimists Club. John had always been able to talk to strangers, but he usually maintained a reserve that wasn't always evident to those he was speaking to but that had always been obvious to Penny. Oddly, she didn't notice that reserve now. He seemed genuinely relaxed, talking and laughing with an ease that surprised her. Then she remembered with a little shock that he had been in Aspen Springs long enough to meet people and build relationships of his own, even if the relationships were temporary.

"I wasn't referring to his baking binge," Susan said, then stopped. "Oh, dear, I hope I didn't let the cat out of the bag. I guess it's supposed to be a surprise." After a quick glance at John, she murmured something about needing to refill the canapé tray and eased through the crowd toward the kitchen.

What was that all about? Penny wondered. A frown crossed her face. Sometimes small towns could be exasperating. Small-town residents made secrets out of nothing and everything. Or they protected secrets better made public. Or they revealed secrets better left private.

Shifting slightly, she located Alice and Dr. Adler in the holiday crowd, laughing at something Wes Pierce had said. They were standing close together, fingers touching, both looking ten years younger than Penny knew them to be. That was a secret Aspen Springs had kept well. Penny smiled, genuinely happy for her mother.

As she turned to look again toward John, her smile became a sigh. The past few days had been difficult for them. She supposed they were both wondering if this was the last Christmas they would spend together as a family. She knew she was. Now that she had quit Santa's Village and made a commitment to herself to return to Los Angeles, she felt less and less sure that John would welcome her back.

Something had changed in the past couple of weeks. He wasn't as tentative as he had seemed when he first arrived. An air of confidence had returned, and with it an excitement she recognized as an indication he was thinking about a deal and eager to get on with it. More and more frequently she had seen a look of distraction in his eyes, and she assumed it meant he was thinking about leaving them and returning to Los Angeles. He had said nothing more about her returning with him.

She pressed her lips together. Maybe this time together had convinced him a divorce was actually the best thing. Her chest constricted and Baby Whosit vaulted through a series of somersaults.

What if she had waited too long? She bit her lip.

If John wanted her back, wouldn't he have said something more about Los Angeles? Pressured her a little? Concentrating, she tried to remember when they had last talked, really talked. They had both been so busy....

At that moment, he lifted his golden head and their eyes met and held. After excusing himself, he crossed the room to her side.

"Penny, are you all right?" Touching her elbow, he studied her expression with a frown of concern.

"I...yes, of course." Reaching deep, she summoned a smile. "I must look awful. Everyone keeps asking if I feel all right."

"You look beautiful," he said softly, his gaze sweeping the green ribbon in her hair, her holiday dress.

It was nice of him to tell her what she needed to hear, even if she didn't believe him. "John—" she drew a breath "—I need to talk to you. There's something I want to tell you."

"There's something I want to tell you, too."

She saw the leap of excitement flash in his eyes and her spirits sank. He was thinking about work. She had seen that look too many times not to recognize it.

But what had she expected? Of course he was eager to return to Los Angeles and work. John wasn't the kind of man to adjust easily to small-town boredom. Witness the peculiar binge of oven madness. If she returned with him to L.A., she had to accept everything that went with that decision. Anything less than total surrender just wouldn't work. They had to do it his way.

For an instant resentment flared in her. Then she relaxed. She loved this man. And that meant accepting him the way he was—ambition, long hours and all. In the end, she knew she would rather live with John in a smog pit and see him on the run than live on a quiet mountaintop with anyone else.

John saw a flicker of resentment in her eyes and immediately dropped her arm. An ache tightened his stomach. He knew what she wanted to tell him. She wanted to tell him that she had learned of his plans for the coffee and bake shop, and it made no difference that he would be living in Aspen Springs. The divorce was still on.

When he dropped her arm, she wanted to weep. It was true then, she had waited too long.

"When would you like to have this talk?" he asked, looking away from her.

"I thought tomorrow night, but if you don't think Christmas Eve . . . ?"

"No, that's fine. Why not?"

They stood together looking toward Alice and Dr. Adler, both aware that, in one of the few times in their life together, they had nothing to say to one another.

IT WAS SNOWING HEAVILY when Penny awoke after sleeping late. After doing her morning exercises, she pulled back the bedroom drapes and studied the blizzard swirling past the windowpanes, glad Lydie had insisted she stay home today.

"You're running on empty, Penny," Lydie had informed her briskly. "You need some rest. Besides, Christmas Eve day should be a light day at the park."

"Liar," Penny had responded, but with a smile of gratitude. "Sundays are our busiest days."

"Not this one. The weatherman predicts the storm of the season. If he's right the highway patrol will close the tunnel and stop all traffic. We'll be lucky to see three people all day. You can sleep in guilt-free and enjoy the day at home."

For once the weatherman was right on target. A heavy white curtain blew past the window, so thick Penny could not see the road looping through the subdivision. Snowdrifts, mounded across the yard like waves, were formed into exotic shapes. The branches of the pine near her window drooped, bowed by the weight of the snow.

They were snowed in for Christmas. The thought delighted her now as it had when she was a child. Penny pressed her face to the glass, watching the blizzard with pleasure.

When she came downstairs Alice was sipping a cup of coffee in front of the windows, watching the snow pile up on the balcony. "This one is a real corker," she said to Penny. "We've got about four inches so far and there's no sign the storm is slowing down."

"Are you worried about Bill?" Penny asked, looking out the windows.

Alice nodded. "He planned to leave for Denver early. I hope he got down the mountain before the worst of this hit. The radio said they've closed the tunnel and traffic is backed up on both sides."

"Why don't you call? You'll feel better. He may not know you're worried. You know how different the weather can be between here and the other side of the mountains." Dr.

Adler was spending Christmas with his son and his son's family in Denver.

"You were right," Alice said, beaming with relief after completing her phone call. Color had returned to her cheeks. "It's only starting to snow in Denver. Bill didn't realize it was so bad up here." This time when she looked out at the blizzard, she did so with contentment. "We have plenty of coffee and snacks, the shopping is finished, there's lots of firewood and Christmas dinner is in the fridge, so... let it snow, let it snow, let it snow."

"'Oh, the weather outside is frightful,'" John sang, appearing in the living room with an armful of firewood. "'But in here, it's so delightful.'" After building and lighting the fire, he joined them in the kitchen for freshly ground Brazilian coffee. "Which one of you ordered the perfect traditional Christmas weather?" he asked with a grin. "Those of us more accustomed to Christmas smog and balmy temperatures thank you."

His smile wrapped around Penny's heart and her throat tightened. The words *too late* rang in her mind. To drown them she turned on the radio and let carols fill the room.

"Perfect," John said, nodding. "I used to imagine Christmases like this."

"You did?" Penny looked at him in surprise. Then the telephone rang.

It was Lydie. "With Ian back East for the holidays, you and I are in charge," she began. "Our new Santa is stuck in a snowdrift somewhere between Frisco and Santa's Village. He called in on his CB and the state patrol is looking for him now. I can't get out of my driveway—it's a sheet of ice. I'm calling to see if you agree that we should forget it for today. According to the radio the plows can't keep up with the snow. The roads are drifting over faster than the plows can clear them. I'm in favor of not opening."

"Lydie, you're the boss, remember?" Penny said into the telephone. She spoke in a low voice so John wouldn't overhear.

"Not until the end of January. Until then, we're both in charge. So what do you think?"

"I think a person would have to be insane to go out in this storm. Don't give it another thought. Do you need some help calling everyone to tell them not to go in?"

"Are you joking? They're calling me! Telling me they can't get out of their garages. Just about everyone is accounted for except Helga and Sims Delacorte. Their lines are busy. I'm guessing they're phoning their people and telling them not to go in."

"So all we have to worry about is Santa."

Lydie laughed. "According to the state patrol, Santa is marooned with the chestnut vendor I mentioned. He told the patrol not to hurry."

"It sounds like you've taken care of everything."

"Unless you can think of something I've missed. Before I say Merry Christmas and get off the line, I want to wish you good luck tonight."

Biting her lip, Penny gazed out the windows at the storm. She lowered her voice again. "I don't know, Lydie. I'm having second thoughts about saying anything to John. It's been so long since he's mentioned anything about—"

"Listen to a friend, Penny Martin. Don't be an idiot. Tonight is Christmas Eve, remember? It's magic, the night all wishes come true." Penny could imagine Lydie's smile. "Besides, I know what you're getting for Christmas. And you're going to like it."

"How could you possibly know what I'm getting for Christmas?"

"The whole town knows. Everyone is waiting with bated breath to see what you'll do."

"Do? I have to do something with this mysterious gift?"

"I know what you'll do, but I'm not telling."

"Lydie Severin, I am so sick of secrets!"

"Then you're living in the wrong place," Lydie said, laughing. "I have to get off the phone and try Helga and Sims again. Have a wonderful Christmas, and I'll see you the day after tomorrow."

"You, too. Have a merry, merry Christmas." After hanging up the receiver, she carried her coffee into the living room and sipped it while she examined the gifts under the tree, wondering which was the one everyone in Aspen Springs knew about. Several of the gifts were lumpy and strange-looking, wrapped with love and yards of tape. Penny smiled. Next year she would have homemade gifts for everyone, too. This year she had broken the agreement. There hadn't been time to make anything.

From the shape of the packages, she guessed Flash had made her a pencil box or a penny bank. At Amy's Brownie party, she had overheard hints of embroidered place mats. She had surprised Alice making mosaics out of rice, beans, dyed macaroni and seeds. That left John's gift. She studied the shape of the container. It looked suspiciously like the containers he had wrapped in red cellophane. Maybe a special rum cake?

None of the gifts impressed her as meriting a town secret. They were precious to her, but not what she would consider as ranking in the "bated breath" category. And she couldn't imagine what she might have to "do" with or about any of them.

"I'm sorry I didn't have time to make anything for you guys," she said as John came up from the basement, the kids behind him. "I promise, next year will be different."

"We understand," John said lightly. Before she could say anything more, he winked at the kids, then looked back at her. "We have been challenged to a game of Go Fish. What do you think? Can we beat this pair of cardsharps?"

"It's a tough job, but I think we can do it," she said, watching the kids' faces light with delight. "Girls against the boys?"

"Oh, no," Amy said, suddenly anxious. She and Flash exchanged a conspiratorial look. "We're a team, and you and Daddy are a team."

"You guys just don't quit. Well, if it's okay with Daddy, it's okay with me," she said, not looking at John.

"I don't know." Teasing her, he pretended to hesitate. "As I remember it, your mother is hopeless at cards. You guys are saddling me with a severe handicap."

For the kids' sakes, she went along with him. "What? I'm a handicap? I'll show you! We'll beat these two so bad they'll plead for mercy."

Laughing, loving it, Amy and Flash informed them they had to sit close together on the same side of the kitchen table.

"Closer," Flash insisted, pushing them. "Partners have to sit close!" When Penny and John were self-consciously arranged to suit their children, Flash looked out the windows at the storm. He tried not to look worried. "Can Santa come in a storm?"

"Hey, this is the best Santa weather there could be," Penny said, shuffling the cards.

"Mommy's right. Santa loves storms like this. Don't worry," John assured them. "Santa's on his way right now, it's a long flight from the North Pole." Neither he nor Penny looked at each other at mention of the North Pole. "And I'll bet he brings you everything you asked for."

Startled, Penny looked up from the cards. John didn't know what he was saying. But then, he hadn't read Amy's and Flash's letter to Santa Claus.

"I'm sure you'll like whatever Santa brings you," she amended, managing a smile. "Okay, the cards are ready. Who goes first?"

She didn't have to glance at the clock over the stove to feel the minutes ticking toward evening. Suddenly she decided it was a bad idea for her and John to try to settle things tonight, of all nights. They should have given themselves one last perfect Christmas.

"Think positively," John said as her hand hovered above the Go Fish pile. "Picture a match in your mind."

She studied him a moment, trying to read his thoughts. "Yes," she said finally. "That's the only thing to do. Think positively."

SNOW CONTINUED TO FALL throughout the day. The intensity of the storm deepened. The radio crackled with road closings and travel warnings. By late afternoon more than twelve inches of snow had accumulated on Alice's balcony. The windows were laced by lovely fernlike tracings of frost.

Inside it was cosy and warm, the air filled with carols and the scent of freshly baked sugar cookies. Penny read and dozed before the fire, smiling at the sounds of cowboys and cowgirls emanating from the basement as two wound-up kids tried to work off a little of the excitement. John and Alice visited companionably in the kitchen as they prepared Christmas Eve dinner.

It had been a perfect restful day, Penny thought, disturbed only by an occasional cramp. The first cramp had occurred about three o'clock and Penny sat up abruptly, letting her book fall to the floor as she placed her hands on her stomach and made herself go still inside. When nothing further happened, she relaxed and reminded herself that she had a history of false labor.

Another cramp arrived after dinner, passing so quickly she told herself she might have imagined it.

"The baby isn't due for another two weeks," she said, cupping her hands over her stomach.

Alice looked up from the pie she was slicing. "We know, dear. Now, who's ready for cherry pie?"

After dinner they watched a Christmas Eve special on television, then Flash and Amy argued over what to leave Santa, cookies or a piece of cherry pie, and where to place it so that Santa would be certain to see.

Then John donned a red Santa's hat and, as he and Penny had agreed, they allowed Flash and Amy to open one present before bedtime, having chosen the presents in advance to make certain they weren't gifts that would excite the children too much and keep them awake. Flash received a color-and-paste set; Amy opened a new Nancy Drew book. Eventually it was time for baths and bedtime.

When Flash ran upstairs fresh from his bath, his face scrubbed and shining, he rubbed his palms over his pajama top and cast a worried look at the fireplace. "You'll put the fire out before you go to bed, won't you, Daddy?"

"Absolutely," John promised solemnly. "We wouldn't dream of singeing ole Santa's beard."

"And you're sure he'll see the pie and milk?" Amy asked doubtfully. "Maybe we should put the tray under the tree..."

"Santa will see the tray on the coffee table the minute he steps out of the chimney," Penny promised, giving her a hug.

"Did you hear that?" Flash gasped, his eyes widening. "Jingle bells!"

Alice laughed. "It's too early, big fella. What you heard was the wind chime on the balcony. Santa doesn't come until all little boys and girls are sound asleep."

Penny took Amy's hand and started toward the basement stairs. Behind her came John and Flash. "Silent Night" played on Alice's stereo; the lights twinkled on the tree. Outside, the driving snow drifted through the night, wrapping the house in a blanket of white. Inside it was warm and lovely with the sights and sounds of Christmas. Tears of happiness glistened in Penny's eyes. She wished she could capture this moment and keep it with her always.

After the children had been tucked in for the third time, the adults returned to the living room for hot spiced wine and a slice of John's Christmas fruitcake.

"This is excellent," Alice enthused. "Usually I don't care for fruitcake."

Penny grinned. "Remember the theory you used to have? That there were only ten fruitcakes in the world, and they were being mailed back and forth to people who kept them in a closet for a year then mailed them to someone else. You were positive no one ever ate them." Baby Whosit apparently enjoyed the story. He chose the moment to perform some spectacular acrobatics.

Alice's smile turned to concern. "Penny? You have such a peculiar look on your face. Is everything all right?"

"I can't seem to find a comfortable position tonight." If she hadn't known she was prone to false labor, she would have thought she was beginning real labor. She'd had several cramps since dinner.

"Would you like a pillow for your back?" John asked.

"Thank you."

Alice studied her thoughtfully while John slipped one of the decorator pillows between Penny and the sofa back. Her gaze turned to the snowy blackness against the windows. The outside lights decorating the balcony rail, a few feet from the windowpane, were a dim shine of color, blurred by the thickly falling snow. "I don't think we've had a storm this bad in years," Alice commented absently, tapping a red fingernail against her throat. "I'd hate to try to go out in this."

"Thank goodness we don't have to," John said, poking up the fire. He was still wearing the red Santa cap, humming with the carols drifting from the stereo.

"The wind comes down the gully behind the house and pushes drifts all down the driveway," Alice continued, looking at Penny.

"I used to love that," Penny said, smiling at the memory. "It meant I didn't have to go to school." She explained to John. "The driveway is about a quarter of a mile long, and with all the drifts we couldn't get the car out until the plow came to dig out the subdivision. The plow usually didn't get to us before noon."

"I wonder how soon they'll have the plows out tomorrow," Alice said, her eyes still on Penny.

"According to the radio, the plows and sand trucks are out now," John told them. "They just aren't doing much good. The snow's too heavy and coming down too fast. They're concentrating on the major highways."

"Which means the loop road is buried under at least twelve inches of snow. Probably more by now. And drifts."

"Alice, what are you worrying about? Are you planning to go somewhere?" Penny asked. Then her stomach tightened beneath her smock and she concealed a wince of discomfort.

Alice continued to study her daughter. "I wish Bill were here instead of in Denver," she said quietly.

John's head snapped up and the ball on the end of his Santa's cap bounced against his shoulder. "Is something going on here that I should know about?"

"Yes, Penny, is there?"

"I've been experiencing some discomfort off and on throughout the day." She dismissed the cramps with a shrug. "It's nothing to worry about. You both know I've had false labor before."

"As I recall, it happened in your seventh month," Alice said into the silence. "Not this close to your due date."

"Penny?" Sitting beside her on the sofa, John tilted her face up to him.

"Honestly, if there was anything to worry about, I'd tell you." She gestured toward the windows. "I'd be insisting we start for the clinic if I really thought this was the real thing."

"I hope you're right," Alice said slowly, staring at her. "Because I doubt we could get the car out of the garage tonight, let alone down the driveway and out of the subdivision."

Penny smiled at them. "Will you two stop worrying? It's nothing."

"You're absolutely certain?" Alice demanded.

"Absolutely." Penny's gaze darted toward the clock. It was almost eleven. If she and John were going to talk . . .

Alice noticed the direction of her glance, then stood and smothered an exaggerated yawn. "Well, I imagine Flash and Amy will be up at dawn. I think I'll call it a night."

John stood, too. "Shall I get more firewood from the garage?"

Penny nodded, realizing too late he was actually asking if she still wanted to talk. For an instant she hesitated, thinking to call him back. Then she bit her lip. Maybe it was best to get it over with. Either he wanted her back or he didn't. She didn't want to spend another night not knowing.

"Before you go, help me up, will you?" she asked Alice, indicating that the sofa had trapped her. After hugging Alice and wishing her a merry Christmas, Penny went into the kitchen to pour fresh cups of hot spiced wine for herself and John.

A hard cramp bit into her stomach and she gasped, grabbing the kitchen counter for support until the clamping sensation passed. When her stomach softened again, she stood beneath the kitchen light staring down at herself.

That had been a contraction.

Not a cramp, not a moment of discomfort. What she had just experienced had been an authentic contraction. This was not false labor; it was the beginning of the real thing.

Automatically she glanced at the clock, then let her eyes travel slowly toward the black snowy windows.

"Oh, my God," she whispered.

At that moment John reappeared, his arms filled with firewood, the red Santa cap pushed back at a jaunty angle. He dropped the wood on the raised hearth, then walked toward her, rubbing his hands together.

"It's cold out there."

A warm gush of water spilled down the inside of Penny's white wool slacks. For a moment she thought she had lost control of her bladder and was suffering the ultimate embarrassment. Then she understood what had happened, and stood helplessly as the water ran out her pant legs and puddled around her feet.

"John, this is crazy, but my water just broke."

His mouth dropped. His expression froze. "Oh, God." They both looked at the snow hissing softly against the windowpanes. Then John came around the counter and held her in his arms, stroked her hair back from her face. "Don't worry, honey. I'll get you to the clinic."

She looked deep into his eyes, telling herself not to panic, then she nodded. "I'll have to change clothes." She looked down at her wet pants and the water spreading across the kitchen tiles. "I made a real mess, didn't I?"

"Don't worry about it. I'll clean up while you're changing." Arm around her waist, John led her toward the stairs. "Tell Alice we'll be leaving in a few minutes, will you?"

Alice flew down the stairs and took the mop from John's hands. "I'll do this. You get on the phone." She gave him the number to call for road conditions. For a long moment she and John looked at each other, then Alice bent over the mop and John reached for the telephone.

A recorded message listed a lengthy number of road closings. The person who had made the recording sounded tired and frazzled. The recording ended with a strongly worded warning to stay indoors and off the roads. Slowly John replaced the receiver.

"Not even emergency vehicles are getting through," he said to Alice.

"The news said this is the worst storm in a decade. John—"

But he didn't wait to hear. He dashed for the stairs and opened the foyer door to the garage, flipping on the yard light as he hurried toward the windows on the garage door. The snow was too thick for the yard light to penetrate more than a few feet into the swirling darkness. But it was enough to see that a four-foot drift lay against the garage door. A series of snowdrifts, like waves tossed up by a violent white sea, ran down the driveway and flowed into the blackness.

"You can't see where the driveway ends and the side ditches begin," Alice said from behind him. Anxiously, she wrung her hands. "The loop road will be impassable."

John looked at the Porsche, cursing himself that he hadn't yet traded it for a jeep. At least he'd installed snow tires. But at this moment, he would have given everything he owned to see a four-wheel drive sitting where the Porsche was.

"I'll dig out the driveway."

"You can't," Penny said quietly.

They spun to see her standing behind them, holding her overnight bag, dressed to leave. She looked out the garage windows at the blowing snow.

"Even if it wasn't still snowing, digging out would require hours," Penny said. Alice nodded. "And the loop road will be drifted over, too."

Alice threw out a hand and steadied herself against the trunk of the Porsche. "We're stuck here." Her eyes rounded and she spoke in a whisper. "What on earth are we going to do?"

Penny and John looked at each other in the snowy light.

"I guess we're going to have a baby," John said softly. He touched the red cap he was still wearing. "It looks like Santa is going to deliver this one."

"I'm a little frightened," Penny said simply.

John came to her and held her gently in his arms. Then he framed her face between his large capable hands and looked into her eyes.

"Almost two thousand years ago tonight, another baby was born without a hospital and without a doctor present. And look how well he turned out."

As little as three months ago he had been so big-city uptight that the present situation would have shaken him badly. He would have been frantic, thinking they could not possibly have a baby without the safety and comfort of a modern hospital. Right now, he was uneasy, yes, but he was not frightened. He felt sure enough of himself and of Penny to give her the support she needed.

"Once upon a time you and I believed we could lick any problem if we faced it together, remember?" he asked, still framing her face between his hands, looking into those lovely large eyes.

"I remember," she said softly. "We forgot that, didn't we?"

"I think we forgot a lot of important things along the way."

A contraction bit down hard and she gripped his arms until it was over.

"We've both been stubborn idiots," she gasped when the contraction released her.

"Darling Penny—"

Alice flung out her hands. "You two are turning me into a nervous wreck! Will you stop talking and go inside? We need to figure out what we're going to do!"

They looked at her in surprise.

"We're going to have a baby," Penny said, laughing.

"That's what we're going to do," John confirmed.

"We used to be a pretty good team," Penny said, smiling up at him. "Think we can pull this off successfully, Santa?"

"When you and I are pulling on the same team, Ms. Claus, there is no stopping us."

They looked into one another's eyes.

"It's going to be all right," John said gently.

"I know." She was still holding onto his arms. "There may be some scary moments—"

"This is one of them!" Alice said, pushing at them. "Will you please go inside so I can have a breakdown where it's warm?"

Chapter Twelve

After John helped her inside and upstairs, Penny warmed her hands in front of the fireplace and drew a breath to steady her nerves. It was going to be all right, she told herself, silently repeating John's words. This baby, her little Whosit, this baby about whom she had felt such ambivalence, had suddenly become very, very precious.

Smothering a gasp, she sat abruptly on the ottoman before the fire and wrapped her arms around her stomach as another contraction gripped her. "We'll be fine," she whispered when the tightening eased and the tug on her lower back loosened.

"Okay," John said briskly. He sounded a hundred percent more confident than he felt. If the birth was normal, he knew he and Penny could handle it. There would be a few shaky moments, and this was a situation neither of them would have chosen, but they could make it work. But if anything went wrong... "Here's what we're going to do." Alice and Penny looked at him expectantly, and he hoped something sensible would fall out of his mouth.

"Yes?" Alice prompted. She spoke in a calm tone but he read the anxiety in her eyes.

"Okay. This is the plan." He exhaled slowly. "Alice, take Penny upstairs and help her change into something more comfortable. Get her into bed. I'll phone Dr. Adler in Denver and find out if we should be boiling water or something."

"Boiling water? I've always wondered what the boiling water is for," Alice said, raising an eyebrow. "Does anyone know?"

"Maybe it's to make coffee and spaghetti afterward to celebrate. We'll find out." John made a shooing motion with his hands. "Scoot. I need to get on the telephone."

Because he didn't want to worry either of them more than necessary, he waited until Penny and Alice had disappeared up the stairs before he turned to the kitchen, poured himself a shot of brandy, then phoned Bill Adler in Denver.

"You said her water's broken?" Bill Adler asked after John had explained the situation. During the long silence that followed, John could hear his heart thudding against his rib cage.

"What does that mean?" he asked when he couldn't bear the silence another second.

"I'd be happier if her water hadn't broken yet."

"What does *that* mean?"

"It could mean things are going to happen pretty fast, especially if the contractions are as close together as you indicated."

"Or?"

"I'll level with you John." There was another pause. "A dry birth can be dangerous."

"Oh, God," John whispered. All the moisture vanished from his mouth and he sat down hard on the kitchen chair.

"For the moment we'll assume we're dealing with the first circumstance. John? Are you still there?"

"Yes."

"Your situation is unfortunate—we all wish it could be otherwise. But Penny is healthy, and she's delivered twice before. According to her records, her previous deliveries were comparatively swift and without complication. There's no reason to assume this delivery will be any different."

"If it's a dry birth—"

"You have plenty of time before that becomes a possible problem. I probably shouldn't have mentioned it."

"No, I'm glad you did. I assume you'll give me signs to watch for and—"

"We'll get into everything. We'll walk you though this, John. The main thing right now is for you to remain calm. Okay?"

He stared at his reflection in the snowy black window. "I was present during the birth of our first two children, if that means anything."

He sensed Dr. Adler's smile. "It means you probably aren't going to faint on us."

"So." John inhaled deeply, watching the snow fly out of the blackness and melt down the windows. "What happens next?"

"Probably nothing except a lot of waiting. Things aren't going to get interesting for a while yet. Meanwhile, I'm going to give you a list of what you'll require and remind you that everything will have to be sterilized."

"The infamous boiling water."

Dr. Adler laughed. "Right. Have you got a pencil?" After he dictated the list, he continued. "I'll phone Dr. James Harrington at St. Anthony's Hospital and tell him what's happening. We'll make sure you have an open line to St. Anthony's. When the time comes, I'd suggest you put Alice on the phone and she can relay any questions or information."

"Where will you be? I think Penny would be more comfortable if she knew you were on the phone. No disrespect to Dr. Harrington, but—"

"I'll leave for Aspen Springs as soon as I get off the phone with Dr. Harrington."

"Bill, wait a minute. The roads are too dangerous. And it'll take you three hours to travel what's usually a forty-five-minute drive to the tunnel. Then, if you manage to get that far, the state patrol won't let you through. The tunnel is closed. If somehow you convince them to let you pass, you're facing another dangerous situation on the other side. And that's before you get to the loop road, which is impassable."

"I can't guarantee I'll get there in time, John, but I promise you I will get there."

John's throat tightened. "Thank you," he said quietly, the words inadequate for what he felt. "I appreciate it."

"As it's likely I won't arrive in time, let's review what you'll need to do. Have you still got that pencil?"

He took it slowly, wrote down every word. "Sounds easy enough," he said in a weak voice when he had copied Dr. Adler's instructions.

Dr. Adler laughed again, his cheerfulness raising John's spirits. "That the right attitude. Now, before I get off the line let's find out how far along we are." He told John what to do.

John placed the telephone on the kitchen counter, stared at it a moment, then he squared his shoulders and walked across the living room to the bedroom stairs.

Penny was in bed, resting against a pile of mounded pillows. Alice had brushed her hair into a ponytail and tied it with a length of red Christmas ribbon. She looked more relaxed than he could believe, considering the circumstances and considering that he was all they had by way of medical assistance.

He swallowed and looked at her, pushing his hands into his pockets, feeling the set of rubber gloves Alice had found for him earlier. "I have Dr. Adler on the phone. He, ah, asked me to..."

Penny and Alice looked at him expectantly.

"Dr. Adler suggested that I...it seems that it's normal procedure to, ah..." He looked at Penny's hands folded on top of the blankets and wondered how she could be so damned calm. "The thing is, he'd like to know how far along..."

A blush tinted Penny's cheeks as she began to understand, then a small smile formed under twinkling eyes. "Alice, if you'll excuse us a moment..."

"Of course," Alice said. "Yes, yes, I see." She gave John a wicked smile, then chuckling, she ducked into the bathroom and closed the door as Penny lowered the blankets and raised the hem of her nightgown.

Blushing furiously, John checked as he had been instructed, then he hastily pulled Penny's nightgown back into place and tucked the blankets around her.

"Who does that in the hospital?" he asked.

"Nurses, the doctor." Penny shrugged and grinned. "The last time we had a baby, I was positive the staff was pulling people in off the street to come up and have a look at me." She laced her fingers together on top of the coverlet and grinned at the red Santa cap he had forgotten to remove. "Well, Santa. Now that you've had a peek, how are we doing?"

He grinned back. "As far as I can tell, Baby Whosit is positioned exactly as Dr. Adler said he should be." In an exaggerated parody of a doctor, he said, "We seem to be dilating nicely, Mrs. Martin."

"We do, do we?"

"I've got Dr. Adler waiting on the telephone. I'll be back in a few minutes."

The moment he stepped outside Penny's room, relief overwhelmed him. He sagged against the wall and offered a silent prayer of gratitude. The baby was positioned properly for a normal delivery. Penny's body seemed to be doing everything it was supposed to be doing.

"Good," Dr. Adler said when John had completed his report. He, too, sounded relieved.

After John had been issued a few more suggestions, he hung up. For several minutes he stood beside the telephone, watching the reflection of the Christmas tree lights blinking on and off against the windowpane. Then he found the telephone book and dialed.

"Hullo?" A sleepy voice answered on the fifth ring.

"Wes? This is John Martin." Even a few days ago he would have sworn there could be no circumstance under which he would telephone Wes Pierce and ask for help.

"Wha' time is it?"

"Midnight. I apologize for phoning so—"

Instantly Wes came awake. "What's wrong?"

Quickly John explained their situation. "I know all the state and county plows are in service, trying to keep the major roads clear for emergency vehicles."

"That's right, son. Even privately owned plows are out helping tonight."

John drew a breath. "Wes, if you have any influence, if you know anyone with a plow—I don't care what it costs— we need—"

"You need a way into the subdivision and a path to your door."

"I'm sorry to disturb you on Christmas Eve and especially this late, but if you could make a few phone calls, I'd—"

"Consider it done. You say Bill is coming up from Denver?"

"He's going to try. Frankly I don't have much faith that he'll make it."

"You gotta have faith, son. Remember the Indian and his snow dance? Remember what tonight and tomorrow is all about? Faith. That's all, just faith."

"So simple. And so hard." That wasn't all that was hard. Placing the phone call to ask Wes's help had been equally hard. And Wes would know it. When this was over, John had an apology to make. He had been a fool to think other people might need help, but not him. Covering his eyes, John leaned away from the storm blowing against the windows.

After a moment he went into the kitchen and made a few preparations. He collected some crushed ice, which he put into a bowl, then carried it and a spoon up to the bedroom.

"How are we doing?" he asked Penny, taking a seat beside the bed and placing the bowl on the bedside table.

"Pretty good, I think. I'm doing my breathing exercises, trying to remember everything else I'm supposed to do."

She lay on her side, one leg almost straight, the other bent at the knee. Another contraction came as he watched, and he fell silent, not wanting to interrupt her concentration as she focused on minimizing the discomfort. When the contraction passed, she gave him a weak smile.

"Are you frightened?" he asked softly, taking her hand.

"A little," she admitted. "Are you?"

"A little."

They smiled at each other, speaking softly so they wouldn't wake Alice who dozed in the rocking chair near the window.

"Do you feel like pushing yet?" John asked, pulling his chair closer.

"Not really." She glanced at the bedside clock, measuring the time before the next contraction. "I think it's going to be a while yet."

"Is there anything I can get you?"

"No. But thanks for the ice. I'll appreciate it when I get the nervous nibbles. As I always do."

They didn't say anything for the next few minutes, but it was not an uncomfortable silence. They listened to the sounds of the storm and to the Christmas carols drifting from the living room.

"Lousy timing, huh?" Penny commented after she had caught her breath following the next contraction. "The good news is the kids will get what they wanted for Christmas. They asked for a baby sister—though, if it's a boy, I'm sure they'll be just as happy." She thought of what else Amy and Flash had asked of Santa. "I'm sorry we didn't get to talk, John," she added softly.

"I realize you're a bit busy," he said. "But I'm just hanging around. Would you like to talk now?"

"Now?"

"It might take your mind off... things."

She closed her eyes and breathed. When the clamping sensation passed, she nodded. "All right. You said you had something to tell me."

"So did you. You go first."

"No, you go first."

"No, you."

"I quit my job," they said in unison. They stared at each other.

"You quit Blackman Brothers?" Penny asked incredulously.

"You quit Santa's Village?" John blinked. "Why? What about the promotion?" Slowly comprehension dawned in his eyes. "Oh, Penny, are you saying what I think you're saying?"

She looked at him from shining eyes, and he thought she was more beautiful than he had ever seen her, wearing a white flannel nightgown and a red ribbon in her hair. She was more beautiful, more precious to him now than on their wedding day. He held his breath, loving her so much he ached, praying he had not misjudged her meaning.

A look of sudden shyness came into her eyes as if she was unsure of his reaction. "I'd like to go back to Los Angeles with you, John. If . . . if you still want me."

Joy burst inside his chest, paralyzing him with happiness. He wanted to scoop her into his arms and dance her around the room. Instead he leaned forward and gently placed his hand on her cheek, tracing the curve of her lips with his thumb.

"No," he said. Then realizing how that sounded, he smiled and added hastily, "We're not going back to Los Angeles, darling." Then, between contractions, he told her about buying the space facing the town square and his plans for a coffee and bake shop.

When he finished Penny said, "So that's my mysterious Christmas gift." She repeated what Lydie had told her and how Susan Galloway had given her a hint.

"For once I'm glad this town can keep a secret. I wanted to tell you myself." Catching her hand, he covered her fingertips with kisses. "So . . . what do you think?"

"John—" she stroked his beloved face "—is this really what you want? A coffee and bake shop in a small town?"

"Are you kidding?" His eyes twinkled. Everything was going to work out. He told her all his plans. "It's the opportunity of a lifetime! And Penny, I promise you—our shop is going to be open from nine to five *only*."

"Maybe until seven during tourist season," Penny teased gently. He was a workaholic; he always would be. But if he could turn his life upside down and move to Aspen Springs, surely she could accept the late nights and an occasional working weekend.

"It's probably too soon to mention this . . ."

"But?" she asked. She was gripping his hand, and gazing lovingly up at him. She had been wrong to think total surrender was the only course. If two people loved each other a compromise could be found. It meant giving in here and there, but good marriages were built on compromise. It was one of the things they had both forgotten.

"But think about this. If the shop is successful, maybe we can consider franchising. Not immediately, of course," he added hastily. "I mean in a few years, like after the kids leave for college."

Penny's laugh changed to a groan as another contraction wrapped around her stomach. When it passed, she was panting, and a light sheen of perspiration had appeared on her brow. "This is hard work," she explained. "That's why it's called labor. It's almost as exhausting as being an assistant manager at Santa's Village."

"I love you, Penny. God, I love you. I can't stand to think how close I came to spending a life without you!"

"I love you, too, John Martin. I love you with all my heart. I'm sorry I was so foolish and stubborn."

He placed a finger across her lips. "Shhh. It's all worked out for the best. And maybe we learned something. One thing is certain. Our lives are going to be better for it."

"Love is enough, isn't it? If you really love someone, the answers eventually come."

The contractions were arriving faster now, the spaces between them shorter and shorter. Penny looked toward the bedroom window where Alice was dozing beneath an afghan. The blackness outside the window had begun to fade toward gray. The storm was easing.

"Are you—" she ground her teeth and tried to remember her breathing exercises "—going to need..." The contractions seemed almost constant now.

"An extra employee?" John had been right. He wasn't the only workaholic in the family. But compromise was possible in this area, too. She could work part-time until the children were old enough not to need her as much as they did now.

"Because if you do—" she was panting, knew it was time to push "—I'm unemployed at the moment. And I've always—" breathe, in and out, slowly "—wanted to work in a coffee and pastry shop."

"Right. But if this is an application for part-time employment, you're hired," John said, laughing. Then he stood quickly as he recognized the signs. Moving across the room, he gently shook Alice's shoulder. "I think it's time," he said softly. "Would you mind bringing the tray I prepared? It's in the kitchen. Don't touch anything. It's sterilized. And Alice, please phone Dr. Harrington at St. Anthony's. He's prepared to stay on the line as long as we need him."

"Part-time only," Penny gasped. She managed a wink at Alice when Alice paused beside the bed to stare at her. "We're working out . . . the terms of our employment."

Alice rolled her eyes toward the ceiling, then shaking her head, she hurried toward the stairs.

"I think we'd better have a look," John said. Leaning, he kissed her perspiring forehead, then gently pulled up her nightgown. She had kicked the blankets off some time ago.

"Good heavens!" Awe transformed his expression. "Penny, we're about to have a baby!"

"Darling, I know that. It's time to push. I need to push!"

"Okay." Mind racing, he returned to her side. "Okay. Now here's what you're supposed to do. Remember? Put your knees under your arms. . . ."

She stared up at him. "You're kidding! Maybe you haven't noticed, but I have this stomach in the way."

"I'll help. Don't push yet. Wait a minute."

"Wait a minute?" Panting, she looked at the ceiling. "Just once, one time only, I wish you could be pregnant!"

Sweat appeared on his own forehead as he lifted her knee and pushed it back where she could grab hold. She yelped, but she grabbed. Then he raced around the bed and pressed her other knee upward.

Penny released a long breath and relaxed a bit as the space between contractions lengthened again now that delivery was imminent.

"There is no dignity in this process, is there?" she asked the ceiling, holding her knees as near her armpits as she could. Then she closed her eyes, gripped her legs and bore down.

"I think it's going to happen," John said as Alice set the tray on the table he had placed at the end of the bed.

"Rubber gloves, Santa?" Alice said solemnly. She spoke to John, but her eyes were on Penny, urging her on.

"Thank you, nurse." After pulling on the gloves, he drew a long breath and bowed his head briefly in silent prayer. "Is Dr. Harrington on the telephone?" At Alice's nod, he said, "Okay, tell him what's going on now. And tell him, for God's sake, to tell me what I need to know." When Alice hurried out of the room, he glanced at Penny. "Keep pushing, sweetheart. Remember your breathing."

"I'll work...the front counter...and do the books... Can you see the baby yet?"

"This baby's got a head of hair you're going to love!" He was watching a miracle! A thrill of joy brought a flood of moisture to his eyes. He blinked rapidly, trying to clear his vision. "If you work the front counter, then I can do the baking exclusively. We'll be a hell of a team, darling. Push!"

"Martin and Martin...franchises all over...the country!" Her face reddened with effort. "But only after...the kids start college."

At the time it seemed to happen very fast. Later they would both remember Alice running in and out of the room relaying messages and questions as the sky gradually lightened outside the windows. Then Penny gave a tired triumphant cry and suddenly John was holding a wiggling infant. Behind him Alice leaned against the bureau and wept with joy. A lusty cry rose from a set of tiny lungs.

Quickly John finished as he had been instructed, while Alice cleaned the baby and wrapped it in a small warm blanket before she kissed Penny and quietly tiptoed from the room. Then John, his eyes brimming with tears, carried the bundle to Penny.

"My dearest Mrs. Martin," he whispered. "Your daughter wishes you a merry Christmas."

Stretching out beside Penny on the bed, he placed the baby against her breast, then enclosed them both in his arms.

PENNY AND THE BABY were dozing and dawn had broken against the frosted windowpanes when John heard a sound outside. Careful not to wake them, he eased from the bed and hurried downstairs, noticing as he passed through the living room that the radio was still playing carols and the Christmas tree lights were still on.

He looked through the window next to the front door and saw that the storm had blown itself out. The wind had finally died, leaving enormous drifts across a sea of white. A few lazy flakes still floated down, but a pale yellow glow stretching up the eastern sky signaled a clear day to come. Then his heart moved in his chest as he saw the blade of a big orange plow swing around the bend in the road and cut up the driveway. It was one of the most welcome sights he had ever seen. Sitting in the cab beside the plow driver were Dr. Adler and Wes Pierce. They waved when they saw him at the window.

John threw open the door as Dr. Adler climbed down from the plow and waded through knee-deep snow toward the porch, holding his bag in front of him.

"How is she?" the doctor called as he hurried up the porch steps, pausing only long enough to stamp the snow and ice from his boots.

"Mother and daughter are doing fine," John said, smiling and clasping Bill's hand. "But I can't tell you how glad I am to see you!"

The weariness vanished from Bill Adler's eyes. "Terrific, John! That good news makes a very long night worth every minute." Talking while he peeled off his coat, hat, muffler and gloves, he quickly sketched how he'd fought the blizzard up the mountain, talked the state patrol into allowing him through the tunnel, and then had found Wes Pierce waiting on the other side with the plow. "It took us almost three hours to get here from the tunnel. The roads are impossible. I couldn't have made it in my car. If Wes hadn't been there with the plow..." Dr. Adler moved past John and started up the stairs where Alice was waiting to lead him to Penny. "After I have a look at Penny and our newcomer, I'd sure like a cup of John's hottest coffee. Wes and I exhausted the thermos hours ago."

John stepped off the porch, his throat working, and he clasped Wes Pierce's hand in a bone-crushing grip. For a moment neither man spoke.

"I don't know what to say," John began, "except that I've been a damned idiot. You spent Christmas Eve sitting in a plow. You didn't have to..." Unashamed tears glistened in John's eyes. His voice thickened around a lump of emotion and he spoke with difficulty. "How can I ever thank you for what you've done for us?"

Wes clapped him on the back and gave him a tired grin. "You can start with a cup of hot coffee. And I'd like to use your phone to call Edith and let her know we arrived safe and sound."

"Wes, I..." He was still gripping the older man's hand, needing to say more, but unable to find adequate words.

Nothing seemed strong enough. "I've said some pretty stupid things. You must have thought I was an arrogant fool. And I was."

"Seems to me the key word there is *was*." Wes returned his handclasp, then stepped up on the porch. "You know, John, I've been thinking. Edith says I'm too set in my ways, too much a creature of habit. So I've been thinking about getting a summer place." His eyes twinkled. "How would you feel about setting me up a park bench in front of your new shop? Next to the aspens?"

John laughed, liking this man and the solid values he stood for. "I'd be honored. And I can promise you a steady supply of the best free coffee you ever tasted." He met Wes's gaze. "Your presence would help launch our new business. I'd be grateful."

Accepting help was never going to be easy. But maybe each time he let himself take as well as give, it would feel a little more comfortable.

Wes smiled and dropped an arm around John's shoulders. "Welcome to the family, son. And welcome to Aspen Springs. Wouldn't surprise me if one day you ran for mayor. Hell, I might even campaign for you."

"Mayor John Martin. It has a kind of ring, doesn't it?"

Laughing, knowing they were beginning a lifelong friendship, they went inside to inspect the new arrival.

AN HOUR LATER, Wes and the plow driver had wished everyone a Merry Christmas and left. When Amy and Flash came running upstairs at seven, horrified to discover they had overslept, Penny was lying on the sofa in front of the twinkling Christmas lights, her face tired but radiant in the light of the fire John had built in the grate.

"Santa came!"

"Oh, Mommy, look! Santa brought me an Elizabeth doll!"

Penny smiled. "Santa brought everything you asked for," she said, her eyes shining as she nodded toward the stairs leading to her bedroom.

John stepped into the living room, wearing his red Santa cap, and holding a red-and-green blanket in his arms. "Look what Santa brought us," he said smiling. Kneeling, he drew back the blanket so Flash and Amy could see a tiny red face and a cap of golden hair. "This is your sister, Holly Noel."

"Wow," Flash said. "She came down the chimney?"

John laughed. "Something like that." He winked at Penny.

"Can I hold her?" Amy asked, her eyes round.

"I think we should let Mommy hold her now. After you've unwrapped your presents you can hold her."

Later in the morning, Penny adjusted the folds of a slim new robe and lay back on the sofa in John's arms. Tears of joy filled her eyes as she listened to Alice and Bill talking together in the kitchen as Alice prepared Christmas dinner. Amy and Flash played with their new toys on the floor in front of the fire. Holly Noel dozed in a bassinet.

Penny gazed around her, radiant with happiness. Everyone she loved was here with her. And nothing else mattered but that. Love. Love would always be enough.

"I just remembered," she said, shifting in John's arms to gaze into his eyes. "I didn't have time to mail this." Reaching into the pocket of her robe, she removed a folded sheet of paper she had placed there earlier.

He raised an eyebrow, then opened the page and read aloud. "'Dear Santa, if you can tear yourself away from the North Pole, Mrs. Claus loves you and wants you to come home.'" John grinned. "Does this mean I can sleep upstairs?" Tenderly he caressed her glowing face with his fingertips before he covered her temples, her eyelids, her parted lips with a dozen eager kisses that left her laughing and breathless.

"Wowee," Flash said, nudging Amy and giggling. "Look at Mommy and Daddy—they're necking. This is the best Christmas ever!"

"The best Christmas ever," Penny agreed, smiling against Santa's lips.

H A R L E Q U I N
American Romance®

A Holiday Message to My Readers....

For most of us the holidays come wrapped in joyful ribbons of home, family, love and friends. This wonderful time of year is a time of renewal, an opportunity to exchange messages with distant friends, a time to express our love through family gatherings and gifts. It's a gingerbread time of baking and wrapping and trimming, surrounded by carols and the scents of cinnamon and evergreen.

But for some there is no home to decorate with holiday greenery. There will be no tree, no sugar cookies, no visit from a generous Santa. For America's homeless, Christmas is just another hopeless day.

Harlequin readers are among the most caring and warmhearted people in the world. Please join me in a commitment to make this a kinder, gentler Christmas for those families less fortunate than our own. If each of us will give one toy, one can of food or one hour of our time, we can make a difference. And we will experience the true joy and spirit of Christmas.

Margaret St. George

MARG-1

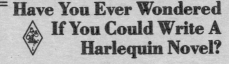

Have You Ever Wondered If You Could Write A Harlequin Novel?

Here's great news—Harlequin is offering a series of cassette tapes to help you do just that. Written by Harlequin editors, these tapes give practical advice on how to make your characters—and your story— come alive. There's a tape for each contemporary romance series Harlequin publishes.

Mail order only

All sales final

Wonderful, luxurious gifts can be yours with proofs-of-purchase from any specially marked "Indulge A Little" Harlequin or Silhouette book with the Offer Certificate properly completed, plus a check or money order (do not send cash) to cover postage and handling payable to Harlequin/Silhouette "Indulge A Little, Give A Lot" Offer. We will send you the specified gift.

Mail-in-Offer

	OFFER CERTIFICATE			
Item:	A. Collector's Doll	B. Soaps in a Basket	C. Potpourri Sachet	D. Scented Hangers
# of Proofs-of-Purchase	18	12	6	4
Postage & Handling	$3.25	$2.75	$2.25	$2.00
Check One				

Name _____

Address _____ Apt. # _____

City _____ State _____ Zip _____

ONE PROOF OF PURCHASE

To collect your free gift by mail you must include the necessary number of proofs-of-purchase plus postage and handling with offer certificate.

HAR-3

Harlequin®/Silhouette®

Mail this certificate, designated number of proofs-of-purchase and check or money order for postage and handling to:

INDULGE A LITTLE
P.O. Box 9055
Buffalo, N.Y. 14269-9055